For Grace and Henry

CHAPTER ONE

I am disturbed at about twenty past two, in the early hours of Saturday morning.

I sleep lightly when Marc is away, noticing the slightest noise in the street, and always position myself in bed so that I'm facing the open door. I leave the bathroom light on too – just bright enough so that I'm able to see out into the hall beyond. My mum says I was fine until I watched *The Woman in White* at a friend's house aged about eight. I'm now thirty-nine, and I still have to make sure I don't accidentally stumble upon any scary TV when I know I'll be sleeping alone.

Jolting awake suddenly, I sit up, blinking. It is pitch-black in the room. Confused, I stare into the darkness, my already panicky brain fumbling around for an explanation. It must be a power cut, but before I can think anything else, I hear a soft click, and a small, bright sun appears on the carpet, to the right of the wardrobe.

I stare at the circle of light stupidly for a second, but as my eyes begin to adjust, I notice a larger, unfamiliar shape above it. I scan the outline rapidly – and freeze.

It's a figure.

Someone is in my bedroom, sitting on the low chair in the corner, watching me.

Jerking up what seems to be a surprisingly powerful pencil torch, they shine the blinding beam right in my face.

'Don't move to turn on the light, and don't try to reach for your phone. I've got it here.' He holds it aloft in confirmation. As I try to focus, the familiar image of my niece – my screen saver – briefly illuminates, along with the 'Slide to unlock' bar. I see the metal rim of his glasses and staring eyes, before the phone returns to standby mode and simultaneously he swings the torch beam down again.

He must be a burglar. I want to scream, but there is no sound as my mouth falls open, just a breathy leak of air from my lips, as if I've been punctured.

The chair creaks as he leans forward. 'Don't, Sophie.'

Oh my God, he knows my name. Hard little shunts of just audible sound begin to gurgle in my gullet.

'Shhh,' he says softly. 'You realize when people hear screams at night, they mostly don't report it? Everyone thinks someone else will. A woman was beaten to death by her husband in New Zealand over a period of several hours, and not one of her neighbours called the police.'

I don't recognize his voice. I know I don't. A confident stranger is sitting in my bedroom, as calmly as if he were out for dinner at a nice restaurant. This isn't the first time he has done something like this.

But what, exactly, is he here to *do*?

Apparently reading my mind, the floorboards groan as he gets to his feet... and I scrabble backwards, thumping into the head-board behind me. I have nowhere to go.

The torch beam bounces around as he starts to move towards me. He is not especially tall, but has the kind of wiry physique other men underestimate – until it's too late. He stops alongside my chest of drawers, reaches into his pocket and pulls out an envelope, before propping it up carefully against the freestanding mirror.

'You're going to open this in front of all of your family and friends at your birthday party.'

My eyes widen. How does he know about *that*?

'You're to read it under the clock in the foyer of the hotel at 8 p.m. precisely – NOT before. My client has other stipulations too. You will not mention to a single living soul that I have visited you here, neither will you discuss the existence of this letter with anyone. And Sophie.' He pauses. 'I *will* know, and I *will* find you. Don't think about not showing up tomorrow night either, OK?'

He takes two steps to the bed and is immediately right alongside me. 'I don't like hurting women. Men, I'm OK with – they mostly deserve it... But someone like you, who has no idea...'

He reaches out and touches my hair. I can feel his fingers shaking with excitement. He's lying – I have no doubt this is a man who relishes his job, and would not hesitate to cause me pain.

He shines the torch up sharply, right in my eyes again, tipping my chin with the other hand to get a better look. He is wearing gloves. 'Pretty,' he says, quietly. 'You look like your sisters – or rather, they look like you. You're the oldest, aren't you?'

My mouth falls open, horrified. I watch him reach into his pocket and pull out another mobile. 'This is your youngest sister, Alice, yesterday.' He holds up the screen, and I stare at a picture of Al holding a thermos and concentrating on crossing the busy road outside her flat. 'See? No mistaking the family tie there. And this is Imogen dropping off your niece at nursery.' He scrolls along, and there is Gen, struggling with a key code on a door while holding a clearly crying Evie in a car seat. 'Here they are arriving back at home later... I know where all of your family live, Sophie.'

'If you hurt them...' I whisper.

He looks up with interest. 'Oh, I *will* hurt them, Sophie. That's entirely my point. If you so much as breathe a word, Alice will wake up to find me standing over her like this. Then I'll go to Imogen's – her husband works late a lot, doesn't he? And I'll finish up at your mum's.' He puts the phone back in his pocket. 'I will be watching you until 8 p.m. tomorrow night. Just do exactly as I've said and you'll have nothing to worry about.'

He abruptly flicks the torch off, and I sense him straighten up. 'Happy birthday. Life, so they say, begins at forty.'

I lie completely still in the stifling silence that follows, eyes wide open in the darkness, not daring to breathe.

Has he left the room? I don't hear the stairs creak; there is no slam of the front door. It must be at least another five minutes before I reach out with trembling fingers and put the lamp on.

I'm alone. The letter is still there but my mobile is gone. So much for always keeping it beside me on the bedside table, in case of an emergency. He must have picked it up while standing over me as I slept, completely oblivious to his presence.

I listen again, but there is no sound at all.

Pushing the duvet back and shivering as the cold air hits my bare legs, I slip out of bed and snatch up the very ordinary cream envelope. The sort you might use to send a thank-you letter. My name – Sophie Gardener – is printed neatly on the front. I turn it over. It is sealed with an anonymous red wax stamp. Nothing else; no clues.

This has to be a mistake.

But how can it be, when it's addressed to me? And that man knew that I would be here alone. Someone told him Marc was away. *My client?* Someone sent him here?

Terrified, I let it fall from my fingers. Dropping to my knees and reaching under the bed for a bag, I drag one out, then quickly make my way to the wardrobe. Flinging the door open, I slide a top that I barely look at off a hanger, and tug at a pair of cords until they also come free. I bundle them both into the holdall and then edge around the letter to my underwear drawer, yanking it open to grab a pair of knickers. Shoving them in too, as well as the bra from the chair, I put on yesterday's jumper over the top of my pyjamas and pull on some socks.

I hesitate, not wanting to touch the letter again, but dart forward, thrusting it into my bag before rushing from the room. I don't stop to turn the lights off.

Pausing at the top of the stairs, and peering down into the dark, quiet hall below, I take a deep breath and, as if I'm plunging into icy cold water, dive down them. At the bottom, by the front door – one hand on the latch – I struggle to shove my feet into boots, grabbing at my coat on the hook, not daring to look behind me, before fumbling to turn the keys that are still in the lock.

Flinging the door open, I run out into the freezing night. Some distant neighbour's dog barks as I hurry down the drive, bleeping the car to unlock it. But wait – is he expecting me to do this? What if he's already in my car, crouched down low in the footwell at the back, poised for me to innocently get in and drive off?

I draw up short, and just stand there, my breath forming clouds as I stare at the dark windows. I run a desperate hand through my hair. Shit – what do I do? *What do I do?*

I exhale sharply and grasp the handle on the driver's side. Feeling like I'm going to faint, I fling it open.

The interior light comes on: the front seats are empty. I scan the rest of the inside, throwing the bag onto the passenger seat, then make my way around the outside of the car, peering into the now-illuminated rear seats – nothing. I straighten up and glance at the boot. It's not that small a space. Someone could get in there. Biting my lip, I move over to the catch and release it, stumbling back as if I'm opening a jack-in-the-box, but he doesn't burst out. There is just Marc's rain mac bundled up in the corner, an empty oil container I keep meaning to throw away, and a candy-striped windbreak.

Slamming it shut, I hurry back to the driver's door and get in, turning the engine on. The wipers start manically swishing – I can't have switched them off the last time I got out of the car – and the windscreen is almost completely misted over, but I lurch blindly out into the road anyway. I just want to get away.

Grinding the gears, like I've completely forgotten how to drive – Marc would be wincing at the sound – I fumble to turn the fan on and the wipers off. I huddle over the steering wheel like an OAP so that I can peer under the fogged-up glass.

As the condensation starts to recede, I manage to settle into a slightly smoother speed to continue the drive to Alice's. The contents of my bag have spilled out everywhere. The letter is lying on the mat, visible out of the corner of my eye. I swallow. Someone broke into my house.

He was *standing right over me.*

Starting to shake, I grip the steering wheel more tightly in total disbelief.

My *client*?

MY CLIENT.

There is only one person who hates me enough to have done this.

CHAPTER TWO

I have never met Marc's ex-wife, Claudine – I've only seen photos.

Isabelle showed me one the first time I met her at Marc's flat. 'This is my mother,' she said, in very precise English, fixing me with a direct stare as she passed me the picture she had carefully taken out of her backpack.

'She's very pretty,' I said truthfully, looking at the grown-up version of the child seated in front of me – except Claudine was laughing. A slim, small, brunette woman, with very white teeth and dark eyes, she was standing slightly behind Marc, her arms tightly around him, on what looked like the balcony of a hotel. It certainly seemed to be a holiday snap; they were both lightly tanned and Marc – seated at a table – was wearing a wide smile, a short-sleeved white shirt and stone-coloured linen trousers. He was also holding a cigarette. He only ever smokes when in hot countries. I've teased him about it before, at which he's shrugged ruefully as if he knows how daft it is, but what can you do? Claudine's hands were resting on his chest, fingers spread, nails painted a just-the-right-side-of-trashy scarlet, her wedding and enormous engagement ring catching the camera flash. Next to Marc on the table stood a mostly drunk bottle of wine, with someone else's hand reaching for a glass, and a half-naked Isabelle and Olivier pulling funny faces in the foreground. A happy family portrait. For a moment it had crossed my mind that Claudine had intended Isabelle to show the picture to me, but I dismissed that as idiotic.

That was in the early days, of course, before I learnt that pretty much *everything* Claudine does is calculated.

'Are you staying here tonight?' Isabelle had watched me from her vantage point on the top bunk like a suspicious kitten, legs crossed on her pretty flower bedspread, the fairy lights, especially threaded around the curtain pole behind her, twinkling.

'No.' I smiled. 'I'm not. You'll be up there and I expect Olivier will be below decks.' I motioned to the freshly ironed pirate duvet cover on the bottom bunk. 'There's no room for me!'

'I don't want to share with Olivier, I want to be in my own room at home.' She swallowed, looking suddenly much smaller than her eight years, and I instinctively stepped forward to take her hand. It must have been horrible for her, dragged over from France and forced to meet some random woman she couldn't care less about. But, understandably, she shrunk away from me. Instead I gently passed back the picture, putting it on the duvet in front of her.

'I've been very excited about meeting you, Isabelle. We're going to have lots of fun while you're in England.'

She hadn't answered, just picked up the photograph and stared at it furiously, tears welling up in her eyes.

Marc came in, carrying Olivier on his back, who had his arms wrapped tightly around his father's neck, his head resting contentedly on Marc's shoulder. Marc's happy smile vanished, however, at the sight of his little girl. 'What's wrong, Issy?'

She said something in French that I didn't understand. Marc glanced quickly at me, then replied, 'Well, we can swap you over if that's better. You don't have to if you don't want to, but remember, we speak English here.'

Isabelle had lifted her gaze and looked at me piercingly. 'So *she* can understand.'

Taken aback by the hostility in her voice, I nonetheless smiled apologetically and shrugged.

'No, not just that,' Marc said smoothly. 'We're in England now.'

Her bottom lip trembled, and she said something else in French, eyes downcast.

Marc knelt down, gently releasing Olivier, and, straightening up, opened his arms out to Isabelle, who clambered into them like a koala bear. 'Because Sophie is my girlfriend.'

Isabelle looked sideways at me, with barely concealed dislike, and I tried to remind myself that everyone had warned me to expect a bumpy ride. It wasn't personal, and I just had to give the children time.

Later that evening, once they were finally in bed – Isabelle on the bottom bunk – Marc got a bottle of wine from the fridge, came over and gave me a kiss. 'Well, I think you did great. The thing you have to remember, Soph, is that I have no idea what Claudine says to the children when I'm not there. I wouldn't put it past her to be telling them a million shitty things like, "We could all be living together again but Daddy only wants to be with Sophie now." She's hardly going to own up to the truth, is she? And, to be honest, I don't want them to know what really happened until they're much older – if ever, actually.'

Marc told me on our first date that he was separated from his wife, whom he'd met while living in Paris on secondment with the London-based corporate law firm he worked for. 'I don't think she realized they only sent me to Paris purely because I spoke French, not because I was some legal hot-shot,' he joked. There was a pause. 'We're in the process of getting divorced.'

I gave him an oblique smile, but felt my heart sink as I reached for my wine and wondered what he'd done.

'She was sleeping with someone else,' he said quietly, reading my mind. 'Claudine fell pregnant just four months after we met. By the time my daughter Isabelle was one, we were married, had a house – Claudine went back to work shortly after that.' He reached for the bread. 'My son, Olivier, came along a year later and we kind of spent the next few years in a sleepless blur. Having small children can test the strongest of relationships, but it was only once the kids were a bit older that we actually realized we just didn't have the foundations to shore us up, full stop. We'd been arguing a lot anyway – Claudine is quite an... intense person. Anyway, she came to a work do with me one Christmas and met Julien, the managing partner of my firm...' He shrugged. 'When their affair finally came to light – Julien's wife told me – I moved out. That was last year. I wanted to stay in Paris to be near the children, but the firm made it clear that Julien wanted me transferred back to London and I was told that my employment had only ever been a "secondment". This was after some seven years' loyal service, of course, but' – he raised a rueful eyebrow – 'you don't argue with a bunch of lawyers. It was come back to London or lose my job, and I couldn't afford to rock the boat because I have responsibilities to the children. Although, to be truthful, Claudine makes a lot more money than me.'

I was completely taken aback. 'I'm so sorry.'

I was actually apologizing for assuming he was the guilty party, but he misunderstood me.

'Don't be.' He took a mouthful of food. 'I had a wonderful time in Paris. I fell in love and have two incredible children to show for it. The hard bit is not being around them now as much as I'd like. Claudine travels a lot with work and sometimes when I speak to the kids and they're at their grandmother's again, or the nanny is putting them to bed or, worst of all, they're with Julien, it breaks my heart. It ought to be me.' He spoke factually and without self-pity, but in the pause that followed, I instinctively reached across the table and quickly squeezed his hand – before realizing what I was doing. He looked surprised at my touch and I blushed, quickly pulling back again.

'Now it's my turn to be sorry,' he said immediately. 'Please don't think I was going for the sympathy vote.'

'I don't.'

He shifted in his seat. 'I just wanted to be upfront about the fact that I have some... baggage... in that I'm still technically married.'

'I appreciate your honesty.'

'That said, I certainly don't want to go on about it – it's all in the past, and everything is in a much better place now.'

'Well, that's great,' I said slowly.

He closed his eyes, cringed and laughed. '*Now* I'm going on about it, aren't I? God, I am so out of practice at this. This is why my friends have been trying to set me up on blind dates. Here' – he reached into his pocket and pulled out his mobile – 'use this to emergency call whoever you've got on standby.'

I looked at him steadily for a moment, then grinned. 'I don't know what you mean,' although I had my best friend, Lou, primed and ready to leap into action with a fake disaster I needed to attend, just in case.

It was Lou who had virtually insisted I have dinner with Marc, having chaperoned me at coffee with him.

'Oh my God.' She'd turned to me the second Marc had apologetically excused himself to take a client call. 'If you don't go to dinner with him, I will.'

'You're married.'

'So?' She'd looked through the window at Marc talking animatedly. 'I'll leave Rich for him. And the kids too – I don't care. He can hold an interesting conversation, he's clearly solvent, has a proper job – and he obviously works out. A full package.' I'd sniggered and she rolled her eyes. 'Don't be gross. I think you should definitely go for it, Soph.'

I'd hesitated and glanced at him through the window of the coffee shop, still talking on his mobile. 'He seems a nice bloke, but...'

'Oh, Lord!' Lou groaned, pretended to thump her head down on the table, then gestured heavenward. 'God's up there right now shouting, "What more do I have to do, woman? I've sent him to your ACTUAL HOUSE."'

'Yes. Let's pause for a moment and remember exactly that. He is a complete stranger, who turned up on my doorstep two nights ago, flyering because he wants to *buy my house*,' I said pointedly.

'That's not why he asked you out,' she scoffed. 'Direct flyering is a very sensible tactic – lots of people bypass estate agents and contact potential sellers directly these days. Anyway, he pretty quickly forgot about the house when you opened the front door, didn't he? What was it he said, when he asked you to have dinner with him?'

'"This could be one of those life-defining moments that if we don't take, we'll always wonder about,"' I repeated doubtfully.

'Very nice indeed.' Lou nodded approvingly, as if mentally entering another positive tick on one of her spreadsheets.

'You don't think that's actually just a bit cheesy?' I picked up my mug. 'Anyway, I'm perfectly happy at the moment – I don't need any complications.'

'It's been *four years* since Josh.'

'Oh, stop it! I've dated since then,' I said. 'You know I have.' I took a mouthful of coffee. 'You make it sound like Josh's dead.'

She snorted. 'I wish. It's only dinner. Live a little. There's a huge difference between being pragmatic and risk-adverse. No, come on. You know you are.'

'Do you not read the news? He could be a raving nutter. You

12

see it all the time – men stalking women online, pretending to be something they're not...'

'*Or* he could just be a normal bloke trying to ask someone out. I feel really sorry for men these days. They're damned if they do and damned if they don't. The poor guy tries to say something vaguely romantic to you and you instantly write him off as a serial killer. You can't live your whole life in fear, Sophie.'

I'd looked at him again. 'It's not that he's not attractive... but what's the catch?'

Lou gave an exaggerated, patient sigh. 'That's completely my point. There doesn't always have to be one, Soph. Lots of men are perfectly nice – you've just unfortunately not met many of them up until now.' Her phone bleeped, she looked at it and tutted. 'Rich can't remember what I said to give the kids for lunch. He's so bloody useless. I mean it, if you don't go to dinner with Marc, I will.'

There's no doubt my life would have been so much easier if I had walked away after that first date. And if I'd known he had a lunatic ex-wife, I would have done. I never expected her to go this far, though.

Pulling up at some traffic lights on red, I sit there at the deserted crossroads, trying to stay calm as I drum my fingers on the wheel with fear, looking nervously in the mirror. 'C'mon, c'mon!' I whisper aloud, willing the lights to change, looking for a car slowly turning out of a junction, starting to follow me.

He said he'll be watching me.

The lights finally go to green and I shoot across the road. It's actually a relief to pass a gang of boys in their late teens hanging around outside a kebab shop, hoods pulled up, trying to ignore a drunken pack of men in their forties, singing and shouting. I don't want to be out here on my own.

I knew Claudine had been becoming more and more desperate, but *this*?

The weird thing is, I was probably the one who was mildly obsessed with *her* at first.

'Don't take this the wrong way,' Marc had said on our second date, 'but it's so nice that you actually enjoy food.'

I paused, fork halfway to my mouth, and looked at him.

'I said don't take it the wrong way!' He'd laughed. 'It's good to see a woman tuck in, rather than pick at it, that's all I'm saying.'

I'd been horrified. Grown women who played hockey and netball as a hobby – rather than being forced to by gender-questionable PE teachers – were the kind of women who *tucked in*. Even worse, after he'd taken me home, he had merely kissed me lightly on the lips: no more than he had done on our first date.

I'd sat down on my sofa, confused and a little disappointed. Didn't he find me attractive after all? Maybe it really was just the house he was interested in. I reached for my phone and found him on Facebook. I had, of course, already looked at his – surprisingly for a lawyer – semi-open profile, but nothing had leapt out at me. Had I missed something obvious? Messages from lots of different women, of whom I was merely one? I scrolled again through his list of friends, finding, to my astonishment, his *eight*-year-old daughter. I hadn't noticed that before. What were they thinking? That was far too young to be on Facebook! Frowning, I had looked through her friends too – and immediately, there was her mother. Claudine Dubois. Marc's ex-wife.

Instantly curious, I clicked onto her profile but, frustratingly, it was completely locked. There was just one, very glamorous – my heart sank – photo of her. She was all smooth skin, red lips and vast, expensive sunglasses. She did not look like the kind of woman who would dream of 'tucking in'.

I became a little gloomily carried away after that. I checked her LinkedIn profile and found that she worked for the luxury division of some huge French parent company that owned several upmarket jewellers and shoe designers. Of course she did. She was beautiful, French and polished. Why wouldn't she also work in fashion? I felt positively embarrassed at the memory of Marc's polite goodnight kiss. I even Googled her, and discovered she had a Tumblr page. I didn't really understand what Tumblr was, bar a collection of photos. It just seemed to be lots of shots backstage at a catwalk show and more in someone's design studio. There was one of her reading the two children a bedtime story, but then under that was a postcard that said, in English, 'Before you judge me, please understand I don't give a fuck what you think.'

I'd raised my eyebrows. How charming. A career woman, and a mother of two. Really? I reread it. Did she actually believe that, anyway? I remembered Marc saying she was 'intense' and shifted uncomfortably. I found people like her – those who really didn't give a rat's arse what anyone else thought – slightly intimidating. Beneath the image of her reading to her children was a really beautiful picture of her on some beach in a bikini – she was probably an expert surfer in her spare time too. I had stared at it, fascinated. Her hair was all sea-salt-tousled, she had good boobs, a totally flat stomach and no visible cellulite. She was also looking at whoever had taken the photo like she wanted to take them straight to bed. I bet Marc had kissed *her* properly on their second date. Yeah... I'd sighed and quietly closed my phone. He wasn't going to be calling me again.

But to my surprise, he did. We went to the Oxo Tower for dinner and sat overlooking the early summer, rosy city skyline, drinking cocktails. It felt decadent. I drank a little too fast and quickly became very chatty, but it was fun, and afterwards we walked along the South Bank holding hands. I felt an odd surge of triumph later, when he took me home and I asked him to come in – and he did. The following morning when I woke up alongside him, I realized I'd been a little drunker the night before than I ought to have been, but I didn't regret any of it. It was the start of a very happy time.

But only about two weeks after that had come the first phone call. It was Friday evening, we were just sitting down to dinner at mine, and I was looking forward to a second, long weekend of him not going home until Sunday night. We'd been discussing careers, and I'd just confessed to Marc why I'd left teaching: 'I had a complete crisis of confidence. I'd been with Josh for nine years, and when we split, I sort of lost myself for a bit. You can't be like that and teach. It's not fair on the kids – and anyway, they smell fear. I'd have been done for.'

He smiled. 'Will you go back to it?'

'Maybe one day. I've always quite fancied being an MP, actually.' I'd said it before I'd realized I was going to, and laughed, embarrassed.

He looked at me seriously. 'What's stopping you?'

'Well, let's see,' I said. 'My geography is appalling, I know very little about economics, I'd make hideous gaffes, I doubt I'd be able to hold my own on things like *Question Time*, and I also cry at the drop of a hat, which would be beyond unprofessional.'

'OK.' He had grinned. 'So what *do* you think you have to offer public office?'

I shrugged, still a bit shy. 'Well, there seems to be a widening gap between the haves and have-nots. The have-nots don't seem to have many people sticking up for them.'

'As good a reason as any.'

'You say that' – I reached for my wine – 'but then I also get pretty nervous when I imagine being under all that scrutiny...

weirdos sending you death threats on Twitter just because you're a female MP, that sort of thing. People can reach you so easily these days – it makes me realize I'm probably *not* cut out for it, after all. There are probably other ways I could—'

His phone started ringing. 'Shit, I forgot to turn that off, sorry.' He reached into his pocket and pulled it out, but as he caught sight of the screen he frowned, worriedly. 'It's my ex. Do you mind if I get it? It must be something to do with the kids.'

'Of course,' I said, expecting him to stand up and take it in the other room, but he didn't.

'Hello, Claudine,' he answered in English. 'Is everything all right?' He listened, then frowned in confusion and glanced at me. 'I can't do that,' he said, then cleared his throat. 'You should know I'm seeing someone now.'

I got up to leave the room, but he shook his head and motioned for me to sit back down. Which I did, rather uncomfortably.

'Yes, I'm serious,' Marc mumbled awkwardly, and I blushed. We'd not even had that discussion between ourselves yet. 'I'm with her at the moment. No, Claudine, I'm not prepared to do that. Anything I have to say to you, I'd rather Sophie heard for herself...' He trailed off and then sighed. 'Yes, that's her— What? No, she doesn't... She isn't, actually.'

I crossed my arms awkwardly, trying hard not to listen – and failing.

'That's insane!' He blanched. 'You can't possibly have expected me to say yes, just like that?' I heard a female voice starting to shout. 'Look, I have to go now, OK? No, please – just stop!' He closed his eyes. 'I'm going to hang up now, Claudine.' He put his phone back down on the table and sat there in silence, looking stunned. Just as I was about to ask him if he wanted to talk about it, he spoke. 'Julien has gone back to his wife. She's made a terrible mistake, apparently, and she wants me to come home.'

The air sucked out of the room. I went very still and just looked at him.

'It's funny,' he said eventually. 'Well, it's not – but you know what I mean... Even though she cheated on me, I was desperate for her to say what she just did for such a long time, and now she has – I don't feel a thing.' He looked up and gave me a slightly shaky smile, then he reached for my hand. 'I just really hope she didn't say all of that in front of the kids.'

I watched as he entwined my fingers with his, and I hesitated. 'But given you do have children with her, Marc, perhaps this is a—'

Before I could finish my sentence, his phone started to ring again. He picked it up and looked at the screen. 'I'm not going to answer. She was already hysterical, shouting and crying...' He put his elbows on the table, then his head in his hands and muttered, 'Shit.'

I looked at the man I knew I was starting to fall in love with and managed to say, far more calmly than I felt: 'Here's the thing. You know I told you my parents divorced when we were all pretty young? Well, although they're both happily remarried to very nice people, it was really hard for my sisters and me for a long time and, even now, it's obvious to everyone who knows them that, twenty years later, they're still the love of each other's lives. They've both told me separately that, at various points, they each asked if they could try again, but for whatever reason the other one didn't think they should. It's so sad, really, and I couldn't bear to be the person who causes that to happen to someone else's family. It's still very early for us – you and me, I mean. I've had a really great time with you, but...'

'Oh.' Marc stared at me unflinchingly, before looking down at his drink in confusion. After a moment more, he said, 'Wow. I have to say I absolutely didn't see the evening going this way.'

'Um, me neither.' I tried to smile, as I heard the echo in my head of my own excited voice saying on the phone to several friends: *I really like him. Ha ha! I know! I wasn't looking for anything and just like that he walks right into my life!* 'What Claudine has said to you is probably something that you need to absorb on your own, though. Let's rain check tonight. Maybe you could call me in the morning or something?'

'But—'

'Really, Marc. It's OK. We both know I'm right.'

He gave me a long, steady look, reached for his phone and got to his feet. 'Don't get up. I can see myself out.' He put a gentle hand on my arm. 'I'm so sorry, Sophie.'

'Hey,' I said, my eyes suddenly shining with tears that I was embarrassed beyond belief not to be able to hide. 'Don't be. And see?' I joked, motioning at myself. 'Told you!'

It would have been easier if he'd just left but, instead, he leant across the table and I automatically closed my eyes as his lips brushed my cheek. I was transported back to my kissing him hard on the mouth, as I had done only two nights earlier in bed, his hands starting to move down my body. I felt like I was as good as sitting at the table in nothing but the new, matching and stupidly expensive underwear I'd so pathetically put on earlier.

After the front door closed quietly behind him, I stared at the half-eaten dinner, sat back in my chair and picked up my wine. I had no doubt I'd done the right thing – for everyone, not just me – and I had no intention of getting involved with a man who had unfinished business elsewhere.

Leaving the plates but taking my wine, I got up and moved over to the sofa, putting on the TV as I curled my legs up underneath me. Flicking unseeingly through the channels, my eyes filled with more tears as the newly hollowed-out feeling inside suddenly became too much. Cross and frustrated with myself for having become so involved already, I set down my glass, dropped the remote, and properly cried.

Except, of course, he didn't go back to her.

He turned up on my doorstep first thing the following morning, after Claudine's 'I want you back' bombshell.

Completely thrown, I just stood there in my PJs and stared at him – partly because I was also mute with horror that he was seeing me make-up-free for the first time.

'I've been up all night thinking about everything, and I don't want to lose you, Sophie.' He didn't even bother with hello. 'You're right, it's not been long, but it's long enough for me to know that I like you. I *really* like you.' He looked up at the sky and gave an embarrassed laugh. 'For God's sake, I sound like I'm fifteen or something... Look, I love my children so much, I really do, and I'm a good dad to them' – his voice broke a little bit – 'but that's because I've worked really hard to get to a place where I've stopped being bitter about what my wife did to our family, and I've stopped obsessing about what I – we – could have done differently. I can't go back, because I have to protect Isabelle and Olivier, give them stability and the best of me, and the way for me to do that is by not being with Claudine. It's too late.' He looked at me desperately. 'I don't want to be with her; I want to be with you.'

Perhaps because my frame of reference was still the nine years I'd spent with Josh – who had told me he loved me *once*, when drunk; referred to me as 'pal' in public; and was, as Lou memorably once described him, 'the most emotionally constipated man' she'd ever met – such frank honesty pushed my buttons.

I didn't even think about it. I simply stood to one side and smiled shakily at Marc. 'You'd better come in.'

Do I regret that decision? No. If Claudine didn't exist, I'm pretty sure we would have absolutely no problems at all.

But she's very much real and, as far as she is concerned, it's not her sleeping with someone else that destroyed her marriage and broke up her family: it's me.

From the moment she realized Marc wasn't going to let me bow out of the picture after all, she has done her utmost to try and convince him – sometimes sober, sometimes very much not, occasionally in tears, often shouting – that *they* are meant to be together, and that he will eventually see that.

A typical phone call will consist of her ranting away in French – she always becomes angry enough for me to hear her from the other side of the room – with Marc saying things like, 'I'm not going to do that,' or, 'That's not going to happen,' over and over. She will, by turns, become cajoling or pleading, then angry and frustrated. It's amazing what you can glean from a conversation you understand less than half of, just from the tone.

As soon as Marc told her he wanted the children to meet me, she took the gloves off completely. She 'lost' their passports, meaning Marc had to drop our plans and go over to Paris at a moment's notice instead. The next time they were too 'ill' to travel to the UK, and once she had run out of excuses, she announced instead that she intended to once again contest the already hideously dragging divorce. It was ostensibly on money grounds, but really it's because she knows all the time that she and Marc remain technically married, *our* lives remain in limbo. I can't deny it's put a massive strain on our relationship, her looming over my happiness like a malevolent black crow.

We did split up temporarily two months ago – I shift uncomfortably, changing down a gear to go around a corner and really not wanting to think about *that* – but we somehow managed to come through it. I assumed Claudine would absolutely flip when Marc told her we'd got back together and, to cap it all, become engaged, but oddly, she had gone quiet.

'Perhaps at last she's got the message,' said Marc hopefully. 'She must realize that she's never going to get what she wants. I think there's a real chance she might give up, and actually agree to the divorce.'

But now I see she was just building up to *this*. She's fully aware it's my fortieth birthday tomorrow because we asked her if the children could come over, and she said no – they already had 'plans' for that weekend and, in any case, the children had no desire to celebrate anything with me. '"The children detest Sophie,"' Marc said incredulously. 'That's actually what she said.'

'Wow,' I said, after a pause. 'That's a really strong word.'

'Hey!' he replied, appalled. 'They don't at all.' He drew me into a hug. 'You know they don't – it's just her being a bitch, Soph.' He sighed. 'Leave it with me. I'll talk to her again when she's calmer.'

Except, of course, that never seems to happen. She is only capable of extreme actions, this woman who I have never met, and who seems intent on punishing me for something I've not done. I didn't wreck her life – she did that all by herself. However sad it is that, as a result, her husband is not coming back, she remains so consumed by jealousy and hatred, all she wants to do is hurt me.

She *really* wants to hurt me.

I think about that man in my room, touching my hair, whispering her threats to me, and shudder. I just want to get to my sister's and make sure she's OK – he said he'd go there first. I simply cannot believe even Claudine can have done something so extreme, so deranged.

I glance down at the envelope, now slip-sliding around in the footwell, with dread.

In all this time she has never tried to contact me directly, until now. What can she possibly have to say that she can only tell me in front of everyone I love best?

CHAPTER THREE

I ring Alice's doorbell repeatedly, thumb on the buzzer for her flat, until, thank God, the grubby plastic intercom crackles. 'Please just go away,' my sister says tiredly. 'For the last time, it's the bottom flat you want, OK?'

'Alice – it's me!'

'Soph?' She is immediately alert. The door clicks and I push my way in past a pile of junk mail and pizza menus on the floor, trying not to knock over a push-bike that someone has left in the hall. The stairs of the Victorian building creak as I try to climb up quietly, although light is still coming out from under the front door of the couple that live below Alice, and I can hear faint music. I check my watch – it's twenty past three in the morning. The irregularity of other people's lives seems completely surreal and somehow only unnerves me more.

My sister is standing at the top of the stairs wearing a spa-ghetti-strap vest, arms crossed over her braless chest, and stripy pyjama bottoms. Her long, dark hair is all over the place, and she has huge smudges of mascara under her eyes. She never, ever takes her make-up off before she goes to bed.

'What's happened?' she says urgently as soon as I reach the top of the stairs. 'Is it Mum – or Dad? Or Imogen and Evie?'

'No, no.' It's such a relief to see her standing there, safe, that I just want to hug her, but manage to restrain myself. 'It's nothing like that. Everyone's fine. Can I come in?'

'Yeah, of course,' she says, dazed, and stands to one side, eyeing my overnight bag as I pass her and put it down on the carpet. She looks at me expectantly.

'I've had a fight with Marc,' I lie, wanting to protect her, imagining the man from the bedroom walking slowly towards my little sister with his black gloves.

'Really?' she says slowly. 'You look like you just found out you're fifty tomorrow, not forty. Oh, except it's today now, isn't it? Happy birthday.'

'Thanks.'

'What did you two fight about?' she asks. 'I thought Marc was away with work tonight?'

'He is.' I try to think faster on my feet. 'We rowed on the phone. How do you know he's away?'

'Oh, Mum told me,' she says vaguely. 'Marc was worried about you waking up on your own on your birthday, so he's asked Mum to go round to yours with a champagne breakfast as a surprise.' She yawns. 'You'd better set a reminder to text her in the morning, or she'll be pretty pissed off if you're not there. I assume you *are* staying?' She nods at my bag.

'Yes, please. If that's OK?'

''Course. Let me just go and put a jumper on, and then I'll make us a cup of tea.'

'We don't have to talk about it all now.'

She looks away, waving a hand. 'Don't be daft. God, it's freezing. I'll be right back, then you can tell me what happened.' She shivers, then shuffles out of the room.

'Do *you* mind setting a reminder to text Mum?' I call after her. 'I can't.' I pause again, trying to think how to explain away the fact that a stranger who knows my name stole my mobile from my bedroom, right in front of me, about an hour ago. 'I've lost my mobile.'

'I thought you said you rowed on the phone?' She reappears wearing an old jumper of Dad's.

'Jesus, Al!' I almost explode, and she looks surprised. 'OK, I didn't lose it! I threw it at the wall and it broke.'

'Right.' She gives me a considered look. 'Well, don't worry. We've all been there. Is it completely fucked?'

I blink. 'It's fair to say it's pretty much unusable.'

She sits down on the sofa. 'I've probably got an old one somewhere here you can use. You brought the SIM with you?'

'Um, no.'

She stares at me. 'Well, it's not like you've got a big birthday and anyone is going to be calling you... dick. Although I suppose you'll see everyone at the party later anyway, and I can tell Marc you've lost it.'

'Thanks.' It occurs to me instantly that that's probably the point of Claudine having stolen the phone: to prevent me from speaking to as many people as possible ahead of tonight. I need to ring the phone company and put a stop on the number, but how am I going to explain that to Alice? In any case, do they even have manned call centres at 3 a.m.? I'll have to use Al's phone to call first thing in the morning.

Alice suddenly cranes to listen, and I tense, terrified. 'What?'

'Kettle's boiled.' She gets up, looks around and picks up a couple of mugs. 'I'll just give these a quick wash.'

I breathe out slowly, trying to calm down. But all I can see in my head is the picture of her on that man's phone, blithely crossing the road, and Imogen struggling with Evie.

She comes back in holding two steaming mugs, one of which she passes to me before sitting down on the sofa opposite and crossing her legs in the lotus position. I go to take a sip of tea and notice a brown tidemark ring just above the hot liquid. Hastily, I make out like I need to blow on it instead, then set it down on the side table.

27

She scowls at me. 'I didn't *lick* the cup – I rinsed it in actual water. It's clean. Just drink it.'

I hesitate, but pick it up again.

'So it must have been a pretty serious argument to make you throw your phone at the wall and come over here at 3 a.m.?' She takes a mouthful of her tea and swallows. 'A "we're over" kind of row?'

'No, it's not like that.'

'Sure? It's only two months ago that you were convinced you couldn't take any more of Claudine and that was it, then out of nowhere he's proposed, you've said yes and it's all happily ever after.'

'Honestly, it's nothing. We—'

'Yeah, I don't believe you,' she interrupts. 'You haven't had another change of heart, have you? You're still sure you *want* to be with him?'

I stare at her, utterly confused by this out-of-left-field interrogation based on what is, after all, a completely fictitious argument. And suddenly, overwhelmed by the last hour of my life, with the realisation that I was essentially trapped with a man who could have killed me then and there, in my own house, I burst into tears.

'Shit! Oh, Soph – hey!' Alice puts down her tea, slopping it over the carpet in her haste, and scrabbles across the sofa to me, wrapping her arms around my tight shoulders. 'Right, that's it. Tell me what's actually happened!'

'Don't, Al.' I pull away from her. I can't. It's too dangerous. That man in my room meant every word he said. 'It's nothing, I promise.'

'Bullshit.' She looks at me.

She'll tell me to call the police, that they'll protect me, and then we'll have to argue about the fact that everyone thinks that there is a system in place when stuff like this happens: that you dial 999 and the cavalry arrives, swinging into action…

when, actually, there isn't. We are all just bloody lucky that 95 per cent of the time, 95 per cent of people decide not to break the law.

'Sophie, you have to tell me. I can't help you otherwise.' My beautiful little sister looks at me earnestly, now very concerned indeed.

'Sorry,' I whisper, wiping my streaming nose.

'Did Marc say something to upset you?'

'No,' I shake my head. 'He's been amazing since we got back together. If anything it's me who...' I pause wretchedly and close my eyes. 'I don't deserve him, Alice, put it that way.'

She frowns. 'Don't be a prick. You've been a bloody saint to put up with—'

'No. I haven't!' I interrupt, starting to get upset again. 'You don't understand!' A jumbled film begins to play in my head: a hazy mass of naked limbs, a soundtrack of theatrical gasps and moans that makes me feel sick – sick to my stomach with guilt. 'I... I cheated on Marc.'

'What?' She stares at me, astonished. '*When?*'

I look at her, completely horrified at what I've just said. It's as if my brain is now spitting out other secrets, overloaded because it can only deal with the enormity of what happened an hour ago. 'You can't tell anyone,' I plead. 'I shouldn't have said anything. It was the day before Marc proposed.'

'OK,' Alice says slowly. 'Well, you were still split up then, so you weren't unfaithful.'

I rub my eyes tiredly. I don't want to patronize her, but that's just a 'Ross and Rachel' technicality. Back in real life, how does she think Marc would have reacted if, right after he handed me an engagement ring, I'd said, 'Yes! I will marry you, but by the way, I had sex with someone else last night. That's not going to be an issue, is it?'

'Er, Sophie,' she says suddenly. 'That's not *why* you said yes when he proposed, was it? Because you were spinning out over what you'd done the night before?'

'No,' I reply instantly. There's a pause – and, as much to my surprise as hers, I add, 'I don't think so.'

'Oh, God...' she says slowly. 'You're not still involved with this bloke, are you?'

I look at the floor and whisper, 'We've been in contact since it happened, yes.'

'You'd better tell me exactly what happened.'

CHAPTER FOUR

It was bang on half past five as I shut my computer down and stared out of the large, uncurtained office windows at the lit-up block of flats opposite. Other people were already arriving home, and I realized I simply didn't have the energy for the gym. I knew I ought to: I didn't feel like going back to an empty house, but then, in all honesty, Marc wouldn't have been finishing until at least eight had we still been together, so I would have been going home alone anyway.

'Done!' groaned Nadia, one of my team, stretching. 'Jesus, what a crap week. I'm going to have the biggest glass of wine in the world tonight. Jude's doing tea and putting Lily down, so I'm *free* – a whole night off! What does your Friday night hold, Soph?'

'Gym, then dinner.'

'Is Marc taking you somewhere nice?' She reached into her desk and pulled out her make-up bag.

I hadn't been able to bring myself to tell people at work that we'd separated. I could already see the pity on their faces, knew that they would immediately be thinking, 'Poor thing, there goes her last chance to have a baby...' There are some bullets that single women past a certain age are just unable to dodge. 'It's dinner at home, actually. Marc's... away.'

'What?' She wrinkled her nose while peering into her compact mirror. 'Balls to that. Come to the pub! It's Ben's leaving-do tonight. Go on, it'll be fun!'

I hesitated. I'd read the email reminder, but I wasn't sure I felt like a shouty night in a packed bar in aid of some bloke I'd barely ever said hello to. Nadia knew him much better than I did. Then again, I had no dependents. I ought to be going out and doing *something*. If I'd planned it, I would be, but spontaneity among my friends was a little harder to come by these days. This was the middle of tea or getting back from swimming, ballet or football and *about* to start tea, or on the way back to take over from whoever else was doing teatime... Pretty much all of my lot would laugh hysterically if I rang now and asked them if they wanted a drink.

Family wasn't an option either. Imogen and Ed, I already knew, were preparing to host an insane dinner party for ten. Imogen was desperately clinging to an insistence that having an eight-month-old wasn't going to stop them living their lives. That left Alice, but I'd already declined a gig in Camden that she had sweetly invited me to.

I looked down at my office skirt and blouse, and wondered if I could reconsider. No, I couldn't, unless I *really* wanted to look like a past-her-sell-by-date-*Mad-Men*-wannabe standing in a sea of Alexa Chungs. So that left Mum and Scrabble; going home alone; or witnessing 'Ben' get drunk enough to insult whichever senior management was stupid enough to overstay their welcome.

'Come on!' wheedled Nadia, sensing I was weakening. 'At least just for one or two.'

I looked at her doubtfully. 'The last leaving do I went to ended up with that bloke from sales head-butting the marketing director.'

'Yes, but in fairness, he *had* been perving over his girlfriend all night, it's just no one realised they were actually going out because she's in HR, and it served the dirtbag right anyway – he's married. So, you're coming then, yeah?'

I sighed. 'Go on. Just for a bit, though.'

'Excellent!' She beamed, and perversely, I felt immediately old, knackered and suddenly *really* wanted to go home. Where was Marc right now? How was he going to be spending his Friday night? I swallowed and mentally shook myself. I had to stop this.

Two weeks had passed since I'd come home later than normal to find him yelling on the phone to Claudine, yet again, in French. My heart had sunk – him having a key to the house had turned into somewhat of a mixed blessing. I'd sat down at the kitchen table, poured a drink and listened to him shouting. As usual, she'd finally hung up on him and I'd listened again when he'd marched in – still in his work shirt and trousers – and ranted to me about how angry he was because she'd taken the kids out of school on some trip to Italy that he knew nothing about. She had no concept of how irresponsible and selfish that was! She never stopped to think, that was her problem. She just did *what* she wanted, *when* she wanted. When was she going to realize that the same rules applied to her that applied to everyone else? It was nothing but attention-seeking, because she knew it was going to get a reaction, that he'd be forced to call her, *that*'s what this was about!

He sat down, rested his head in his hands in frustration, and before I even knew what I was doing, my mouth said, 'How are you supposed to move on with your life when you're still married, Marc?'

He looked up in astonishment. 'You know how hard I've been trying to get her to agree to the divorce.'

'I'm not talking about the piece of paper.'

He frowned. 'What *do* you mean, then?'

'One of the first things you said to me when we met was that you were in a good place with your ex-wife. Eight months further down the line, I don't know how you'd describe it now, but it's certainly not good for me.'

He leant forward with energy. 'I don't like the situation any more than you do, but I *have* to speak to her. I have children with

33

this woman. Children that I love more than anything – or anyone,' he added warningly.

'Hey!' I said, hurt. 'And that's exactly how it should be. I'm not saying *that* for one moment.'

'Then what are you saying? Christ!' He leant back in his chair and closed his eyes. 'I've just had a row with her – do I have to have one with you now, too?'

My mouth fell open. There was the problem, right there, in a nutshell: I was always the second in line. 'You really don't get it, do you?'

'No, apparently I don't.' He sighed crossly. 'Look, I didn't realize we were on a timescale here—'

It was my turn to frown. 'That's not what I meant, either.'

'Really? You're sure about that? I've told you I love you. You've met my kids... What else did you want to have happened by now? You want me to move in? Fine, I'll move in!'

There was a long pause. 'Wow,' I said eventually. 'That was romantic. Yes, please...'

He exhaled slowly. 'OK, I'm sorry. I didn't mean it to come out like that. It's not that I don't get it... I know that you're thirty–nine, and—'

I gasped, blindsided. 'Excuse me?'

'Oh, come on,' he challenged wearily. 'So I'm wrong? That isn't what this is about?'

'I should just shut up and be grateful for whatever I get, you mean?' I stood up. 'You know what, Marc? Claudine's welcome to you.'

I was so angry with him, I meant it.

'Sophie, I'm not your ex,' he said clearly. 'It's not my fault he was a gutless bastard who didn't have the balls to tell you he wasn't ever going to marry you—'

If that was his attempt at being conciliatory, it was way, *way* off the mark. Managing not to wince at such a pinpoint-accurate summation of Josh, I steadied my voice and said quietly, 'The implication that I've been waiting for a Mr Right to deign to marry me before it's "too late" is offensive in the extreme. For your information, I am complete already.'

'Oh, God.' Marc rolled his eyes. 'I don't want the Germaine Greer lecture either. I never said you weren't "complete". You're "completely" over-reacting.'

'That's *exactly* what you said. And as for Josh, no one ever really knows what goes on in someone else's relationship except the couple concerned. Don't be so arrogant as to assume you get what happened with Josh and me, based on what little I have chosen to tell you, because you don't.'

'But *you*, on the other hand, understand the situation perfectly with me and Claudine?' He was beginning to flare up again. 'I can't let her go, I'm still in love with her... That's what you think? Never mind I've been working my nuts off to get a divorce!'

'I think you're still very angry with her for what she did and—'

'This is bullshit.' He stood up suddenly and grabbed his jacket. 'I don't have to listen to you patronizing me.'

'And I'm not prepared to be anyone's second best!' I shouted after him, then stood there, waiting... but the front door slammed. He didn't come back that night.

Or the following night.

I refused to let myself call him. Not only was I hugely hurt, I genuinely felt I deserved an apology and I really meant what I'd said: I didn't want to feel like the consolation prize. That was a road I had no intention of going down ever again. But I felt less resolute the next morning when I received a text, which read simply: **I'm sorry, but I can't do this. I need to be alone.**

Everything we'd been building over the last eight months, the layers of our lives that had delicately woven together, ripped straight down the middle. I couldn't believe what I was reading. What the hell kind of message was that to send after the best part of a year together? He needed to be alone permanently? Was that what he meant? Or he needed space to think? I immediately tried to call, but he didn't pick up. Confused, I didn't leave a message.

Either way, he very obviously didn't want to speak to me.

I rang Lou instead. 'So what do I do? Just wait? How long do you give someone before you have to accept that's it?'

'If it were me, and I hadn't heard from him in another couple of days, I'd walk away.'

'Really?' My eyebrows flickered.

'Oh, my darling Soph.' Lou sighed. 'Yes! That's what most people do when someone treats them badly. They don't hang about for the next decade waiting for things to get better. I could *kill* Marc for doing this to you!'

There was a pause. 'It wasn't like that. I told him I wasn't prepared to be second best. I made that very clear.'

'Well, that's something at least.'

'But I think I might give it a little longer than a couple of days, and see where the land lies then.'

'Why not.' She said it with an exaggerated patience that I deliberately didn't rise to. 'Whatever you think best.'

But, incredibly, two weeks passed, and nothing...

Two weeks and one day, to be precise.

I looked around the packed pub while Nadia hopefully waved a twenty-pound note under the nose of a bored-looking barman, who was nodding his head slightly to the overpowering beat as he confidently filled several stacked pints from the tap. The couple of large glasses of wine we'd already got through were starting to kick in, and I was feeling rather proud of myself for not slinking off home.

'Excuse me.' A suited arm reached over our heads to pick up two of the lagers, some of which slopped over my wrist and hand in transit.

'Careful!' I turned, frowning – to see Rich, Lou's husband, looking down at me in surprise.

'Soph!' he said, holding the drinks a little wider as he leant in and gave me a quick kiss. I smelt a mixture of booze and sandalwood as his stubble scratched my cheek. 'Sorry about that.' He nodded at the stain on my sleeve. 'I thought I was about to get an earful then.'

I grinned. 'As it's you, I'll let you off. What are you doing here?'

He gave me a deadpan look. 'The shortlist for the Elite Awards was announced today, recognizing the achievements of our sales persons who have outperformed their targets.'

I pulled a face.

'Exactly. We've brought them all out to "celebrate" in advance of the proper winner announcement next week. Actually, it's a pretty good gig. Twenty of them from the worldwide offices, and their wives or husbands, get taken off to some exotic location for a long weekend – five-star hotel, golf, spas, that kind of thing.'

'And senior management tag along for the jolly?'

'Yup.' He winked. 'Although Lou is already saying she doesn't want to come this year.' He sighed. 'It's in New York and she says that's too far to be away from the kids. She was meant to be here tonight too, but the babysitter didn't turn up.'

Hmmm. That old get-out clause. More like Lou couldn't be bothered and now had her PJs on with her feet up in front of the TV.

'It was actually quite important that she came – not so much to *this* bit, admittedly – but all of the other wives are here. She said she's going to try and find someone else and still make it, but...' He shrugged.

If anyone was capable of dredging up a last-minute sitter from nowhere, it was Lou. She would have if she'd wanted to.

I smiled and remained diplomatically silent.

'Anyway, how are you? Sorry to hear about you and Marc.'

My smile slipped. I'd specifically asked Lou not to tell anyone. 'Thanks.'

'I think you're well shot, to be honest, Soph,' he said matter-of-factly. 'The guy was an arse. What are you drinking?'

'I'm fine, thanks. My friend is getting them.' I nodded over at Nadia, who was now deep in conversation with the person standing next to her, still holding the twenty-pound note.

'Hmmm,' Rich said doubtfully. 'Well, I'll get you one to have in the meantime. Sorry, mate, and a glass of champagne, please,' he called over to the barman, who nodded.

Rich turned and handed his pints, and the remaining ones on the bar, to someone else, then passed me my glass. 'Here's to freedom and fresh starts. Right, I'd better go and do the work schmoozy bit.' He suddenly looked gloomy. 'Lou's so much better at this bit than me. Bloody babysitter... See you later!' He bent and gave me another kiss and then began to cut through the crowd.

Nadia appeared instantly at my shoulder. 'And that is—?'

'Rich.'

She gave me a suggestive look.

'God, no.' I laughed. 'Lou's husband. My best friend, Lou?' I elaborated as she looked back at me blankly.

'Blimey.' She turned and looked at Rich's departing back. 'He's a bit familiar for a best friend's husband, isn't he?'

'I've known him for years. We were all at university together. In fact, I dated him before Lou did.'

'Ah,' she said in satisfaction, as if I'd just solved a puzzle for her.

'When I say dated, I'm talking no more than a two-week thing. And everyone dated everyone then. Four of my friends from one house shagged the same bloke at various points – he just kept turning up at breakfast. But you do that sort of thing when you're twenty, don't you?'

'Well, obviously you did!' She laughed. 'The things you learn about people…! Anyway, I've got your drink.'

I hesitated, then took it with my free hand.

'Look at you!' Nadia remarked. 'Mrs I'm-only-having-two. I didn't realize you meant one for each hand. Marc needs to let you out with us more often!'

I stiffened briefly, and then took a large mouthful of my champagne. I wasn't going to think about Marc. Interesting that Rich had said he thought he was an arse, though. I'd never once got that impression from him.

The more drunk I became on my empty stomach, the more his comment played on my mind. An arse in what way, exactly? I got to my feet abruptly, leaving the shrieks of shot-fuelled laughter from our collective tables, and wove off in search of Rich and some answers.

I couldn't see him anywhere, though. The crowds had thinned out slightly and I decided he must have left. Disappointed, I was about to return to the work lot when I suddenly noticed him sitting in a dark booth talking to a pretty redhead who was most certainly not my best friend. They were sitting very close and both drinking champagne. It looked extremely cosy indeed. I thought of Nadia's earlier comment about his familiarity and, without a second thought, I marched over to them.

'May I have a word?' I said frostily, as they both looked up in surprise.

'Sure,' Rich said easily, and got to his feet.

I strode off, bumping into a table as I careered across to the other side of the room so that we would be out of earshot, at which point I swung around furiously, only to realize he was *laughing*.

'Are you all right, Soph? You looked like you were trying to dodge a crocodile for a moment there.'

I stared at him, completely thrown. 'What?'

'A crocodile,' he said, yawning slightly. 'They can only run in straight lines, so if you need to escape from one, you zigzag. And you were zigzagging a-plenty just then.' He swayed slightly.

'You're pissed,' I said. 'What the hell are you talking about, crocodiles?'

'It's true,' he protested. 'Google it. And I'm not the one cannoning off the furniture.'

I blinked. 'Yes, well, we're not talking about me. We're talking about *you*, flirting with little Miss Hendricks over there, like Lou doesn't exist.'

His smile faded. 'Sorry?'

'I'm not blind, *Richard*,' I retorted. 'I could see exactly what was going on. Finish your drink and go home to your wife.'

'Fuck off,' he said suddenly.

Shocked, I took a step back. 'What did you just say?'

'I said fuck off,' he repeated angrily. 'You don't know the first thing you're talking about. How bloody dare you, sitting in your ivory tower like you have all the answers. "Go home to your wife"? How patronizing can you get? Who the hell do you think you are?'

I was stunned – he was *really* angry. And also the second man in as many weeks to tell me I was patronizing. My eyes pricked with tears as the confrontations with Rich and Marc drunkenly morphed into one. I gave a sob, turned and fled back to my colleagues.

Nadia, pale and shakily looking as if she was about to puke, was being led off to the loo by two girls from Accounts, as everyone else chanted 'Ben! Ben! Ben!' at the man of the moment as he downed several Jägerbombs back to back, retched slightly, tried to sit down and completely missed his chair.

In the gales of laughter that followed, no one noticed me pick up my coat and bag. I barely looked at the two bouncers who said, 'Goodnight,' and held the door open for me.

Rushing out into the cold February air, tears streaming down my face, I looked around desperately for a cab to take me to the station. There wasn't one, and I just stood there stupidly for a moment, unable to think what to do.

A couple of blokes smoking by the door started to eye me with inebriated curiosity. Shit, one of them was starting to come over. I edged away nervously, willing a taxi to appear with all my heart. I just wanted to go home.

'Soph!' I heard a shout behind me and turned to see Rich clattering down the pub steps. The random bloke shrugged and turned back to his mates as Rich hurried over.

I deliberately turned my back and started off up the street. As he chased after me, another of the men cat-called, 'Don't think you're getting it tonight, mate. I wouldn't bother.'

'Soph, wait!' Rich panted up to me. 'Where are you going?'

I actually had no idea.

'Jesus, you walk fast.' He grabbed my arm.

'Get off!' I tried to pull myself free.

'You're crying?' he said, surprised. 'Oh, shit. Sophie, I'm really sorry. I didn't mean it, I—'

But it was too late. I burst into yet more noisy, pissed and snotty sobs, like my heart was breaking.

'Come here!' He pulled me into a warm hug and wrapped his arms tightly around me, making us both almost wobble over. 'I'm sorry. I'm so sorry. I wasn't flirting with her, though. I wasn't doing anything, I swear!'

My tears soaked into the lapel of his overcoat as he began to pat my back, and then rub it.

'Can you not do that?' I said after a moment. 'It's making me want to be sick.'

'Sorry,' he said again.

I pulled back and looked up him exhaustedly, squinting slightly as some prat in a parked car over the road from the pub accidentally put their lights on full beam. 'I want to go home.'

'I'll get you a cab.' He took my hand and began to drag me up the street. 'I'm sure we'll find one up here,' he said confidently.

I sat down on a bench and put my head in my hands as everything began to spin slightly, while Rich tried to hail a taxi by standing in the middle of what was quite a busy main road and shouting, 'Oi!' I realized I'd had way too much to drink and silently pleaded with God to make me feel better.

'Soph!'

I roused myself and opened my eyes to see Rich standing next to a mini-cab with the back door open. I began to protest about safety but he waved an arm. 'I'll take you all the way back to yours, and then go home from there. What? Of course it's not too far! I'll just expense it. C'mon.'

We both flopped in, the door closed and we lurched off, slipping around on the badly fitting velour seat covers. The cab smelt strongly of pine needles and stale fags. Rich's head was already lolling forwards onto his chest. I closed my eyes and tried to focus hard on not being sick as my stomach sloshed around inside me like a wet blancmange. I think I came to halfway home, blinking and peering out of the window in confusion, not really recognizing where I was. I turned to look briefly at Rich, who now had his head back on the seat and was snoring.

A vague memory of waking up next to him twenty years ago, us lying in my single student bed, stirred somewhere in my head, before I closed my eyes again.

'I said EXCUSE ME!'

I woke with a jolt to find the taxi driver shouting at Rich and me, and realized to my surprise that we were holding hands.

Rich pulled away and began to fumble around in his wallet for some cash.

I climbed out unsteadily into the cold air and began to stagger up the small drive. I tried to find my keys for what felt like an age, and then couldn't get any of them into the lock.

'Here, I'll do it.' Rich, who was now, for some reason, standing behind me, reached over and took them. I looked at him in confusion, and realized the cab had gone. 'S'not the right ones,' Rich said conclusively, and my attention returned to the more pressing conundrum of getting in, as I wordlessly took them back and tried again, then again.

The lock was briefly illuminated as a sudden bright light flashed on, making Rich swear and painfully scrunch his eyes shut, although I *almost* managed to get the key in… but then it went off again just as abruptly, plunging us back into darkness.

'Just put it back on, so you can see,' Rich slurred.

'I didn't do anything. Next door's cat must have set off their security thingy.'

'I'm telling you, it's not the right key—'

'It's *my* house.' I glared up at him mutinously and had another go, at which the door swung open. 'Ha!' I turned back to him triumphantly.

He gave me a strange look, then suddenly ducked his head and kissed me on the lips.

'What are you—' I gasped, but before I could say anything more, he was kissing me again. I automatically closed my eyes and, as we tumbled in backwards through the door, it felt as if we were beginning to hurtle in reverse on some sort of manic theme park ride, like I was rushing past streams of bright lights, falling back twenty years to the tiny bedroom in my halls: Rich frantically stripping off his white, tight T-shirt to reveal his gap-year tanned torso, and me wriggling out of my denim cut-offs... Only somehow we weren't there after all, we were in my hall at home, and it was my blouse coming off and Rich's work shirt. Then we were already in bed, and it wasn't the single one I'd had back then, but mine and Marc's. I was gasping again, while vaguely aware that we were both naked and, before I knew it, we were having sex.

That much I'm certain of, but as for the specifics, I don't know if we actually managed to do it for more than a moment, or if he came... I don't really remember any of the details at all.

I don't tell Alice that last bit, of course. It's a) too shaming, and b) I'm her big sister. 'He was much drunker than I realized, too,' I say instead. 'When he went to go, I noticed we'd left the front door slightly open – that's how far gone we both were.'

'Oh God, Sophie!' is all Alice can say.

'I know,' I whisper. 'I know. He took off at 3 a.m. I'm not even sure how he got home. It was awful. We both woke up and just didn't say anything. We couldn't. We lay there, about as far away from each other as we could possibly get, and then he suddenly said out of nowhere, "I'm not making excuses, but Lou and I haven't slept together since Tilly was born... But then I expect you know that already, don't you?"'

'Did you?' Al asks, curious in spite of herself.

'No! Lou doesn't talk about that sort of thing with me. I knew she had a rough time having Tilly, but I had no idea they'd not had sex in three years.'

'Jesus!' Al says. 'Poor guy! I mean, he's still a complete shit, but, wow... That's a long time.'

'Yeah, well, *I* don't have any excuse, do I?'

'No,' Alice says, after a pause. 'No, you don't.'

'I'm disgusted that I can have done this to Lou, and Marc. When Lou wanted to start seeing Rich at uni – which was ages after we'd broken up – she came and asked me if I was OK with it, and said she wouldn't start seeing him if I minded, because my friendship was more important to her.' I hang my head. 'I mean, yes, I was horribly drunk, but I know she wouldn't accept that as any kind of excuse, and as for Marc...'

'You're not going to tell them, are you?' Alice interrupts incredulously.

'Of course not! Do you know the devastation that would cause? Rich and I agreed no one must *ever* know. I shouldn't have even told you.'

'So what happened with Marc the next day, then? You contacted him, I guess?'

'No. He came round to the house that afternoon,' I say quietly, looking at the engagement ring sparkling on my third finger. 'Just turned up out of the blue – didn't call first or anything.' I take a deep breath. 'He said he was so sorry for the last two weeks, he was very grateful for my understanding, and that I knew him well enough to know how stressed he'd been, that he really needed some space to properly work everything out, but he'd given everything a lot of thought. He could see where I was coming from, and he'd considered carefully what he was going to say to me next... And that's when he went down on one knee.'

'Bloody hell,' says Alice.

'I know. I felt absolutely...' I stop and swallow. 'I felt heartbroken, actually,' I say, after a moment's pause. 'He explained how hard he's found it to learn to trust someone again, that it's not just him he has to think about, it's the children. That they've already had to cope with so much…' I look up, my eyes full of tears.

Alice reaches out and takes my hand very tightly. 'Are you in love with Rich? You must be, or you'd never have let this happen. It's completely out of character for you. Maybe *that's* why you got so angry when you saw him flirting with the woman at the—'

'Al, I'm not in love with him at all! It's been twenty years. If we still had secret feelings for each other, they would have come out well before now. It was a unique set of circumstances and I know how indefensible this sounds, but… I really was just completely out of it.'

'But you accept you might have said yes to Marc because you felt overwhelmed and guilt-tripped into it?'

'Well…' I feel exhausted all of a sudden. 'Possibly, but…' The letter is just sitting there over in my bag, on the other side of the room. 'It's certainly not something I can think about right now in any case, and—'

'No, Sophie!' Al cuts across me. 'You don't understand.' She suddenly looks furious, muttering, 'I *knew* it! I told him it was a bad idea.'

I stare at her, bewildered. 'Told who… what's bad?'

'I have to tell you something. They're all going to go crazy but I can't not – particularly after what you've just said. It would be totally wrong not to.'

'What are you talking about?' I say slowly, for an insane moment thinking that *she* knows something about the letter. 'Tell me what?'

Al takes a deep breath. 'The party later,' she says. 'It's not a birthday party. It's a wedding. *Your* wedding.'

CHAPTER FIVE

I stare at her in disbelief. 'What are you talking about? Of course it's not a *wedding*.'

'Marc said he wanted to do something really romantic for you.' Alice looks at me, frightened. 'He's organized the whole thing.'

'No,' I say slowly. 'You're wrong. We can't get married. He's not divorced from Claudine.'

Alice nods. 'Yes, he is. It came through last month. He called Mum, me and Imogen and took us out to dinner. He said he'd had an idea and wanted to know what we thought. He wanted to surprise you with a perfect wedding on your birthday. Imogen practically started crying on the spot. She was all, "Oh my God – that's like something out of a movie".'

'But you can't just book a wedding on someone's behalf!' I exclaim. 'You both have to give your notice to marry in person to the registrar for it to be legal.'

'That's what Mum said too, but Marc told her you'd already done that. After you went to look at Goldhurst Park as a possible venue…?'

I remember the day she's talking about instantly, and gasp aloud as I realize she's right.

'It's perfect,' Marc had said to the wedding co-ordinator, as I'd wandered around the art deco ballroom open-mouthed with delight. 'Once we know what date we want, I assume we just put a deposit down?'

'We're already booked for the rest of this year and quite heavily into next, actually,' she'd replied apologetically. 'We do sometimes get last minute cancellations though, and I know it doesn't sound terribly romantic, but if you're certain you want to hold your wedding here, it might be worth applying for your licence now anyway. Just in case something comes up.'

'Can you do that?' Marc frowned.

'Oh, yes,' she said breezily. 'You just tell the registrar's you've got, say, the third of September booked here, or some other date. They grant your licence, which is *venue* specific, but then you can use it for any other date that comes up here for another year.'

It had sounded sensible, so we'd made our appointment at the registrar's, only to be told that Marc needed to supply written proof that his divorce was concluded.

'My ex-wife *has* agreed to proceedings,' Marc said confidently.

'I'm sorry,' the registrar insisted. 'We need the actual paperwork. I can go ahead and process Sophie's application, but I'll have to put yours on hold, Marc, until you can get the documents to me.'

'Actually' I remember aloud, 'Shortly after that was when Marc told me Claudine had called off the divorce again. I didn't bother to tell the registrar to cancel my application. To be honest, I just forgot about it.'

'Well, Marc didn't.' Alice says bluntly. 'When Claudine finally did give him the divorce, he checked, discovered yours was approved and just waiting in the system, and applied for his! You should have seen him – he was beside himself with excitement. By the time we had lunch he'd already got the date booked at Goldhurst Park, sorted a florist, auditioned bands... even looked at dresses for you.'

'But he doesn't have the first clue what size I am!'

Alice nods her head again. 'Oh, yes, he does.'

I start to feel faint, and have to lean forward to put my head in my hands.

'He sent out the invites last month. He's got an RSVP at don'ttellsophie@gmail.com. He's invited all of your friends. Imogen and I helped him do the guest list.' Alice is confessing everything in a burbled rush. 'He nicked your phone while you were asleep to get all their numbers—'

Jesus – *I* don't even know who is in my contacts list. My mind has gone utterly blank. I can't believe what I'm hearing.

'He's asked Mum to book you in to have your hair and make-up done. He's got the rings – the works. He's organized it *all*. Lou's helped him a lot too,' she adds, wincing.

I sit up again and stare at the wall in front of me, on which is hanging a print of Klimt's *The Kiss*.

'I'm so, so sorry, Sophie,' says Alice. 'If I'd had any idea about you and Rich, I'd never have gone along with it. I mean, at first I said to Mum I thought the whole thing was a bit control-freaky anyway, to be honest, but then, as she said, Marc can't help being all lawyer-ish and detail-obsessive, and like *Imogen* said, it's not as if you hadn't wanted to marry him at some point at Goldhurst Park anyway. Plus, you had such a massively shit time with that anal-retentive Josh, who practically wet himself if you so much as tried to hold his hand... Imogen said she thought you deserved a grand public gesture, and I thought, yeah, you know what, if her fiancé wants to show everyone how much he loves her, and give her a day she'll never forget, that's got to be a good thing, surely? He wants to just throw open the doors once you arrive for the "party", and the aisle will be there in front of you...'

'I'm getting married later today,' I manage eventually.

'Yes,' she says, in a small voice. 'It never occurred to me for a moment that you ought not to be marrying him, or that something was going on. You'd just got engaged! I—'

'It's not your fault. Where is Marc now?' I ask, dazed. 'Not in Berlin on business, I take it?'

She shakes her head. 'He said that in case you rang him and got the international tone. He's gone to France to get Isabelle and Olivier. I *shouldn't* have gone along with it. I don't know what I was thinking! You're a grown woman, so why we have assumed that you—'

But I'm not listening to her, because everything is falling into place with a horrible, juddering thud. 'So Claudine knows what's happening later?'

'Yes. Don't worry, he's done it all properly and discussed with her how to tell the children – all of that sort of thing. He said that when she realized you two really were going to get married, she just stopped fighting it.'

I stare at Alice incredulously. Someone like Claudine doesn't just *give up*. This woman has spent the last seven or so months making my life as difficult as she possibly can. They honestly thought she'd roll over, just like that, while wishing Marc and me a lifetime of happiness together?

I am getting married in less than twenty-four hours and my fiancé's ex-wife has sent me a letter that I am only to open in front of everyone I care about most.

'I feel dreadful,' says Alice. 'What can I do to help? Is there someone you want me to call? Or should I just leave you to have a think about how you want to play this, and what you're going to say to Marc?'

Don't even think about not showing up.

I WILL find you.

I reach out urgently and grab my sister's hand. 'I don't want you to tell anyone that I know about the wedding. It's really important. It would kill Marc when he's worked this hard. No one need be any wiser that I knew all along.'

She looks shocked. 'But you're not going to go through with it? Sophie, you can't! You slept with your best friend's husband two months ago! I'm sorry, but that's huge. It's—'

'And I'm going to need your help to make sure that no one suspects I know a thing. Not Imogen, not Mum — especially not Mum! No one, OK? Promise me?'

'But you just admitted to me that you're not sure you said yes to Marc for the right reasons!'

I look at her desperately. No wonder she's panicking — I would be too, if the situation was reversed. But she doesn't understand. I *have* to be there. I have no choice.

And she really doesn't have anything to worry about. Claudine has no intention of allowing the ceremony to go ahead — that much is clear to me. She must be certain that whatever is in that letter, it is powerful enough to halt a wedding.

CHAPTER SIX

I lie in bed next to a fitful Alice, waiting for her to slip into deep sleep, my wide-open eyes staring up at the ceiling in the dark. Marc has arranged our marriage, and his psychotic ex-wife has just delivered a letter to my house via some thug who had pictures of my baby niece on his phone.

I don't know how to process any of this.

What the hell is *in* that letter? I know Claudine wants him back – she's made that clear enough on numerous occasions. She must be either poised to humiliate Marc, so that I will want to walk away, or it's got to be something that she believes is going to make Marc refuse to marry me.

My heart stops.

Rich.

But how can *Claudine* know what we've done? I've never even met her, and she lives in France. Until tonight, I'd not told a single soul what happened.

Unless Rich told someone… But he wouldn't have done. He has even more to lose than I do. Lou and the children are everything to him.

I glance across at Alice's alarm clock, shining away in the dark. The neon face reveals it is 4.20 a.m. I *have* to know if he's told anyone. I glance across at Alice, now peacefully sleeping, and very quietly, so as not to disturb her, I peel back the duvet and slide out of bed.

Picking my way around the obstacles on the floor of her room – an upturned hairbrush and discarded books among them – something else occurs to me, and I tiptoe around to her side of the bed to get her mobile, before padding towards the door and squeezing through the gap into the hall beyond.

In the sitting room, I flick the light on, push the door shut behind me and look around.

Alice's flat is fairly chaotic: there is a spread-out pile of magazines on the carpet, mixed in with some unopened post and a pair of her kicked-off shoes, next to a discarded dirty plate and glass, but I spy her laptop next to the sofa on the rug. I pick it up, sit down and open the lid. As it starts to whir into life, I dial 150 on Alice's mobile and, after a few automated selections, I get through to the lost and stolen option.

Someone asks me how they can help me with my account today – as if it isn't 4 a.m. at all.

I'm about to say that my phone has been stolen, when I suddenly realize that this may trigger the need for a crime reference number, which will also mean reporting it to the police – and I can hardly do that without explaining the circumstances. 'Hello, yes,' I say quietly. 'I'm calling because I can't find my phone anywhere, and until I can – and on the off-chance that it *might* in fact have been stolen – can you put a block on it, please? It's not the number I'm ringing from.'

I give them the first two letters of my password, which is Mum's maiden name, and then they ask me if I want to block all incoming and outgoing calls on the SIM, or just all outgoing calls and messages, and do I want to put a block on the handset too?

'Er, can you do all of it, until I find the phone?' I don't want that man to be able to see my messages. WHY didn't I put a more obscure passcode on it than the first four digits of my date of birth? 'No calls have been made since last night, have they?' I ask, dreading the answer. But, surprisingly, they tell me the last number dialled was at half-past ten last night, which was me calling Marc to say goodnight, so perhaps the passcode has done its job after all.

I block everything and, once I've hung up, I turn back to the computer, which thankfully doesn't require a password. I tap Facebook into the search and it comes up, already logged on as Alice.

My sister and I need to become considerably more security-minded.

I sign in as me instead, and then type 'Richard Hendersen' into the 'Search for people, places and things' box.

Rich's picture is a shot of him with the girls and Lou, taken on their last holiday in Spain. They are all smiling happily.

I hit 'Message'. **You haven't said anything, have you?**

Definitely no kisses. I frown and read it back. I'm not putting anything more than that. I have no intention of incriminating myself in writing, and if by some God-awful chance Lou were to see it, we could just about explain it away.

I sit back and stare at the screen. Well, there's nothing more I can do now. I may as well go back to bed. Yet I hesitate, and type in 'Claudine Dubois' instead.

She's changed her profile picture. This time, she's in some over-sized comedy pink glasses, sipping a cocktail – the woman who hired someone to break into my house. I wouldn't have the first clue how to go about contacting a professional like that. I presume you can't exactly Google 'hitman'. She obviously knows someone, who knows somebody else... Given that she works in a world that also encompasses yachts, private planes, very wealthy contacts and customers, I'm pretty sure the circles she moves in are used to operating at a level well above the law. Marc once told me how, when he hadn't been with her for very long, one of Claudine's bosses had invited them aboard his yacht for a day's sailing in the south of France. Everyone was snoozing and sunbathing after a lunch prepared by the on-board chef when Marc got up to look for a loo – and witnessed the boss calmly slipping a laptop overboard into the depths of the sea, as the yacht cut majestically through the waves.

'What did Claudine say when you told her?' I'd asked, fascinated.

'Um.' He'd tried to remember. 'I think she just said, "It happens."'

I'd pulled a face. 'Not if you're a normal person. I wonder what secrets were on that laptop?'

Marc had looked at me and laughed. 'All right, Jason Bourne. It was probably just dodgy tax stuff.'

'You say that,' I replied, 'but the other day I read an interview with some It girl. A gangster called her, demanding that she pay off her ex-husband's drug debts, or he'd pay her a visit. *She* then called a family friend who had connections in – and I quote – "the business of making people disappear for good". Half an hour later, the first bloke called back to apologize, saying he'd never bother her again... Claudine's boss could have had life or death information on that computer.'

Marc had snorted. 'The socialite's making it up. Anyone who actually did that is hardly going to blab it to a national newspaper.'

'Well,' I replied, 'I've said it before – the gulf between the super elite and everyone else is getting wider and wider.'

'I don't deny *that*'s true.' He'd stretched and yawned. 'People who have vast financial resources *do* approach life in a different way to you or me. It's the same attitude that makes clients think if they pay £450 an hour for my services, they have a right to call me any time of night or day, at the weekend – whenever they feel like it. Money can certainly buy you freedom, silence *and* anonymity.'

'Have you had to deal with some shady stuff for your clients?'

Marc had tapped the side of his nose, but then turned serious again. 'Of course not. All solicitors in the UK adhere to a strict code of conduct. We're obliged to uphold the rule of law and the proper administration of justice. If I commit a crime, I can't practice any more – it's as simple as that. No client is worth taking that risk for.'

Marc is a man who values honesty very highly. I realize I haven't deleted my message to Rich, and return guiltily to it, watching the evidence of contact vanish.

I close the computer and just sit there. This is not me. I have never, ever behaved like this before. Marc is out there somewhere now, having gone to collect the children, all of them excitedly anticipating the wedding.

I have to close my eyes to force the picture away.

Outside, I can hear the first stirrings of the dawn chorus and, glancing tiredly at the thin curtains, I can see it is already starting to get light.

I lean my head back on the sofa. Marc will have told Isabelle she can be a bridesmaid, I know he will. I rest my fingers on my temples and think about Issy when I last saw her – only a month ago – running happily into her and Olivier's new room at the house to check that the shoal of four little fish we made together was still hanging up. It was my mother who helped me find something we could bond over: at her suggestion, I bought some rainbow felt, sequins and coloured beads, thinking we could make Isabelle a bag – but Issy had had other ideas, hence the fish, now suspended from the ceiling. She'd giggled as I stuffed them with balls of cotton wool, only for one to pop out of a gap in my inexpert stitching. The sound had lit me up inside, making me smile, and she'd grinned shyly back at me. They are now the first thing she rushes to see whenever she arrives. Sometimes I go in there and just look at them, sequins shimmering in the dark as they catch the street light outside, twisting quietly in the otherwise still room, waiting for her to return.

My insides knot up. This is all going to happen in front of the children. Has Claudine not considered that, if nothing else? It's one thing to annihilate me – she couldn't be about to expose me if I hadn't done something wrong in the first place – but to let her kids witness this? Has she not thought about the damage this is going to do to them?

And Marc. Oh my God – Marc.

Little things over the last two months are starting to make sense now: why he insisted we should have my birthday party at Goldhurst Park – 'It's the ideal opportunity to test-run them and check if the service is really as good as everyone says it is'; he suggested it should be black tie too – 'No one ever gets dressed up these days. You ought to have a really glamorous night.'

I'd been a bit carried away with that as an idea, and mused that maybe it would be fun to have a forties theme. 'You know, forties dress – I'm forty.'

'Yes, I get it.' He'd smiled. 'But I wouldn't. People hate all of that fancy dress stuff. It's a faff. Play it safe.'

He's even bought me a dress – the man who denounces shopping as 'the ideal way to flush a perfectly good afternoon down the lav'. I've always assumed wedding-dress shopping would include me coming out of a changing room in a gown that would make my mum and sisters well up, but the image of him thoughtfully selecting something for me instead makes *me* want to cry. This is going to devastate him.

How, *how* can Claudine be willing to do this to Marc all over again? Does she actually believe that if she stops the wedding he will go back to her? Or is this simply spite: *'I can't have him, so no one will.'*

My heart flutters with sudden panic. It's not an actual letter *bomb*, is it? I snatch up the computer again. The first search result I read says:

> Note the size of the package. Letter bombs can be small, but flat or thin envelopes are unlikely to contain them. Letter bombs are usually bulky, with irregular lumps. If there is an opening or tear, can you see any protruding wires? If so, or if there is any oil seeping through the package, then immediately move away.

Protruding wires? This isn't serious advice, surely? It sounds virtually cartoonish. Still, the envelope *is* flat and thin. I start to calm slightly, realizing that in any case, Claudine is hardly likely to send me something that might explode when I open it, given there's every chance Olivier and Issy might be standing next to me when I do. She's not that mad.

I rub my eyes. I am exhausted, but there is no chance that I'm going to be able to sleep. I reach for a blanket, cover myself and curl up on the sofa, my mind inevitably turning to Lou and *her* children.

What is my best friend going to do when she finds out, publically, that I have slept with her husband? I think about Rich again – us holding hands in the taxi. Was that me? Did I do it and give him the wrong idea? Or was it him? Did he intend to start it up again, all along? I shudder at the thought of him getting out of my bed, naked. I might have gone for his tall, lanky look when I was younger – hence my original crush on him, I suppose – but that was then, for Christ's sake. Marc is broader and stockier: a by-product of his regular gym routine and rugby training. I like that I always feel tiny and safe when I'm wrapped in his arms.

'You are safe.' He laughs every time I say it to him. 'I'll always look after you.'

The thought of him, such a man's man, bashfully confessing his idea to my mother and sisters over dinner is heartbreaking. It was just the three of us girls and Mum for such a long time, so the way he has so sensitively handled this – essentially asking their permission – is absolutely right and fitting.

How the hell could I have been so *stupid*? It was one thing to believe that Marc had walked out, but to then fall into bed with *Rich* of all people? I'm not a teenager any more – I don't need that kind of validation. What will I say to Marc and Lou? That I was drunk? That explanation would never mean anything to them, and I'm not even sure it does to me. All Marc will see is what Claudine did happening all over again, but this time with me. And Lou will think something must have been going on for years, and that her whole married life has been a lie.

Claudine must have had me followed. It's the only conceivable explanation for her finding out. If she's mad enough to hire someone to break into my house in the middle of the night, she's probably crazy enough to do that too.

I shiver. By this time tomorrow, I'll know for sure. It will have all unfolded and played out.

It will be over.

CHAPTER SEVEN

'Ding dong, the bells are going to chime!'

I blink and turn my stiff neck. Alice swims into view, standing over me apprehensively, holding a steaming cup of tea. 'What you doing out here on the sofa, you lemon?' She holds the drink out, expecting me to take it. 'Oh no, was I snoring?'

I heave myself up and, shivering, reach for the mug, burning my hands slightly. 'No, you were fine. I couldn't sleep.'

She climbs onto the end of the sofa, hugs her knees to her chest and looks at me. 'Not surprised. You're still sure you want to do this?' I nod and she inhales slowly. 'Absolutely certain, Soph?'

I give her a bright smile. 'No doubt in my mind.'

There is a pause. She sighs and says helplessly, 'OK. Well then, happy wedding day. Are you going to take his surname?' She shifts position suddenly, jogging my foot and slopping some of the scalding tea into my lap. 'Oops, sorry. Or will you just use Turner for domestic stuff and keep Gardener professionally?'

'I don't know.'

'I actually had no idea there was so much stuff to change – your bank cards, passport – although you need to change that anyway, FYI. Your picture is appalling.' She claps her hands over her mouth, horrified. 'Oh God, what's wrong with me? It's like now I've broken the seal, I've turned into some verbal incontinent. I know *nothing* about your honeymoon. Anyway,' she says hastily, 'I've told Mum and Marc you're here and that you've lost your phone.'

'Are they OK?'

'Yeah. Marc just texted back to say he's going to ring you in a bit, and Mum was a bit arsey about having got the champagne breakfast just for you and her when I told her to bring it here instead, but she's fine. She'll be over in about half an hour.'

'What time is it now, then?' I feel dazed.

'Half eight.'

My heart thumps. Already? I only finally closed my eyes at 6 a.m., which feels like it was about five minutes ago.

'Once she's here and we've eaten,' Alice continues, critically inspecting something on one of her fingernails before turning back to me, 'she's probably going to want you to go back to yours for some other stuff she's organized. Just so you know.'

'What sort of other stuff?'

But Alice shakes her head firmly. 'No, I'm not telling you anything more. I've let more than enough of the cat out of the bag as it is – there's pretty much only its tail left. You've got to have *some* surprises today.'

I'm pretty sure I've already got that covered, thanks, Al.

'Can I borrow your laptop?' I ask, and she nods, getting off the sofa. ''Course. I'm just going to nip to the loo. I'll leave my mobile here too in case Marc rings.' She reaches into her dressing gown pocket and pulls out her phone, before balancing it on the sofa arm. 'The computer is just there.' She points to where I left it when I switched it off about three hours ago, and wanders out of the room.

I hurriedly put down my tea and reach for it.

It takes what feels like an age to load up and, once it does, I scramble immediately to my Facebook messages.

He's replied.

Of course not. Delete this now.

Alice's mobile phone buzzes into life on the sofa arm, making me jump out of my skin.

Soph's Marc shows on the screen. Still holding the laptop on my knees, with Rich's message in front of me, I reach over and answer the phone. 'Hey Marc, it's me.' I try to sound as normal as possible.

'Happy birthday to you, happy birthday to you! Happy birthday, dearest Sooooophiiie, happy birthday to you!' he sings. 'Morning! How are you?'

'I'm very well, thank you.'

'Apart from losing your phone,' he says sympathetically. 'What happened? You're normally surgically attached to it. Well done for reporting it, though. I called it this morning right before I got Alice's message, and it said the number was unobtainable.'

Well, that's a relief, at least. 'Good,' I manage to say.

'The last thing you want is someone else finding it and racking up a great big bill that you're liable for,' he says. 'So, excited about the party later?'

'Very.'

'Me too. I can't wait, in fact!' He sounds incredibly happy.

I close my eyes briefly and shrink back into the sofa. 'How's Berlin?' I practically whisper, because I would ask, I think, if I didn't already know what I do.

'Oh, it's fine,' he says dismissively. 'The only thing is, my flight times are a little tighter than I realized. I know this is a bit much, and I really, really wanted to see you on my own first, but I think I might have to go straight from the airport to the party. Is that going to be OK?'

'Of course,' I say automatically. He'll want to get the kids sorted, I suppose, and greet the guests before I arrive.

There's a pause. 'Really?' He sounds a little surprised. 'You don't mind?'

I sit up a little straighter. 'Well, it's a little bit James Bond-esque' – I quickly inject a pretend wry annoyance into my voice – 'but

63

there's hardly much I can do about it. You'd better have bought me a good present, that's all I can say.'

'Trust me,' he says delightedly. 'You won't be disappointed.'

Now I know to look for it, I can hear that he can barely keep the excitement from his voice. Has it been like this for the last six weeks and I just haven't noticed? Or is it just that now the day has arrived, he is struggling to hide it?

'I love you, Sophie,' he says suddenly. 'You know that, don't you? You make me happier than I ever thought I could be.'

I glance at Rich's message and hit 'Delete', as if Marc might be able to see down the phone line. 'I love you too. I'd better go. I think Mum is coming over for breakfast or something, and I'm not even dressed yet.'

'Well, you have a really lovely day,' he says. 'Enjoy it, and I'll see you later, OK?'

'Thanks. Safe trip back.' I hang up and then exhale sharply. That was horrible. Really, really horrible. Everything I say just feels like another sticky strand that I'm somehow wrapping around myself in this bloody web I didn't even realize I'd become trapped in.

'You made up then?' Alice smiles, walking back in to find me still holding her phone.

I look up at her dumbly.

'That *was*, I take it, your husband-as-of-this-evening?' She frowns at me. 'You are actually awake, aren't you?'

'Yes, yes, of course I am...' I shake myself. 'Listen, do you think I could have some coffee? Would that be OK?'

She shrugs. 'Help yourself.'

'Can you make it for me?'

She raises an eyebrow.

'Please?'

She tuts. 'Only because it's your birthday...'

I turn quickly back to the laptop once she's left the room.

I know about this evening being a wedding. Please do whatever you can to make Lou miss it.

That's as much as I feel comfortable in saying. I have to be there, but Lou doesn't. The very least I owe her is to ensure she doesn't discover my and Rich's betrayal in front of the rest of our joint friends; although what could possibly convince her to forgo her best friend's wedding, I don't know.

'Here you are.' Alice reappears, holding yet another cup out to me. 'Don't you think you'd better get off Facebook and get dressed?'

'Obviously Lou and Rich are invited tonight, aren't they?'

She nods and sinks onto the sofa.

I don't answer. How on earth can this all be happening to me, when last night I watched a Sky Plus episode of *The Good Wife* over a bowl of Alpen, then went to bed like normal?

Alice sits there looking at me worriedly. The insane thing is, whatever scenario is now going through her head – Rich jumping to his feet, as if in some bad soap opera, when the registrar says, 'Does anyone have any reason why this man and woman should not be joined in matrimony?' – isn't anywhere near as bad as what is actually going to happen when I open the letter that's sitting in my bag.

The sudden sound of the door buzzer makes us both jump, shocking Alice out of her reverie. 'Mum,' she says in dismay. 'OK. Let's not panic. We'll think about this Rich and Lou situation. Don't say anything to her – not that you were going to!' she adds hastily, at the sight of my face. 'We can sort this, Soph. Don't worry. All right, Mum!' she shouts, as the buzzer growls furiously again.

I can hear Mum snapping crossly at Alice as she comes up the stairs, and then she's there, in charge of the room immediately, as usual, although slightly puce in the face having lumped up a large wicker basket, out of which is sticking the neck of a bottle of champagne. Her handbag is slipping from her arm, which is obviously irritating her immensely. Setting everything down, she barks, 'Hello, darling, happy birthday,' before straightening up and smoothing her hair. 'So.' She smiles tightly at me. 'Why are you here and not at your house?'

'Don't bollock her, Mum. It's her birthday; she can do what she likes.' Alice nips in behind her like a feisty terrier and whips the bottle out of the basket. 'I'll open this, shall I?'

'You'll need to chill it again first,' Mum says, adding pointedly, 'I had a rather longer than expected journey. You were saying, Sophie?' She looks at me and waits.

'She wasn't saying anything,' Alice replies, before I can even open my mouth. 'She went out for some birthday drinks in town, got a bit tiddly and came here afterwards because it was closer.'

Mum raises an eyebrow. 'But your car is outside.' She turns to face me with the full weight of her stare. 'You drove while *drunk*?'

'She came here first and then went into town,' Alice says smoothly. 'Let's just have that drink, shall we?' She pulls a 'Gah!' face behind Mum and dashes off to the kitchen.

'Well, at any rate, it's fixed now,' Mum says starchily.

I frown at her. 'What is?'

'Your car,' she replies impatiently. 'The man was just leaving as I arrived. He said to tell you everything seems to be running smoothly, but it'll need keeping an eye on for the rest of the day. He said you'd know what he meant, and he'll be dropping the invoice off at your house shortly.'

The man... I blanch immediately and hurry over to the window, peering down into the street below from behind the net curtain. All I can see now is an elderly couple going into the greasy spoon two doors down.

Oh my God... he really *is* watching.

'You look very tired, Sophie. You didn't think yesterday that, as you knew you were having a big party tonight, you might just have given yourself an early night?'

He was within touching distance of my mother, just moments ago.

'*Sophie?* Hmm, it's not often I say this, but today I think the hair of the dog might actually be what you need. Ah, and here's the champagne. Oh, for goodness' sake, Alice, these glasses are revolting.' Mum glares at my sister – who shrugs as she passes me one – before ordering, 'Small sips, Sophie. You want to keep a clear head.'

She has no bloody idea.

'In fact, if you're going to drive us all back to your house after this, you'd better have no more than half that.'

I grit my teeth and put the glass down. 'We don't need to go back to mine.' I don't want any of us in that house, which he got into so easily. 'I've got clean clothes I can wear with me here.' I reach into my bag on the floor and pull out my hurriedly grabbed cords and rather scrunched-up top.

Mum stares at me in disbelief. 'We're not going to a *farm*, Sophie. Anyway, the appointment we have is *at* your house.'

'But—'

'Why is this a problem?' Mum demands. 'I don't understand.'

Both she and Alice stare at me curiously, and I realize I've got no choice. Protesting like this just looks weird and the more I resist, the more suspicious they will become.

'Fine,' I say quietly, standing up to look for my shoes and my car keys. 'I'll get dressed now and we'll go.'

Mum looks at her watch. 'We've got about ten minutes. Imogen said she was on her way, but she always fibs and says she's left when she hasn't.'

I whip my head up. 'She's going straight to mine and she might have already left?'

'Apparently,' says Mum.

'We have to go now!' To their evident surprise, I quickly take off my pyjama bottoms so I'm standing in just my knickers, and yank on the cords. What if he's already on his way there? I can't have my sister arriving at the house alone. She's a mother – I'd never forgive myself. 'No, don't worry about your drink, Mum.'

'But we've got pains au chocolat, too,' she protests.

'Just bring it with you! We'll eat it in the car!'

'Sorry, Soph, but what's the rush?' Alice looks at me, utterly bemused. 'Can't I even—'

'No, you bloody can't!' I explode. She frowns at me in a 'What the hell?' sort of way, but gets up nonetheless and marches off to her room, muttering something about us all being mad. She reappears slightly sulkily two minutes later, also dressed, with shoes on and carrying a bag. 'Come on then,' she says. 'Let's go.'

We've barely driven more than half a mile before Mum looks at me, astonished. 'Just slow down. What on earth is the matter with you?'

'Yeah, Soph,' Alice says warningly from the back seat. 'What's up?'

'I…' I trail off, then say pathetically, 'I don't want to be forty.' It's the best I can manage. I see Alice frowning at me in the mirror and steadfastly ignore her, focusing on the road in front.

Mum softens, however, and reaches over from the passenger seat, pats my knee and says kindly, 'I know, darling. I know. It's very hard.' There's a pause, and she adds, 'How do you think it feels knowing that you're old enough to have a daughter who's forty?' She turns and looks out of the window. 'Not very marvellous, I can tell you. By the way, I meant to say to you about tonight and your father. I know he's bringing –' she pauses and says, as if there is now a bad smell in the car – 'Margot.'

'Of course he is,' says Alice from the back. 'She's our stepmother.'

'No, she isn't,' Mum says briskly. 'She's your father's second wife. There's a difference.'

Alice sighs.

'I'm talking to Sophie, thank you,' snaps Mum. 'I just want to say that if there is any requirement for us to be in any *photos* together, I'm quite happy for that to happen, but—'

'MUM!' barks Alice.

Mum rounds on her furiously. 'Alice, will you kindly put a sock in it? I just want to say, I have no problem with being in a photo with your father and Margot – I think she's a perfectly nice woman, actually – but I'd rather she wasn't in *all* of our family shots.'

'I really wouldn't worry about it, Mum,' I cut in. 'It's not like there will be an official photographer there. Why would there be? It's just my birthday, isn't it?'

There is nothing, of course, that she can say to that without entirely giving the game away, and the rest of the journey passes in comparative silence.

When we arrive at mine, the drive is mercifully empty. My sister hasn't arrived yet.

I turn off the engine without taking my eyes from the house. Imogen wouldn't have been able to get in without me, of course, but that's not the point. Everything looks exactly as I left it; the curtains are still pulled like we've gone on holiday and are trying to pretend the house is occupied to deter burglars.

Mum starts to climb out and I say sharply, 'Just wait here, Mum.'

'Why?' she asks, not unreasonably.

I ignore her and, reaching for the bag that contains the letter, clutch it to me tightly. I feel my heart start to thud as I walk up the path to the front door. There are no visible signs of any forced entry at all: no scratches, the door is closed, and my key slides into the lock easily.

I take a deep breath and push it open, staying on the doorstep as I look up the stairs in front of me. The lights are all still on. I glance down the corridor to the kitchen. It all looks completely normal...

'For goodness' sake, Sophie,' says Mum, suddenly right behind me. 'Are you sure you're not still drunk?' She steps neatly around me and marches off down the passageway. 'I'm going to put the oven on and warm these poor pains au chocolat before they go completely stale.'

'Mum, wait!' I call desperately as Alice appears next to me, looking confused. 'I think there might be a gas leak!'

She stops and spins around, now really cross, slamming the basket down before sniffing the air violently. 'It's absolutely fine.' She frowns at me. 'What is it that you don't want me to find?'

Alice steps forward urgently. 'Mum, leave it. There's nothing. No one's here, OK?'

I round on Alice in astonishment, who instantly clutches her mouth like she swallowed a wasp, as Mum says quietly, 'Who said anything about there being *someone* here?' She turns her head slowly and fixes me with a furious glare. Before I can say anything, she marches towards me, pushes past us, and stomps off up the stairs.

'You stay there,' I instruct Alice, and run up after Mum, petrified. 'Mum, wait! Just stop, please!'

She ignores me and bangs into Isabelle and Olivier's room, then re-emerges and turns straight into our bedroom, before yanking the wardrobe door open. I am almost sick with relief when it, too, is empty. Turning on her heel, she stalks off to the spare room – still ignoring my pleas to stop what she is doing – then finally checks the bathroom and even the airing cupboard.

'Mum! Have you gone mad?' I grab her arm.

'You've been acting bizarrely since the moment I arrived at Alice's. Who were you expecting to be here, exactly? I'm not a fool, Sophie.'

Oh God – she thinks I've got a lover hidden away up here? Hiding among the towels? It might be quite funny, in a bedroom-farce sort of way, if it wasn't completely terrifying for reasons she can't possibly appreciate.

'I'm not Dad,' I shoot back. 'I haven't done anything wrong! I don't know why on earth Alice said that. Who the hell else would be here except me or Marc?' I'm starting to shake slightly.

She scans my face. 'I don't believe you. Something is going on.'

I open my mouth, but fear catches in my throat. What if while he was in the house last night that man bugged it, or fitted a camera? He could be listening to every word we're saying *right now*. I need to be very, very careful. I clasp the bag, and the letter within it, to my body more fervently.

'I know I'm getting married today,' I blurt, my only defence being attack. Mum goes as white as a sheet. 'I found out about two hours ago. Is it any wonder I'm a little on edge?'

She takes a step back, the wind taken right out of her sails. 'Who told you?' she whispers.

I can't drop Alice in it. 'A friend emailed to say she can't make it because of an emergency. She must have thought she was sending it to Marc, but it came to me.'

Mum closes her eyes briefly. 'I told him it wouldn't work, that someone would make a stupid mistake like that. Oh, that poor, poor boy – he's going to be devastated. He's worked so hard.'

'He doesn't have to know,' I say quickly. 'I can pretend if you can.'

'Are you two all right up there?' calls Alice from downstairs.

I squeeze Mum's arm. 'You can't say a word to anyone. You promise me?' As I'm saying it, I know it's a ridiculous request

– tantamount to a house of cards, built on sand, in the middle of a gale. Mum is the least subtle person I know.

She uncharacteristically bites her lip, but then draws herself up a little more proudly. 'I won't breathe a word.' There is a glint in her eye as she challenges me to disagree. 'After all, I've managed to keep it successfully from you this far. Now go downstairs and tell Alice. I'll join you in a minute.'

I nod, and hasten to do as I'm told. Alice is waiting in the hall, and I yank her forcibly into the sitting room.

'I know, I know!' she bursts out, before I can say anything. 'I didn't think – my mouth just said it. You arranged to see Rich because Marc was away, didn't you? You were terrified we were going to find him here.'

I pause, then exclaim in exasperation, 'Of course not! I told you, nothing is going on like that!'

She looks at me sceptically. 'Well, I'm still really sorry. I'm spinning out a bit, to be honest, that you can be so sure that you want to go ahead with tonight...' She shakes her head. 'And when he and Lou are going to be there too! It's really messed up. But I'm not going to say anything else. If I don't calm down, this is all going to go tits up before ten o'clock. I get it.'

'Thank you. And I'm going to sort him being there, OK?'

'Sort who being where?' says a light voice behind us, and we both spin around to see Imogen standing in the doorway.

Alice, true to her promise, immediately steps up. 'Oh, hi Gen,' she says nonchalantly. 'Sophie is worried Marc isn't going to get back from Berlin on time for the party.'

'Of course he will,' says Imogen brightly, entering the room. She is fully made-up and her hair is immaculate; she's wearing a tea dress and heels, and carrying a basket not dissimilar to Mum's. She looks like Dorothy minus Toto, only in her mid-thirties, a bit too thin and with visible shadows lurking under carefully applied

Touché Éclat. 'Anyway. Happy birthday, Sophie! I've made you some birthday cupcakes!' She reaches into her basket and pulls out a bright pink cake, on top of which is a giant sugar paste – and very orange – flower. It looks like a Mr Men drawing. She inspects it anxiously, before holding it out.

'Thank you.' I manage to take it, feeling like someone has smashed me over the head with a baseball bat and no one else has noticed.

'I know what you're thinking,' she says proudly. 'But it's actually just a Wilton 2D nozzle and a standard bag.'

Alice stares at her. 'I'm pretty sure that's not what she's thinking, Gen.'

Mum appears behind us, once again cool, calm and collected. 'Hello, darling.' She kisses Imogen, then looks at her watch. 'You didn't leave when you said after all, then?'

Imogen flushes and says tersely, 'Liza's back is out and because we are now effectively her employers, we're having to pay her sick leave, which means I can't afford a babysitter, so Ed is having to look after Evie all day on his own. I had a lot to organize and leave out for them before I could go.'

'I'm not criticizing, Imogen,' says Mum airily. 'Just remarking. That's wonderful that Ed is looking after her all day. You *are* brave.' Imogen looks stricken, but Mum has already turned away, only to spy me holding the cake. 'I don't think so,' she says. 'Put it down.'

I hand it to Alice in silence, who shrugs and starts to eat it.

'We want to be able to fit into our party frock later, don't we?' Mum looks at me pointedly and gives me a huge theatrical wink, but luckily neither of the other two notice: Alice is licking icing off her fingers, and Imogen is fretfully texting Ed, presumably to ask him if he's *sure* he can cope.

What I really want to do, more than anything, is escape them all, so I can try to think. There has to be something I can do, something that will—

'Now, Sophie.' Mum appears right next to me, taking my elbow like I'm an invalid, before guiding me towards the sofa. 'We have a little treat for you. We've arranged for a very nice lady to come to the house and give you a treatment. It's a detoxing sort of thing. Very good for drainage.' The doorbell suddenly rings. 'Ah, that will be her now.' Mum smiles brightly. 'Do you have a bus to catch?'

I have no idea what she's talking about – what bus? Where? I stare at her dumbly.

'You're still holding your bag.' She motions patiently to it. 'Put it down, and do try to relax.' She says the last bit with emphasis before turning to my sister. 'Imogen, go and answer the door, will you, dear?'

I look around, trying to decide where is going to be the safest place to keep the letter. I don't want to let it out of my sight. I can't run the risk of losing it. I'm still holding the bag, paralyzed with inaction, when Imogen reappears carrying a huge bunch of flowers. 'It wasn't her – it was these.'

'Ahhh!' chorus Mum and Alice. 'Good boy, Marc,' Mum adds approvingly, which makes me blush in spite of myself.

Gen passes me the bouquet of white lilies and chrysanthemums, and I put the bag down at my feet so I can open the card.

'I love you, Sophiiiiieeee,' teases Alice, watching me read it. 'You're so beeeauutiful.'

But there's actually nothing on the card at all. It's completely blank. I turn it over in confusion, and then look at the envelope. It simply has **SOPHIE GARDENER** printed on it. I look up at Imogen. 'Was there nothing else with them?'

She shakes her head. 'No, I don't think so.' She looks at the lilies. 'Bit funeral flower-ish, aren't they?'

'Imogen!' scolds Alice. 'Don't be so rude!'

'I'm not! Everyone knows that about white lilies.'

'*I* didn't. They're just nice flowers.'

'No, she's right. They *are* traditionally funeral flowers. Especially chrysanths,' Mum confirms.

'There must have been something else.' I search in among the cellophane as Imogen taps away on her phone, then exclaims, 'Ha! See, Alice? I *am* right.' She begins to read aloud: 'Lilies are a symbol of death, and at one time were placed on the graves of young innocents and…' she pauses briefly, presumably for another page to upload, 'in Europe, including France, Italy and Spain, chrysanthemums are only used for funerals, similarly in China and Japan, white chrysanthemums represent lamentation, while in other countries they mean honesty.'

'Read that bit again,' I say slowly.

'They mean honesty.'

'The bit before that.'

She looks puzzled. 'The bit where it says they're used for funerals in China and Japan, and Spain and France?'

Marc didn't send these.

She did.

You didn't need to sign the card, did you, Claudine? I get the message.

CHAPTER EIGHT

'You didn't notice which florist it was?' I ask Imogen, as calmly as possible.

'No. I know it's frustrating not to know who's sent them, but...'

I exhale. With a company name, I could call them and ask for the details of the sender, although I'm sure I'm right. It just sums Claudine up: a beautifully packaged, heavily scented threat. Funeral flowers? That's a truly horrible thing to send. And what am I supposed to infer from the 'honesty' connection? She's about to tell me the truth – or she knows I'm a liar.

'You didn't see which company it was on the side of the van, or when they asked you to sign for delivery?'

'He didn't ask me to sign anything,' says Gen. 'He just said, "These are for Sophie Gardener" and I took them.'

'What?' I say sharply. 'A man just gave them to you? What did he look like?'

'Oh, *I* don't know!' she says, exasperated. 'He can't have been attractive, or I'd have noticed.'

'Tell me exactly what he said to you,' I persist, trying to keep the urgency out of my voice.

'He said, "Delivery for the birthday girl."'

The hairs on the back of my neck prickle. 'How did he know it was my birthday? Did you tell him?'

'I don't remember. I suppose I must have done. I said, "She's not very happy about it," and he said, "Well, life begins at forty."'

My mouth goes dry. That phrase again – the last thing he said to me before he left my room. It's him. I'm sure it's him.

I rush over to the window and scan the street, looking as far as I can, up and down the road. There's nothing but parked cars in driveways, and no one is driving away.

I turn and sink down onto the sofa. I understand. The flowers are actually another reminder that, true to his word, he's still here, watching…

Stick to the plan, because I can reach out anytime I like and touch you… I let the bouquet fall slightly in my hands.

'Careful!' says Mum sharply. 'The pollen will drop and stain the carpet. Here, give them to me.' I hold them out. 'I'll go and put them in a vase.' She turns and makes her way off to the kitchen.

'I'd better do something with these, too,' Imogen says, lifting up her basket. 'Have you got a cake stand?'

If I'd had even the slightest idea that Claudine was capable of this…

'Sophie?'

I don't look up. 'No, Gen, I haven't. Sorry.'

'Oh,' says Imogen uncertainly. 'Well, never mind. A plate will do, I suppose.' She disappears off after Mum.

Alice comes over and sits down next to me. 'It was him, wasn't it?' she whispers.

My mouth falls open, and I turn to her, terrified. How on earth does she—

'I don't understand why you can't you just be straight with me? You're blatantly still seeing him. He was supposed to meet you here and us arriving has messed it all up.'

'Al. It wasn't Rich at the door. You think if we were having an affair he wouldn't have told me what Marc had planned for today? He'd never have come here the morning of my wedding!'

'Unless he's planning something to mess it up. I was

watching you – you looked scared shitless. You weren't just trying to find out who the flowers were from because you were curious, or you thought maybe the card had got lost. You were on a mission. And how am I supposed to help you unless you're honest with me?'

I hesitate. Should I just let her believe she's right? Isn't it better that way? It might be safer to let Alice think she's worked it all out – especially given that that bastard really *was* outside my house, talking to Imogen, just moments ago.

I'm convinced it was him. I know there's a slight chance that it was all perfectly innocent – Imogen might well have told some delivery bloke that it was my significant birthday, and he simply answered with a stock phrase that everyone uses all the time. And any number of my friends could have sent me flowers today; someone who can't come tonight, perhaps? The florist could have been in a rush, got distracted when she was about to write the message on the inside of the card and just sealed it up acciden-tally without actually doing it. I could well be reading too much into something that has a very simple and logical explanation.

But I know I'm not.

First the man 'fixing' the car. Now this. He is just as real as the letter sitting in my bag.

'Everything considered, I think it's just a lot safer if Rich doesn't come tonight.' Alice chews her lip.

'Oh, you think?'

'Don't be like that. I'm trying to help. I could call Lou and tell her you're ill or something and the wedding's off? By the time she finds out it was bullshit, it'll be too late.'

'Maybe,' I say, to placate her. 'Let me think about it for a bit.'

She nods with determination, ready to leap in and do battle for me, to protect her big sister. It brings a lump to my throat and I reach out suddenly to take her hand. 'Love you, Al.'

'I love you too!' she says, surprised. 'Hey, don't worry, Soph, we *will* sort it – I promise.' She squeezes my hand. 'You wait till you find out where Marc's taking you on honeymoon...'

'Don't tell me!' I try to smile through tears, which I quickly wipe away.

'I won't, but you're going to love it.' Alice looks at me, bewildered. 'Please don't cry. I've got something for you.' She reaches into her pocket and pulls out an old mobile. 'For your SIM. It should work fine – it's all charged up. You don't think you might want to just—?'

The doorbell rings again. '*I'll* get that,' she says, shoving the phone into my hands. Jumping to her feet, she rushes out into the hall.

This time it really is the woman who has come to give me a home treatment. Within ten minutes I am lying face down in my living room, on a portable massage table, curtains drawn and lights on: I'm naked, apart from some paper knickers, with my thighs being smeared in the same cold, gluey goo that is plastered over the rest of my body. It smells revolting and isn't improved by the beautician beginning to wrap me tightly in what appears to be cling film.

My mother and sisters are calmly sitting on the sofas beside and behind me, eating a selection of pastries and neon cupcakes, as if this is a perfectly normal way to spend a Saturday morning, while I am quietly going out of my mind, now that I finally have five seconds to think.

Can Claudine really have had me followed? In the cold light of day, that seems so extreme and outlandish, but I can't see any other explanation.

'So what are you going to wear tonight?' twinkles my mother merrily. I can practically hear her thinking: 'See? Look at me keeping up the act! Told you I'd do it!'

'I bought a new dress last week,' I mumble through the hole in the table, as I stare down at the carpet.

'Where from?' says Imogen. 'What's it like?'

'Black, and Jaeger.'

'Very nice,' says my mother approvingly, as my sisters chorus, '*Jaeger?*'

'Christ, Sophie! Did you get a matching jacket, shoes and structured handbag to go with it?' says Alice, appalled.

'Like the Queen!' says Imogen. 'Did you know that when the Queen wants to leave an event and go home, she puts her handbag on the table? That's like her secret signal to her staff that she's had enough. And when she's bored of talking to someone, she moves her bag from one arm to the other?'

'You need to stop reading the *Daily Mail*,' says Alice.

'I think your dress sounds *super*, darling!' says Mum.

I suddenly feel my stomach ball up with frustration. Please shut up! All of you! What does it matter? We all know I won't be wearing it anyway! I assume the dress Marc has bought for me is hidden in the house somewhere, ready for one of them to bring out later.

'I don't mean to be rude, um, Lydia,' I say to the woman, who is now busily wrapping my right foot – surely the only weight issues my feet have is holding the rest of me up? – 'but how much longer is this going to take?'

'I'm going to cover you in a foil blanket, then the hot towels that I'm about to get out of your tumble dryer, and after thirty minutes under all of them, you'll be done!'

Half an hour? My frustration twists over into panic. I don't have time for this! I need to—

'Lydia is going to give you a lovely manicure after that, too!' says Mum from somewhere on my right side, whereas moments before she was sitting on the sofa to my left. I can hear her starting to pick things up and then setting them back down, which is unnerving. 'What are you doing, Mum?'

'I'm just looking at this wedding invitation up here, that's all.' She appears to be inspecting the contents of the mantelpiece. 'Whoever wrote this is a very repressed person – and not to be trusted. It all slants to the left.'

'You're such a loony, Ma,' says Alice from behind me, and I hear the flick of the page of a magazine.

'Who is this Rupert and Harriet, anyway?' says Mum. 'I don't remember you mentioning them.'

'A bloke Marc knows from work.'

'Lawyers as well?'

'He is. She's an accountant, I think.'

'Well, there you are. Can't be trusted, you see?' she says.

I don't say anything to that. I'm now worrying that I shouldn't have put the letter – sitting upstairs in my underwear drawer after I was actually allowed to go to the loo, alone, before the treatment started – out of my sight. What was I thinking? I imagine Mum trotting off up there, opening the drawer, *whistling* while rummaging through the knickers and bras before calling down to me, 'Sophie, darling! There's a letter here for you – I'll just open it for you, shall I?' I swallow – which is not easy to do while lying face down. My pulse starts to speed up too. I want to go and check it's still there.

'Marc's father has a very full head of hair, doesn't he?' Mum remarks. She's obviously moved on to photographs now.

'I've never really thought about it.' In fact, I *really* want to sit up, full stop. The ridge I can feel forming on my skin where my face is pressing down through the hole is starting to itch, and my nose is beginning to run.

'Haven't you?' She sounds surprised. 'It probably means you'll have quite hairy babies—'

Oh, please *stop*! There is simply no question in my mother's mind that I will have children. She has pointedly told me hundreds of times how much easier it was with Alice – when she was a much older mum – rather than with me and Imogen, because she was so much more confident as a person by then.

'With genes like that on both sides, it's a foregone conclusion. You had a full shock of black hair when you born. It was most disconcerting. Everyone told me it would fall out, but it didn't – it just stuck straight up in the air. I couldn't do a thing with it except tie a ribbon around it. You looked like a coconut. That reminds me, I have told you Grandpa can't come tonight, haven't I?'

I'm sniffing hard now in a frantic effort to stop my nose from actually dripping on the floor. 'Someone please get me a tissue!' I stick my left arm out and wiggle my hand around. The letter won't have gone anywhere. It is still in the drawer. Calm down, *calm down*!

'Here,' says Imogen, and I feel a tissue push into my fingers. I stretch my arm around the massage table, but I can't quite reach. It's such a small thing, but the inability to wipe my own nose tips me over the edge. I try to get up, and simultaneously all four women shout, 'Don't!'

'For fuck's sake!' I explode, lying back down. 'I need to wipe my nose!'

'Sophie!' says my mother, appalled. 'There is absolutely no need for that kind of language.'

'Here!' Alice appears suddenly underneath the table, holding a tissue. 'I'll do it for you.' She dabs at my nose ineffectually.

'That hasn't helped,' I say through gritted teeth, and sniff loudly again.

'Well, obviously it won't if you do *that*.' She pinches the tissue around either one of my nostrils. 'Big blow – as Rich said to the bishop,' she adds in a whisper.

I stare at her, shocked.

'Oh, come on – they didn't hear,' she teases, and pulls back out from under the table.

But Alice, this isn't funny *at all*. Despite the towels weighing me down and the fact that they all start shouting again, I begin to clamber up. One minute Alice is saying she isn't going to let Rich ruin anything, and in the next breath she's making stupid jokes like that? I can't just lie here as if this is all somehow going to fix itself. It isn't, time is running out, and *all I want to do is go upstairs and make sure the letter is still there!*

'Get this off me, now!' I say, trying to lift up my tightly bound arms. I feel crazily hot all of a sudden – my face is on fire, and my heart is thudding in my chest, practically pushing against the cling film, like it's trying to escape my body.

'She's shaking.' Imogen frowns. 'Is that normal?'

'Um…' says Lydia uncertainly.

I try to swallow. 'I can't breathe properly. Everything is feeling really tight.' I reach up instinctively and touch my neck.

'She's gone bright red,' Alice says, alarmed. 'I think we'd better get this off her.'

'My throat feels like it's closing up,' I pant.

'Oh my God.' I hear Lydia's voice behind me. 'She's having an anaphylactic reaction to the wrap!'

'We need scissors,' I hear Mum instructing. 'It'll be quicker to cut her out rather than unwrap her. Alice, look in the drawer there. Sophie, listen to me! Don't panic. You're going to be fine.'

'I'm going to call 999,' cries Imogen.

I think I start to laugh incredulously. This can't actually be happening. My head suddenly becomes very, very light… I feel myself toppling to one side like a plastic tree, unable to bend my arms or legs properly to break my fall because they're bound together…

And then there is nothing.

CHAPTER NINE

'Sophie? Can you hear me?' Mum's face looms into view.

I stare at her. I appear to be lying on the floor or, more accurately, the large tarpaulin Lydia placed under the massage table before she began the treatment. I flap my newly freed limbs around, like the Little Mermaid, and attempt to sit up. Alice and Lydia have to help me but, when I finally manage it, a searing pain stabs through my head, just above my right eye.

'Ow!' I wince, and lift my hand up to my face. 'What happened?'

'Don't.' Mum pushes my hand away. 'You fainted. Don't *touch*! Just let me look.' She peers closely at me.

Imogen and Alice are staring too. 'She *was* unconscious,' says Alice uncertainly. 'She must have...'

'I must have what?' I ask.

Mum sighs crossly. 'Alice and I were looking for scissors, Imogen was reaching for her phone, and Lydia,' she says icily, '*thinks* you hit your head on the edge of the massage table, but she can't be sure... I can't actually see anything – there's no obvious cut. I think you're all right. At the very least you're not in anaphylactic shock.' She glares at Lydia, who is sitting rigidly on the edge of the sofa, mouth slightly open. 'I think you had a panic attack, that's all. You're probably dehydrated too, and that didn't help with the fainting. Any weight loss she has from the treatment would be water-based, wouldn't it?' Mum looks at Lydia, who nods mutely.

I don't say anything either. My head is absolutely pounding.

'Let's go and get all this washed off you while Alice finds some paracetamol. Imogen, go and put the kettle on. Sophie needs sweet tea.' Mum stands up. 'Come on.' She holds her hands out to me. 'Try to keep the towel wrapped around you so you don't drip everywhere.'

We start to pick our way up the stairs, me moving gingerly partly because everything aches, and also because I'm trying to do as Mum says and not splatter the stairs with foul-smelling gunk.

'That's it,' Mum says encouragingly as we reach the upstairs landing. I brace myself for her inevitable questions – what is wrong with me? Why am I behaving like this? What is it she should know? – but, oddly, they don't come, and I follow her obediently into the bathroom.

Once the shower is running, she leaves me to it, closing the door quietly behind her. I step under the hot needles of water, which bruise my newly delicate skin. I let my thumping head hang as the paste dislodges from my body, slips into the shower tray and whirls away down the plug hole.

What the hell am I going to do? I stare at the bland white tiles. I don't see how I can do anything to prevent it all from coming crashing down around me.

At university, I had a friend who joined the graduate programme for the police. He and I carried on being good friends for about three or four years after we left, despite him being sent to various odd locations up and down the country on placements. I'd ask him how work was going whenever he was back and we met up for dinner in town, but he'd always cleverly dodge answering in specifics; apart from once, when he arrived looking exhausted, haunted and frightened. When I asked him if he was all right, he had shaken his head and said, 'Not really. But I can't talk about it, so please don't ask.'

'I won't tell anyone,' I had promised. 'You can trust me.'

He'd picked up his pint and said, 'Soph, if I told you – if I *really* told you what goes on – you'd never sleep again.' He drained it and said, 'Ignorance is bliss, believe me.' We lost touch eventually, but I can see now that he was right.

Ignorance *is* bliss.

I simply don't know how to handle this. What the hell should I do?

'You will not mention to a single living soul that I have visited you here... I will *know, and I* will *find you.'*

Suppose the police even bothered to come out – that man will see them and know instantly I've broken his 'conditions'. Going to a police station won't be any better. He's already watching the house – he'll simply follow me and find out that way.

What exactly would I say to the police anyway? 'A man was in my room last night. He threatened me – and left this letter.' The first thing they will want to do, in the absence of any actual evidence of a break-in, is open it. And then what?

My head is throbbing so badly , it's actually quite hard to concentrate, but something else occurs to me suddenly: suppose that I'm wrong, suppose it's not about me, and *Marc* has done something – maybe illegal. If the police find out, Marc will be struck off. He'll lose everything.

'Sophie?' Mum is calling outside the bathroom door. 'Are you all right in there?'

The letter could be a trap for Marc. Does Claudine *want* me to show it to the police? No, that can't be right – she'd have sent it straight to them herself. Why would she go to the trouble of involving, and threatening, me?

'Sophie?'

Unless she deliberately intends *me* to be the person that ruins Marc? Wouldn't that be satisfying for someone as toxic as she is?

But that thug specifically said I had to be the one to open the letter, and it doesn't make sense that Marc would have done something that could endanger his career. He's fully aware of what a heat-of-the-moment reaction would cost him. No, this has to be about me and Rich. Claudine knows exactly what buttons will push Marc.

'SOPHIE! Answer me!'

My confused thoughts scatter away like dandelion seeds on the breeze. 'Mum, I'm fine!' I call desperately. 'Please, just give me two more minutes and I'll be out. I promise I'm OK.'

'You don't sound it. Come out right now, please!'

I exhale in frustration as I turn the tap off, pull back the shower doors and, shivering, climb out onto the bath mat. Grabbing a towel off the rail, I wrap myself in it, then open the door.

Mum looks visibly relieved to see me standing in front of her. 'Right, let's get you sorted,' she says, turning slightly so I can walk past her down the hall into my and Marc's room.

I now *really* want to check the letter is still there. As I approach the chest of drawers, however, I'm overtaken by a wave of wooziness so intense I almost lose my balance completely, and have to sit down on the bed at once.

'Are you all right?' Mum says sharply.

I nod. 'Just feel a bit wobbly.'

'Let me look at you,' she says, but not unkindly, and tips my face gently up towards her. 'There's barely a mark there,' she reassures me. 'The photos later will be fine.' She lets my chin go. 'How's your headache now? Better or worse, or about the same?'

Is she trying to work out if I need to see a doctor or not? It's Saturday – that means A&E and a wait of hours, especially if I say the wrong thing and wind up being given precautionary tests. I *have* to be at that hotel tonight. 'A bit better.'

'And your vision? It's not blurred?'

'No,' I say truthfully.

'OK,' she says slowly. 'So can you stand up now?'

I take a breath and get to my feet. 'See? I'm fine.'

'Hmmm,' she says. 'Well, let's get you dressed, shall we, and go from there.'

Mum turns away from me, and I sink back down onto the bed for a moment, closing my eyes. I feel really, really sick, but then I haven't eaten today, and that stupid treatment can't have helped. In fact, it's probably that, not smacking my head on the table, that's to blame for how rough I'm feeling.

'I think if I have something to...' I begin, trailing off in horror as I look up to see Mum reaching for the top handle on my chest of drawers.

'Your knickers and bras are in here, I take it?' she says.

'*Mum!*'

'Oh, Sophie! Whatever it is, I'll have seen it all before!' she says, yanking it open and peering in. 'Nothing seems to match,' she says, puzzled, and then she actually picks up the letter, throwing it carelessly on top of the chest of drawers so she can rummage through properly.

I almost faint on the spot. 'Stop!' I shout, pushing past her so I can scoop the envelope up and shove it back in the drawer. My heart is pounding so loudly I feel sure she must be able to hear it.

Extremely surprised, she steps back and says quietly, 'Fine, you do it. I'll give you a moment to get dressed.'

I lean on the closed drawer for a second once she's gone, then wriggle into some knickers and a bra before collapsing back onto the bed for the third time, shaking slightly.

It's still there. It's safe. I *have* to calm down.

Mum knocks on the door and then comes back in. She's monitoring me for sure. 'You know, I think you do look a little thinner, actually, after that wrap.' Her tone is deliberately light, and I see her notice I'm trembling. 'Although God knows where Marc and Alice got that Lydia girl from. Now in a bit, we need to get going to lunch. Our table is booked for 1 p.m., and we've got the hairdressers at half past two. I doubt we'll be back until five and then I thought we would all get ready to go together from here. Imogen and Alice are bridesmaids, by the way, although I'm sure you've realized that.'

I sit there dumbly. We are all going to pull up together to Goldhurst Park. Everyone gathered excitedly, waiting... Oh God...

Mum eyes me keenly. 'Sophie, I *am* a bit worried about you. I know you don't want to go to hospital and I can see why, one hundred per cent; but Marc and everyone else will understand if we need to have someone check you over. Your health is more important than anything else, even a wedding.'

'I'm fine,' I insist and smile brightly.

'You promise? And you promise that you'll tell me if you start to feel unwell?'

'Mum, I'm just a bit upset at having whacked my head on my wedding day, that's all.' I avoid answering her. 'Can I look at it?'

Mum passes me a mirror. I peer at my face. There's barely a mark.

'You see?' Mum says. 'In years to come, when you and Marc look back on today, you'll not even remember you bumped your head.'

I glance down. How *will* I feel when I look back on all of this?

I want Mum's version of events – not the reality lying in wait for me.

'Oh, come on!' she says gently, but firmly. 'You're all right. This is going to be the happiest of days. Marc has worked so hard to make everything perfect for you, and that's all you need – the love that has made that happen. Get dressed, and we'll go and have a wonderful lunch – just us girls, OK?' She pats my leg and gets up. 'Now, Imogen is just getting the dresses out of her car to put in your spare room, so can you give it another moment or two before you come down, and don't go in there?' She lowers her voice. 'Imogen may not have hidden them very well... I must say, this is all much easier logistically now you know about the wedding. Don't be more than five minutes, though, or I'll be sending a search party up to make sure you haven't collapsed in a corner.' She smiles worriedly, looking tired and older than her sixty-four years.

I nod, and she disappears off downstairs.

I get dressed slowly, pulling on a pair of jeans and a checked shirt. As I'm doing up the buttons, I hear footsteps on the stairs, a swish of cellophane and hushed whispers, then a suppressed giggle as my sisters creep back out of the spare room and down stairs again. That'll be the dresses done. Alice gives a sudden hoot of laughter at the bottom of the stairs – presumably at something Imogen has said – and the sitting room door bangs, as if they've whirled in and slammed it shut behind them like two naughty little kids not wanting to get caught stealing sweets.

The happiest of days...

I can't think of a less apt description. While I know ultimately I have only myself to blame, like a cat playing with a mouse, Claudine is determined to have her cruel fun, no doubt relishing the fact that we both know the killer blow is about to come.

CHAPTER TEN

I mogen offers to drive us to lunch, and once I've carefully locked the front door, we make our way to her Volvo estate, which is parked on the kerb in front of the drive.

Alice climbs in the back as I scan up and down the street anxiously, before getting in after her. There is no one obviously parked, watching us.

'Ah, this is so cute!' Alice starts fiddling with one of Evie's toys that she's found lying in the baby car seat, as I clip in my seat belt and peer out of the window again. The thing is, if when we start to move a car pulls out and begins to follow us, what exactly am I going to do anyway?

'You all right, Soph?' Imogen asks.

'Hmmm. Fine!' Caught off-guard, I smile widely at her reflection in the rear-view mirror. At least Mum, if not Alice too, is going to expect me to start getting more and more hyped up now, and I need to start playing my part properly. It's hard to channel delirium, though, when I'm trying to work out exactly how Claudine is going to pull this off tonight.

'This is really clever, isn't it?' Alice says to Imogen, looking interestedly at a mirror strapped around the headrest to her left. 'So you can keep an eye on Evie without having to turn around?'

'It's essential,' Imogen says, checking her side mirror. 'I have to be able to see what she's doing while I'm driving.'

If I could have told Marc when it happened, I would have, but it wasn't just about us. Suppose he'd told Lou too, and destroyed their family as well? But I shouldn't have said that I would marry him. That is now very clear to me.

'Surely all you need to be able to see is the road in front of you?' Mum says to Imogen, getting comfy alongside her in the front. 'Evie's eight months old. She's hardly going to open the door and climb out.'

Imogen glares at her. 'I know *that*. But if I can't see her, I can't tell if her hat's fallen down and is covering her eyes, or something like that.'

Mum raises an eyebrow.

'What about if she's eating a rice cake or something?' Alice says. 'With the mirror, you'd know if she was choking. See, Mum?'

'Darling, you never, ever give a child of Evie's age something to eat in a car,' Mum says crushingly. 'If she did start to choke, and Imogen saw, she couldn't do a thing about it if she was driving. By the time she *was* able to safely stop, it would probably be too late. Isn't that right, Imogen?'

'Er, yes,' says Imogen.

I should have broken it off. He would never have needed to know what really happened. I think about Mum furiously crashing around my house today, as if trying to catch my father out all over again. It doesn't seem you can ever fully return to being the person you were before you were cheated on. Marc has risked so much to be with me. How could there be any way back for us after this?

'You *don't* ever give Evie food in the car, do you?' Mum says slowly.

'Of course not!' Imogen starts the car hurriedly. 'Let's stop faffing and just go, shall we?'

I glance behind us again as we pull away. No one is following. We reach the T-junction and Imogen turns left before going another hundred yards down the road. Still no one there... We safely reach the main road as I realize suddenly that the truth is that Marc and I were over the moment I wound up in bed with Rich. Did I know that even then? Was my saying yes to Marc's proposal not just about guilt, but playing for time? Delaying the inevitable? I turn quickly and pretend to look out of the window, my eyes spiking with tears. I didn't want to hurt him, or the children. I wouldn't want that for the world. I really do love them.

'You sure you're all right, Sophie?' Imogen asks. 'Got enough leg room?'

'Uhh hmm,' I manage. 'Plenty, thanks.'

So, ironically, Claudine is right: this wedding shouldn't be happening. But does it really have to implode so publically, and painfully? There's got to be a way I can spare us all that, at least?

'It's very spacious, this car, isn't it?' Mum says admiringly.

'Very!' Imogen agrees. 'Although I still struggle with it not having a handbrake – just a button instead! I can't say I don't miss my Audi, though.' Her smile starts to fade slightly. 'I mean, this is a much heavier, safer option – you can't go far wrong with it. It's got loads of space... and it's very practical and reliable. But I really did enjoy nipping around in the A3...' No one says anything and she stares out of the windscreen and adds more quietly, 'But there you go. Things change...'

'Jesus wept,' Alice exclaims. 'Remind me to start hiring you lot out to funerals, won't you? Put the bloody radio on, Gen. We're supposed to be celebrating!' She turns to me. 'So what do you want your fortieth year to bring you, Soph?'

'In fact, it's her forty-first,' Mum corrects.

Alice rolls her eyes. 'You know what I mean – don't be so pedantic.'

I clear my throat. 'I don't know, really.'

'I expect you and Marc will get married, won't you, depending on his divorce *finally* coming through?'

'Maybe,' I say gamely.

'Where do you think you'll do it?' she asks innocently. 'Here, or abroad?'

'Well, I don't know. We both want our families there, so not abroad, I shouldn't think.'

'Really? *In*teresting,' she murmurs. 'Then again, beach weddings are lovely – and everyone either gets married in some dreary hotel or in a marquee in the pissing rain in this country. I think you should tell Marc you want to go to somewhere like Barbados.'

Don't overdo it, Al. I shoot her a warning glance and she grins wickedly back. 'Can Gen and I be bridesmaids when you do get married?'

'No,' I say firmly. 'You can't.'

She narrows her eyes at me. 'What sort of dress will you get, do you think?'

She's really starting to push her luck.

'I don't know.' I pretend to muse. 'Depends on what sort of do it is. Nothing too tight, or tarty.'

'White, or do you think you're a bit old for that? What do you think about coloured dresses—'

Imogen swerves slightly.

'You'd probably look really nice in a—'

'Alice,' interrupts Mum sharply. 'Do you have anything to eat in your bag?'

'Er, yeah, I think so. Some mints. Why?'

'Put some in your mouth and stop talking, please.'

'Oh my God! Listen!' says Imogen suddenly, and turns the radio up. 'It's Granny and Grandpa's song!'

Alice finally falls quiet. 'I haven't heard this in ages...'

We all listen carefully to Nat King Cole's voice, promising to be near each time we call, and simply asking for our love, for ever, in return.

'Not since her funeral, in fact,' whispers Alice.

'Don't you think that's bizarre that it should come on now, while we're all in the car together like this?' exclaims Imogen. 'It's a sign! She's wishing you a day full of happiness and love, Sophie.'

It's such a lovely thing to say that I loosen my seat belt so I can sit forward and squeeze her shoulder, before looking at Mum, who is staring furiously out of the passenger window. I reach for her hand. She takes it very tightly in hers, without looking around.

'She was so proud of you – her girls.' Her voice is slightly choked. 'Imogen's right – I'm sure she's thinking of you today, Sophie.'

I kiss Mum's hand briefly and let it go, before sitting back. The painful sense of our loss and the empty space, as strong as the day my grandmother died, is tangible; yet somehow made just about bearable by the warmth and love I feel at hearing the music that instantly makes me remember just what it was like to have her standing in a room, right next to me. I can practically smell her perfume and feel the softness of her hands. She had particularly elegant fingers, my grandmother.

If she's up there aware of what's going on, she's *not* going to be happy with me right now. I lean my head back on the headrest and look out the window.

Which is when I notice a white transit van sitting in Imogen's right side mirror.

It's about two car lengths behind us, and something makes me lift my head up and peer at the reflection more closely. I can't see the driver, just the wing. I look around quickly to gauge where exactly we are on the bypass. We're about half a mile away from the next junction.

'Are we coming off here?' I ask.

'I can't tell you that,' Imogen says playfully. 'You'll have to wait and see! God, I'm *so* hungry! I might even have a pudding today... And don't say I ought not to, Mum, because I want one.'

'I wasn't going to say anything,' Mum replies archly.

I watch carefully as we approach the junction that leads to the popular industrial estate where most Saturday drivers will be going in search of sofas or computers or DIY tools. Certainly somewhere a white van might be heading.

It doesn't turn off.

I shift forward in my seat. 'Do you think you could put your foot down a bit?' I try to keep my voice steady.

Gen looks in the mirror at me in surprise. 'Why?'

'Just feeling a bit ropey.'

She pulls a worried face. 'You're not going to be sick, are you?'

'Can you just hurry up?'

She does as I ask, and we surge forward. She's right: for a heavy car, it's still quite powerful. We overtake a couple of estates and a Berlingo van. I glance in the mirror. The van is nowhere to be seen, and I start to exhale slowly. But then, right at the last moment, as we begin to slow on the approach to our turn-off, it slips back into view and resumes its former position.

It's following us.

Mum turns to face me. 'Is your headache worse?'

My mouth has gone dry and I struggle to think straight. What should I do? Let Gen carry on to the restaurant? At least it will be busy there, with lots of people around...

'Sophie?' persists Mum. 'Talk to me, please!'

'I'm fine,' I manage. 'Just a bit queasy.'

'Look, I'd rather just stop for a minute if you're going to vom,' Imogen says bossily, taking the exit slip road, then driving up the hill and onto a long, leafy road lined with neat, set-back houses. 'I'll just pull in here for a second.'

'No!' I exclaim in fear, as I see the van appear behind us once more. Gen swerves slightly and Mum frowns. 'Sorry.' I try to smile. 'I mean – can you just keep going. Please?'

'OK, OK...' Imogen, needled, falls silent. Mum continues to survey me for a moment longer, then slowly turns back in her seat. I deliberately avoid meeting Alice's quizzical gaze, concentrating only on the traffic in front of us. Mercifully it's unusually clear, and we sail straight into the centre of town, towards the same car park that we always choose.

'Go to the bottom level,' Mum says, just as she always does. 'There'll be plenty of spaces down there.'

We slow to approach the barrier and, swallowing, I can't help but look in Imogen's wing mirror. The van is now right up behind us, practically touching the bumper. I inhale sharply and hold my breath. All I can see is headlights, nothing else.

Gen opens her window, sticks her arm out, swipes the ticket and pulls away. I loosen my seat belt and slide forward so I can look in her rear-view mirror. The barrier comes down behind us, in front of the white bonnet, but because we're driving into comparative darkness, I can't make out the driver's face properly. Only as Imogen turns the corner to take us onto the lower level do I think I get a flash of a man's face in glasses.

It's him. It *has* to be.

The others start to argue over which space to select, Imogen insisting she can't get in one that Alice tells her is wide enough for a bus. My hands start to sweat. I wait for him to pull slowly down behind us. What's he going to do – park too? Get out and follow us? But I haven't done anything wrong! I haven't said a thing!

To my surprise, however, the next car down, as Gen begins to slowly back into a space, is a red mini, followed by a BMW.

'Sophie? I said, "Have you got any change?"'

I turn back to realize we have stopped, and they are all staring at me, waiting.

I shake my head and there's a pause before Alice says slowly, 'Yeah, I think we probably just need to get her something to eat.' She turns and opens her door.

My hands are shaking as I fumble with the door handle on my side, and we all simultaneously climb out.

I look around me anxiously as they begin rummaging in their bags for money, but there is nothing but row after row of neatly parked cars.

No movement at all.

He is nowhere to be seen.

CHAPTER ELEVEN

We're seated at our table and the others are listening to a waiter trying to remember the specials while I attempt to calm down. He's not here. It *was* him, but he's not here now. I have to steady myself...

There is a delighted 'Hel-*lo*!' behind me, making me jump wildly, as we all turn to see Lou standing there, a huge smile over her face. 'The birthday girl in person – what a treat!' As I get to my feet automatically, she gives me an enormous hug.

'What are you doing here?' I gasp, giving Alice a brief, horrified glance over Lou's shoulder, but she is staring studiously at the table, unable to meet my eye.

'We arrived a bit too early for our hotel check-in, so we thought we'd come back out for a cheeky lunch first. Got to make the most of the in-laws having the girls for the night!' She turns to my sisters and Mum. 'This is our first weekend away together in I don't like to tell you how long!'

I can practically hear Alice thinking: 'Three years?'

'I was just paying while Rich is in the loo, when I looked up and saw you all! Such a lovely surprise! Can I get you all a bottle of something to get you started?' She turns to the waiter. 'Some champagne for the ladies, please.' He nods and scuttles off.

Rich is going to appear any moment now. This can't be happening. My request that he keep Lou away from the wedding is obviously not panning out.

'No, it's absolutely *my* treat!' Lou holds her hand up firmly at Mum's polite insistence that she will get it. 'Sophie's the first of our gang to hit the big four-oh! Flying the flag for the rest of us, eh, Soph? So what have you got planned for this afternoon?' Lou gets out her purse as the waiter returns with a bottle and five glasses. 'Lots of lovely girly fun, I hope. I haven't told Rich, but I actually still have to get something to wear. It's so shameful, but I realized everything I've got, *this one*' – she nods at me, smiling – 'has seen. And I've been so manic recently, I literally haven't had five seconds to get to the shops.' I watch Mum's eyes narrow, and she sits back in her chair. 'So I'm hoping it won't be the old adage, "You can never find something when you're looking for it." No, not for me, thank you.' She stops the waiter, who is about to fill the fifth glass. 'Oh, all right, just a taster, then. Well, here's to the birthday girl!' She takes the glass and gives me a knowing smile. 'May this be a day you remember for ever...'

I ignore her heavy-with-intent meaning and go to take a mouthful of the champagne, remembering at the last moment that I probably ought not to, what with my potential head injury, and needing to keep a crystal-clear head. As Lou's not looking – busily knocking hers back – I surreptitiously place the glass down untouched.

Imogen blinks. 'Why aren't you drinking?'

'She's hung over, that's all,' Alice says quickly.

'It's never stopped her before,' Imogen says suspiciously. Her eyes widen suddenly. 'Oh my God! You're not... *pregnant*? Is THAT why you've been so pukey all morning?'

Lou's mouth falls open.

'No!' I say immediately. 'Don't be ridiculous! Alice is right, I had a bit too much last night.'

Lou looks stunned. 'Wow!' she exclaims, after a moment's pause. 'How incredibly exciting!'

Great. Now she's going to be hurt and pissed off that I haven't told her about this mythical pregnancy...

'Look at me,' I begin. 'I am *not*—' But further denials die on my lips as I see Rich appear at the back of the room, casually casting around for Lou. He glances over, does a double take, and just for a spilt second I see the horror on his face as he clocks the situation, before he manages to smile, wave and make his way between the tables towards us.

'Hi, Sophie.' He takes his place alongside Lou and gives me an odd little wave. 'Happy birthday! Hello, I'm Richard, Lou's husband.' He turns politely to my sisters and mother. 'I see the celebrations have started. Quite right, too!' He gives a jolly, over-loud laugh.

'Yes, sorry, we really ought to leave you to it,' Lou says, gathering herself. 'Standing here cluttering up the place like we haven't got better things to do. Good news, darling–' she turns briefly to Richard – 'we're going dress shopping now.'

'Oh, excellent,' he says heartily.

'I knew you'd be pleased.' Lou turns back to the rest of us. 'I'll be coming out of a changing room in a bit, and regardless of whether I'm wearing a bin bag or not, he'll tell me it looks wonderful. I never know if that's a good thing or not.'

There's a heartbeat's uncomfortable pause, then Rich says quickly, 'You always look great to me.'

I can't look at him. How can it be that the last time we saw each other he was leaving my bed?

'You're too kind, my love. Right!' Lou gets out her credit card. 'I'll settle up for this at the front, so don't let them charge you as well!' Reaching out, she hugs me again, then blows kisses to Mum and the girls.

Rich is forced by convention to lean over and kiss me briefly too. While I'm glad he does – because he always has and it would look very odd if he didn't – it's intensely uncomfortable for both of us. We don't make eye contact and he hurries after his wife without a backward glance, choosing to wait in the street while she pays.

'She's so nice!' Imogen takes another delicate kitten sip, waving cheerily at Lou as she disappears through the door.

'She's a little madam,' Mum says archly. 'You're forty, I'm not. I haven't had time to buy a new dress because I've had more important things to do…'

'You *are* a shit judge of character, Gen, to be fair,' says Alice. 'Look at your husband, for starters.'

'Hey!' says Imogen, annoyed.

'*Do* you think that, Mum?' Alice turns to her.

'He's slightly weak-chinned, but he loves Imogen very much, and that's all that matters.'

'Not Ed!' Alice says. 'Lou.'

'She won't age well.' Mum shrugs, and reaches for her champagne.

I sigh. 'She didn't mean to be rude. It's just the way she comes across sometimes.'

Mum raises an unconvinced eyebrow.

'She's a full-time mum with two small kids and a part-time job. Most of the time she's just knackered, and it can make her seem a bit short.'

'Is it possible she knows?' Alice interjects.

'Alice!' I hiss, glaring at her furiously. She's no better than Mum, she really isn't.

'Knows what?' Mum says instantly.

'Soph borrowed something belonging to Lou, which she accidentally broke. She didn't tell Lou at the time, though, and now Lou might have found out for herself.'

'Shut. Up,' I say, livid. 'And as for you' – I turn to Imogen – 'what the hell was all that "Are you pregnant?" crap? While I'm obviously delighted to hear how nice and slim I must look at the moment, I'm *not* having a baby. I felt rubbish in the car, that's all. Now we're here and I'm going to eat, I actually feel a lot better. Maybe it's psychosomatic, I don't know, but anyway – I'm totally fine. Now, can we *please* just talk about something else?' I reach for my glass of champagne and knock it back in one. 'See? Not pregnant.'

Alice watches me. 'You're psycho-something, I'll tell you that much.'

'I mean it, Alice. Be quiet.' I rest my head in my hands, elbows on the table as I massage my temples, eyes shut.

She's wrong. Lou has no idea, I'm certain of that, but I can't believe we just bumped into each other like this...

I lift my head up and stare into space for a moment. No, that's lunacy. So now my friends are following me too, are they? There just aren't that many nice restaurants in our home town, that's all. Lou only had a choice between about three. I snort in disgust at myself. Alice is right – I'm starting to lose it. I'm slipping into total paranoia, and I can't afford to go to pieces.

I sit back in my chair. 'I'm sorry,' I announce, after a moment's pause. 'I'm feeling a little shaken up. This morning has been a lot to... absorb.'

'Bird on the line.' Alice reaches for her very loudly ringing mobile, ignoring the irritated stares from nearby tables. 'Hello! Yes, of course you can. She's right here... It's Marc.' She passes the phone to me.

'Hey!' I say, trying to sound warm and carefree. Imogen and Mum smile indulgently, before picking up their glasses and turning to each other to chat. Only Alice continues to watch me. 'Everything all right?' I ask him, trying to ignore her.

'I'm fine.' He sounds really concerned, almost agitated. 'Are you, though? Why aren't you answering your phone?' For a moment I feel like I'm in a parallel universe. I did tell him I lost it, didn't I? I'm sure we had a whole conversation about it this morning! 'I got your text and tried to ring you,' he continues, 'but there was no answer.'

All of the noise in the restaurant, the chatter around me, the scrape of knives and forks on plates, the hiss of a coffee machine, fade away like someone turning down a volume dial. I am only concentrating on him. 'What text?' I say slowly.

'The one that says you don't want to have to hurt me.'

My mouth falls open. 'Read it back to me,' I whisper.

'That's it, Soph, that's all it says. "I don't want to have to hurt you." Umm' – he laughs uncertainly – 'what's all that about then? I thought you'd lost your phone?'

A message for me – *from my own mobile*?

'I...' I start to scrabble around for an explanation. 'I found it. And that's a message I sent to Alice earlier – she was winding me up about something. At least I thought I did. How on earth did I get you by mistake?' I swallow and clear my throat. 'That must have been surprising!'

'Just a bit,' he says, sounding very relieved.

How the hell is Claudine *doing* this? She's got my phone now?

'You know, the handset's been really playing up,' I say. 'I might just switch it off. If you need me, ring Alice again instead, OK?'

'OK.' He sounds puzzled, but doesn't question it. 'I probably won't now though, because I'm going into another meeting soon, and then later I'll be on the plane...'

'OK, OK, that's fine,' I say quickly, desperate to get off the phone and call my mobile company to find out why, and how, my phone has been reconnected when I barred it myself last night. 'Safe trip.'

I hang up without telling him I love him and turn to Alice

quickly. 'Can I use your mobile again?' I don't wait for the answer, just dial 150, as I did some eight hours earlier, back at her flat.

'Didn't the old handset I gave you work then?'

'Not really,' I say, distracted, trying to navigate the automated options. 'Kind of. The SIM wasn't registered or something. I'm going to try and sort it out now. Oh, hi?' I get up from the table, the chair scraping behind me, and walk towards the front of the restaurant. 'I phoned last night to bar all activity on my phone because I lost it, but somehow it's been reconnected again – my fiancé just had a text from me, which is really odd, given I haven't actually found it yet, or requested that it be unlocked.'

'OK,' says the woman pleasantly. 'Well, let's take you through security and I'll see what I can do to help you. What's your full name?'

'Sophie Gardener.'

'And are you the account holder?'

'Yes, I am.'

'And is this the phone number for the account you are calling about?'

'No, this is my sister's phone. I give her my phone number. 'I can't call you from my phone because, as I've said, I lost it.'

'Can I have the first and second characters of your password, please?'

'K and E.'

'Thank you. Is it OK to call you Sophie?'

'Yes, of course.'

'Sophie, I'm happy to pass you through security. So you say that you lost your phone?'

'I reported it at about 4 a.m. last night and asked for it to be barred,' I repeat. 'But, like I said, my fiancé called about five minutes ago and said he'd had a text from me. I don't know how that's happened, because I haven't found my phone.'

She pauses. 'I'm reading back through the notes on your account and they say you contacted us today at 8.30 a.m. to request that the blacklist be lifted on your phone. You correctly supplied the IMEI number, and so—'

'Wait, I didn't ring you,' I say. 'And I don't even know what an IMEI number is.'

'It's a number unique to each handset – it's on your phone. We ask for it in conjunction with your security details to verify the handset every time a blacklist is lifted.'

'So whoever rang you must have physically been holding my phone at the time?'

'Not necessarily. They could have been given the IMEI by someone else who has the phone.'

I turn cold. 'If a man contacted you, supposedly on my behalf,' I ask quickly, 'could he have requested that be done?'

'No. We have to speak to the account holder.'

So it must have been a woman who called them, pretending to be me. I start to exhale slowly. 'Does it say what number the call came from? Was it in France?'

'I don't have that information, I'm afraid.'

So for the last few hours, Claudine – possibly via that man – has been getting all of my texts, will have had access to my emails, my Facebook phone app... I freeze. I deleted Rich's message, I'm sure I did... Though I think it's about more than that, anyway. She wants me to see how powerless I am – how far her reach is.

This is about control.

'Please will you blacklist my phone again, and not reinstate it until further notice? And I don't really understand how someone could have got access to my account in the first place, without having to give my password?' I add pointedly.

'There aren't any notes to say that unsuccessful password attempts were made. Perhaps you'd like to change your password to something more obscure?' she says politely. 'It's not a good idea to use information like your mother's maiden name, or a configuration of a date of birth – people can get hold of that information very easily if they know where to look.'

'OK,' I say, chastened. 'Let's change it to...' My grandparents' song pops into my head. 'Kingcole. All one word.' It doesn't come much more obscure than that.

'OK, Sophie, I've done that. Now, if you think someone might have found and stolen your lost phone, you need to report this to the police and obtain a crime reference number. Can I help you with anything else?'

'No, thank you.'

'Well, thank you for calling, and I hope you have a good rest of the day.'

I hang up, but as I turn to walk back to the table, Alice's iPhone vibrates in my hand. A new text message has arrived and I look down to see who it's from.

Me.

All you have to do is open the envelope tonight, as per instructions.

My skin prickles with fear. How the hell is she doing this when I've literally just blacklisted it again!

Although I suppose that message might have been sent just before the bar came into effect. And it's not as if she knows I'm holding Alice's phone...

My stomach contracts. Does she? Can she – or he – see me *right now*?

I whirl around, wildly scanning the faces of animated, happily talking diners. I may have only ever seen pictures of Claudine, but I'm sure I would recognize her, and as for him... I knew it was him in that van. I'm never going to forget his impassive features staring blankly at me in my bedroom.

I inspect each and every table, aware that Alice is still watching me and is starting to look concerned. They're not here.

As Alice gets to her feet, I turn my back to her, walk to the front of the restaurant, open the door and hasten out into the street to look up and down it; but there is no figure suddenly darting away, or just slipping around the corner out of view.

I stare at Alice's phone again, the text from 'me' still sitting on the screen. I have to know that the blacklisting has now kicked in, that they won't be able to send any more messages. I need proof.

Holding my breath and calling my own number, I almost expect the sound of a distant phone to start ringing somewhere, but, to my huge relief, it goes straight to an automated message: 'I'm sorry, but the person you are calling is unavailable. Please try again later.'

If only that were true. I've never felt more exposed in my entire life.

CHAPTER TWELVE

'How is your head feeling now, Soph?' Imogen asks me kindly as we sit in reception at the hairdressers.

Like it's going to explode. She actually threatened me from my own phone. Claudine is not just pushing beyond all reasonable limits; she's annihilating them.

'You look a bit pale,' Imogen continues, concerned.

'I'm fine, honestly.' I force a smile as my hands reach to check, yet again, that the letter is still with me. I feel the edges of the envelope, and then rest the bag back on my feet.

'Good. I am *so* looking forward to a decent wash and blow-dry.' Imogen is palpably excited. All four of us apparently have an appointment at my mother's upmarket salon. She walked in proudly, us following her, as if she were the Queen Mother, and had clearly gone to great pains to organize it: everyone was shooting covert glances at each other and me – the whole staff seemed to be in on the secret. It was unnerving, despite knowing what they were all grinning about.

'Ladies! Hello! Hello! Now, someone has a significant birthday today, I hear?' My mother's hairdresser appears dramatically from somewhere at the back like a pantomime dame ready for the audience participation element of the performance. A large man called Carl, he's dressed in a white, slightly straining shirt and indigo jeans. His hair is excessively bouncy and curly, like a lamb's, razor-trimmed around his rather pink neck and offset by very pointy sideburns that protrude quite a distance onto his face. Somehow they accentuate his very heavy, square-framed glasses, behind which sit two beady little eyes. 'Hello, Maura, my darling.' He kisses my mother. 'I refuse to believe you can be the mother of a forty-year-old. It isn't possible.' As Mum blushes happily, he turns to me. 'And you must be the birthday girl! I gather we are going full-out glamour this evening – diamonds and tiaras, ahoy!' He winks at me. 'So you'll be wanting an up-do, won't you?' It's a pre-order, rather than a question, and he whisks me off to be seated at the mirror, the other three trotting obediently sheep-like behind us.

Without asking if he can, Carl whips my hair-band out and rakes his fingers through my hair. 'When *was* the last time you had it cut, sweetheart?' he asks quietly, as if it's perfectly obvious to us all that I've let myself and everyone else down but he'd still like to hear me say it out loud anyway.

'Um, about three months ago?'

He doesn't say anything, just starts to fan out my hair, then quite abruptly twists my head this way and that to get a proper look at me. It makes me wince, partly in pain at the sudden movement, and also because him forcing my head evokes the stranger in my bedroom touching me.

I instinctively shrink away from Carl's touch and he stops and blinks a couple of times, pushing his glasses firmly back on his nose as he stares at me in the mirror. 'I bumped my head today.' I look away, finding the silence uncomfortable. 'It's a bit painful.'

He regards me impassively again for a moment, then seems to spring back to life. 'Right, away from me.' He waves his hands at Imogen, Mum and Alice. 'I can't do anything with you three hanging over us like you've lost your cauldron. I'll come and brief your stylists in a minute, but in case they get any funny ideas, you two' – he points at the girls – 'are going upsweep too, and Mama – you're a low chignon.'

They disappear dutifully, and he turns back, gathering my hair very gently in his hands, twisting it lightly before letting it drop. He reaches out for the chair next to me, pulls it over and sits down. 'Your mother has given me some pins,' he explains. 'I've got them waiting out the back – they're very art deco. I do agree with her that they would look beautiful wound into your hair. You've got a very elegant neck and your face shape can carry off most hairstyles, but...' He pauses. 'It's *your* big day. What would you like?'

I go very still. What *would* I like? My big day... I somehow never imagined it like this. 'Oh, I don't know,' I mumble, trying to smile.

'We've got plenty of time,' he says kindly – at which I give a frightened little bark of laughter. He gets up again and stands behind me. 'I promise, we really have. Do you want to be softly romantic, or something more sophisticated and sleek?'

I hesitate, and then I confide: 'I know very little about the wedding dress that has been chosen for me.'

His eyes widen, but he takes it in his stride, shooting a glance in the mirror at my mother and sisters, who are all at the basins, before murmuring, 'I've seen a picture. It's *incredible* – and you'll look stunning. Do you trust me to do something that I know will complement it, and you?'

'Yes.'

He smiles, pleased. 'We'll get you over to the sinks once the others are done. I'll do it myself – I'm not having one of my cack-handed juniors maul you around.'

He washes me with the utmost gentleness – it feels almost ritualistic – having fussed around putting supports under my back, and lowering the sink so I can lean back without it hurting. He asks me several times if I'm comfortable, and if the water is the right temperature.

'It's perfect.'

'Close your eyes then,' he says. 'Your poor little head must be going crazy right now. Have some peace for yourself.'

If he only knew... I try desperately to empty my mind as his fingers tease lightly through my hair, but instead see myself walking slowly down an aisle towards Marc, as he turns delightedly, dressed in a morning suit... only for him to morph into Rich. I stop dead and his smile fades. He looks desperately sad and holds out his arms, starts walking towards me, but I pull back, turn and *run* – as fast as I can! It's a church I burst out of – one that backs on to very green fields and a cloudless, brilliant blue sky. I pick up the skirt of the big, ultra-traditional white dress that I appear to be wearing, my bare feet pushing down into the soft earth, and the further away I get, the more powerful my legs seem to become.

A sudden strong, heady and almost cloying scent interrupts my thoughts, surrounding me, dragging me back to the salon. 'This is a treatment designed to calm both the body and mind,' Carl murmurs, in a this-is-the-voice-I-use-when-I'm-being-soothing tone.

I'm filled only with a sudden sense of despair. In just six hours' time, I will be arriving at the hotel.

'Right, we're all rinsed and done, my darling,' says Carl. He brings me upright, tucking a loose corner expertly into my towel turban. 'Right, over here, my love.' Ushering me gently across the salon as if I'm made of glass and may splinter at any given moment, he sits me down in a chair well away from everyone else and murmurs under his breath, 'OK, you *have* to tell me – who caved and sang like a canary?'

I shake my head. 'I can't say.'

'Well, for what it's worth, I would do *exactly* what you're doing if I were you. Maura says hubby-to-be has worked *so* hard to make this perfect. What's a little white lie? Needs must when the devil drives, and all that.' He winks at me again in the mirror. 'I can totally see why you don't want to ruin it for him by letting on that you were in-the-know all along, although *I'd* be uber pissed off with the person that put their foot in it. I suppose he must be at the hotel now, getting everything all ready?' Carl starts to brush my wet hair, then pauses and sighs before resuming his detangling. 'I don't think I've ever heard of anything so romantic, I really don't.'

'He's on his way back from France. He's got two children from his first marriage who he's gone to collect.'

He stops and pulls a face. '*France?* And you're getting married in' – he checks his watch – 'under six hours? He's cutting it a bit fine, no pun intended. You know you have to marry the best man if he doesn't show? Don't tell me – you don't even know who the best man is!'

But I'm staring at myself in the mirror. He's right. What happens if Marc doesn't make it to the wedding? *I'll* still be there to open the letter at 8 p.m. – it meets all of the conditions…

My heart leaps with a first flicker of hope. The guests would be pretty bloody confused as to why Marc had apparently bottled the wedding he arranged, but they wouldn't say a thing to me, given that I'm not in-the-know, would they? And while Claudine would be cheated of humiliating us in public, is that really the crucial bit for her, in any case? Surely as long as we don't get married, she'll have got what she wants, won't she?

Only – I deflate again – there's no way Marc will miss the wedding he has painstakingly organized all on his own. It would have to be a matter of life or death, and I can hardly have my own fiancé arrested, or kidnapped.

'Right, I'm going to blast you dry and back-comb you for some height, OK?' Carl switches on the hairdryer before carefully tipping me forward, shouting, 'I'll be mindful of the head trauma, though.'

I go very still. My injury. If I were taken seriously 'ill' and was in hospital, wedding or not, Marc would drop everything to be there, I know he would. I feel a real prickle of excitement at this, the slightest possibility of there being something I might be able to do to protect Marc and the children. If I fake it becoming worse and go to A&E, while he is en route to the hospital, might I somehow slip out and get to the hotel for 8 p.m. to open the letter?

'Head up now, sweetheart. You've actually got very thick hair, haven't you? Not long and we'll start pinning, OK? Hello? I've lost you, haven't I? Wondering about tonight?' Carl rolls his eyes. 'It must be so weird being clueless about everything he's planned. It's like that *Don't Tell the Bride* on TV – except even the women on that know their husbands are doing it all, and the wedding itself isn't secret.'

I realize suddenly he's right. This is *insane*. This whole situation is complete madness. I shift in my chair in frustration. I'm starting to feel very hot; the noise of the dryers going, the salon chatter and the throb of the background music is all pounding in my brain. Except there *was* a man in my house! A man who knew me and who had been hired to come and find me. That *is* real – and however impossible it feels, it's happening.

If I don't do exactly as I'm told, he will hurt us.

The only answer is to keep Marc away from the hotel. There is no other solution. My breath starts to quicken, and I crane my neck, trying to look to see what stage Alice is at. 'Do you think I could have a quick word with my youngest sister?'

'Of course, darling.' He puts the brush down. 'I'll have her sent over. And do you want a coffee or anything?'

No! I just want to speak to Alice *now*! I shake my head.

'Back in a jiffy.' He pats my shoulder, and I watch him walk over to Alice's chair and say something to her. She gets up, smiling, her dark hair sticking out all over the place like she's had an electric shock, but at the sight of me her expression changes and she hurries across the salon.

'What's happened?' Sitting down quickly in an empty chair and scooting it up close, she takes my hand. 'Take a deep breath. That's it, and another. It's him, isn't it? What's he done now?'

I know she means Rich, but I just ignore her. 'I think I might have a way to protect Marc from a situation I really don't want him to be in this evening.' I grip her hand tightly. 'I'm going to need to get him away from the hotel, so that he—'

'What? How are you going to have a wedding if Marc's not there?' Alice interrupts.

I hesitate and pick my words very, very carefully. 'There's not going to be a wedding, Alice. Are you, me, Mum and Imogen meant to travel from my house to the hotel together later, before the service?'

She nods, looking shocked.

'OK. I'm thinking about my head injury becoming so bad I need to go to hospital, so Marc leaves Goldhurst Park and comes to me.'

Alice sits back in her chair slowly. 'I really don't get this. This morning you said you would be at the hotel come what may, and now...'

'You don't need to "get it". Perhaps if I'd have just known about this bloody wedding in the first place...'

'That's a bit harsh, Soph. We didn't exactly know you'd boffed Rich, did we?' She lowers her voice. 'I understand that having the two men you've slept with over the last two months in the same room together tonight, especially when the registrar says, "Does anyone know any good reason why this man and this woman shouldn't be married" is far from ideal, but what is it that he's—'

'I mean it – this really doesn't need to make sense to you, because it can't,' I say desperately. 'All I need to know is that if I have even the smallest chance to prevent several people's lives from being ruined, I should take it, shouldn't I?'

She looks at me, confused.

'I'm actually asking you, Alice!'

'I don't know, Sophie!' she says, bewildered. 'I suppose so... yes.'

'Will you help me, without asking any more questions?'

She hesitates for a moment. 'Tell me exactly what it is you want me to do.'

CHAPTER THIRTEEN

'OK, so after this we're supposed to be going back to yours to do our make-up. They're going to bring out the dresses, then we'll be going to the hotel,' murmurs Alice, her hair now pinned up in a glossy roll that sits pertly on the back of her head. 'You should probably start showing a few signs of something being wrong soon.'

I nod, tucking my bag up on my shoulder. Carl is faffing around with his phone, insisting on wanting to take photos of the four of us all finished, for his 'look book'. 'Do you think you could Google symptoms of a head injury on your mobile?' I ask anxiously. 'Just so we don't mess it up?'

'Ah! I've done it!' exclaims Carl. 'It's working again. Right, girls, line up!' Obediently, Alice and I are flanked by Mum and Imogen, and I try to focus. I haven't told Alice anything that compromises her. Besides, she would have thought it bizarre if the whole Rich 'drama' had suddenly fizzled away into nothing. Oddly, this is now all somehow more plausible, as far as she's concerned.

'Smile, Sophie!'

'Sorry,' I say automatically. If I'm going to have enough time to get to Goldhurst Park by 8 p.m. from the hospital, I'll need to give them *all* the slip – Alice included. What about if she goes to get Marc? That will get her out of the way, but it still leaves Mum and Imogen...

'Such beautiful girls!' Carl exclaims. 'See?'

Everyone goes 'Ahhh' as they crowd around the camera looking at all of us smiling for the wedding I'm not supposed to know about – and isn't going to happen. I stare at myself. The sleek upsweep style of my hair, pinned firmly in place with the two glittering art deco pins, is unfamiliar, and looks very odd teamed with my casual clothes, but no one else seems to notice my obvious unease.

Mum even gets a little teary, saying out of nowhere as we walk back to Imogen's car, 'I just want you to know I am so proud of you all and the wonderful women you have become.'

'Blimey, Mum,' says Imogen. 'How much champagne did you have at the hairdressers, for goodness' sake?' Imogen herself is pretty giggly, if only with the excitement of someone who feels they are back at a party they'd been forced to leave early, and against their will. 'It's so bloody nice just to be able to switch off for five seconds.' She sighs. 'I love Evie dearly, but I can't pretend it's not great to have a break. I actually can't wait for this bit to be over. That's dreadful, isn't it?' She looks in her bag for the car keys. 'I just feel that when she's a bit older, say five or so, we might genuinely get our lives back, instead of just pretending. Ed and I may be able to do things like leave her with one of you and go away for a holiday, just the two of us again. And by the time she's in her teens, she'll be practically independent of us.'

'Oh, Imogen,' sighs Mum. 'You really think *this* is the hard stage? When Evie's seventeen and you're beside yourself at midnight because she hasn't come home, even though she promised she'd be back at eleven, you'll long for what you have now – the security of knowing she's upstairs asleep, safe and sound in her cot. It *doesn't* get easier, I'm afraid. You should never wish anything away.'

Imogen's face falls completely as she stares at Mum, blipping the car open on auto-pilot.

Mum opens the front passenger door, adding cheerily for good measure before she climbs in, 'Being a mother to the three of you has been wonderful, but completely terrifying in equal measure. You *never* stop worrying.'

I climb into the back of the car feeling like the world's biggest bitch, given I'm about to frighten Mum senseless with a completely fake emergency dash to the hospital. On cue, Alice silently passes me her phone, on which there is a huge list of symptoms for severe head injuries, including unconsciousness (either very briefly or for a longer period of time), difficulty staying awake, slurred speech, stiff neck, vision problems, bleeding from one or both ears, a lasting headache since the injury, vomiting since the injury, irritability or unusual behaviour and visible trauma to the head.

I'm slightly disconcerted to realize I actually do have three, if not four, of them, especially when I read: *If any of these symptoms are present, go immediately to the A&E (accident and emergency) department of your local hospital, or call 999 and ask for an ambulance.*

Alice takes the phone and then types something onto the screen and hands it to me.

You know you actually should go to hosp now, according to this? Not just because of your wacko plan?

I ignore that and silently pass the phone back. She tuts, and looks out of the window crossly.

The remainder of the journey home is a quiet one all round: thanks to Mum's crisp annihilation of the rest of her life, Imogen has fallen mute; Alice continues to stare out of the window; and even Mum seems to be having an introspective moment, suddenly saying out of the blue, 'Later, *can* we make sure we get a photo of the four of us... with your father, too? Would that be all right?' I wait for Alice to lighten the mood with one of her quips, but she doesn't say anything and Mum's comment hangs sadly in the air for longer than is comfortable for any of us.

It's not even a relief when Imogen finally pulls up the drive at mine and we all get out. My little terrace has been a constant since I bought it when I was twenty-seven. I'd no intention of returning to the town I'd grown up in, but after meeting Josh in one of the pubs there on a weekend back visiting an old school friend, I suddenly very much wanted to be local again. Quickly ditching my rented London flat share, I had eagerly hurried off to Mum's, then just as quickly bought my own place, as if that's what I'd been planning all along.

I'd almost sold it after Josh moved out: the absence of him in every room was too much to bear. I'd lie in bed alone, looking out over the rooftop view from our bedroom window, and the familiarity would transport me straight back to the last time he'd slept there. He'd told me on an otherwise ordinary Thursday evening that, despite nine years together, he felt he was no longer able to give me the commitment I deserved, and he didn't want to prevent me from meeting the man who *was* right for me. While it wasn't exactly a surprise, the shock of him finally saying it aloud had made me beg him to stay one more night, even though he'd said it would be better if he left straight away. I suppose I thought I could make him change his mind. He had, humiliatingly, moved my desperate hands back to his chest once we were in bed, and firmly turned over. I'd spent the whole night awake and in silent tears, wrapped around his familiar body as he slept deeply, with a mounting sense of dread as it started to get light outside, because I knew I was never going to hold him like that again. The second he woke up, the spell would be broken...

It was Mum who convinced me not to make any rash decisions when I kept crying every time I so much as opened a drawer that had been his, as I tried to reorganize the space in my life.

'It *will* get easier,' she said. 'I know you don't believe me, but there will come a time when you think of Josh and you'll remember what loving him felt like, but it will be more like an echo that won't hurt like it does now. Moving house won't help. Leaving your job is bad enough. You need constants now, not more change.'

She was right. I didn't notice when it happened but, eventually, coming home to the house on my own became comforting after a long day, rather than something to dread. Even during Marc's and my temporary split, the house was a refuge.

But now, Claudine has successfully achieved in one night what all my experiences of the last few years have failed to do. She's made me feel unsafe in my own house. The man she hired has violated everything.

I hate her for that.

'I'll put the kettle on,' says Alice, as I push the door open cautiously. Everything feels alien, as if the house is in on a secret that it has no wish to share. I try to shrug off the hostility along with my shoes, glancing up the stairs warily, as I grip the strap of my bag more tightly with one hand and slip the other into it to feel for the edges of the envelope.

Still there.

'Sophie, a bit of hair is coming loose.' Mum steps towards me and tweaks it. 'Honestly, I shall have words with Carl. We've only been home five minutes. Come on, upstairs – we need to pin that back and spray it before anything else escapes.'

I follow her up reluctantly and sit on my bed, waiting for her to start fussing.

'It's not really coming apart at all. I want to know how you're feeling.' She sits down on the chair where *he* was sitting only hours ago, and I have to look away. 'Don't try and avoid the question, Sophie. It's important. As I said to you earlier, wedding or not, if you feel unwell, you *must* tell me.'

I can't miss this opportunity. 'My neck feels pretty stiff,' I confess, glancing at her and feeling dreadful as a flicker of concern flashes across her face. 'But I expect that's just from leaning back when I was having my hair washed.'

'Anything else?' she says lightly, leaning over and flicking an imaginary piece of lint from the duvet cover.

'My head is still hurting.' This is horrible. 'It's a bit worse, I think.'

'You have seemed a little disorientated. I wonder if we ought to call a doctor, just to ask him or her to—'

'No!' I turn back to her instantly. It's much too early yet. 'I'm fine, Mum. It was just at the hairdressers I—'

Alice and Imogen appear in the doorway. 'Tea or coffee?' asks Alice, as Imogen sits down on the bed next to me, balancing on her lap what looks like a large hat box, which she unzips happily.

'Make-up time! We can't have five-star hair and B&B faces. I'm going to do us all. You can go first, birthday girl. So, who have you got coming tonight?' she adds innocently, as if she hasn't helped prepare the guest list. 'Can you put your bag down, Soph? You've been glued to it all day. What have you got in there? The crown jewels?'

I stare at her, frightened. 'Of course not!' I get up and drop the bag behind the chair, where none of them can get at it, before sitting back down again.

'All right! No need to bite my head off. OK!' She beams at me. 'Turn this way. You can't see where you bumped your head at all, you know,' she says encouragingly.

'Really?' I ask anxiously. That's hardly helpful.

'She's just being nice,' says Alice. 'You've got a very visible lump there.'

'Alice!' exclaim Mum and Imogen in unison.

'I think you're crazy not to be getting it checked out,' Alice says, and I almost smile gratefully. 'Aren't you supposed to be older and wiser as of today?'

'Leave her alone.' Imogen glares at Alice, then turns back to me. 'Don't worry, Soph. By the time I've finished, you won't be able to see a thing.'

'I hardly think blinding her is the answer,' Alice says.

'Can you just go downstairs and make that coffee?' explodes Imogen, looking incredulously at Mum as Alice gets up and marches out of the room. 'She's seriously starting to get on my nerves. What's wrong with her?'

'Nothing is wrong with anyone,' Mum says soothingly. 'Everything is just *fine*. Now, Sophie, you were starting to tell me something else about being in the hairdressers and not feeling well?'

'Close your eyes,' instructs Imogen. 'I'm just going to give you a quick wipe.'

'I'm sure it's nothing,' I reply, flinching as she scrubs my skin. I hope she's not as rough with poor little Evie. 'I felt a bit pukey, that's all.'

Imogen stops and I open my eyes just in time to catch her pulling a face at Mum, before she composes herself again. 'You're absolutely sure you're not pregnant?' she says. 'You don't just get morning sickness in the morning, you know – it can be any time of day. For lots of women it's worst at night. With Evie it was brushing my teeth that did it. I'd be standing there at the sink and—'

'Were you actually sick?' Mum interrupts.

I swallow nervously. 'Yes,' I lie.

Mum gives a sharp intake of breath.

'I haven't been since,' I add quickly. 'I'm all right Mum, honestly. It's my fortieth birthday, I got drunk last night and I've been feeling crappy all day, that's all.' I turn back to Imogen. 'Keep going, but please don't make me look like a transvestite.'

Imogen looks insulted, adding quickly, 'You want fake eyelashes though, surely? I've brought loads.'

Alice comes back into the room holding her phone out to me. 'It's Marc,' she says. 'He'd like a word.'

Imogen and Mum smile and get to their feet, as if they have been expecting this. I look between them and uncertainly take the phone. 'Hello?'

'Hey!' He sounds slightly breathless, as if he's rushing somewhere. 'You OK?'

'Yes, I'm fine. Where are you?'

'On my way – don't worry! Are you at home right now?'

'I'm sitting on the bed with Imogen, who is about to do my make-up.'

'Excellent,' he says. 'Right, well, I'd like to give you your birthday present from me.'

'But you're not here.' I look around me, panicking suddenly. 'Are you?'

'No,' he says. 'I'm not. But it's something I want to give you for tonight.'

Oh, God – here goes. The dress. I take a deep breath. Remember, you don't know you're getting married, so even if it's white, don't say anything...

'Can you tell your mum to bring in the main present?' he says.

'Marc says can you bring in the main present?' I say faintly, and Mum, beaming with delight, disappears next door into the spare room.

'Is she back yet?' he asks.

'No, she's— Oh my God! Marc!' I gasp.

Mum has reappeared in the room carefully carrying a full-length, shimmering silver silk gown. It's only as I stand up and move over to touch it incredulously that I realize that what is catching the light are hundreds of tiny strung beads on an elegant, sweeping fringe that falls like water from the nipped-in waist, over a long skirt and from the wide neckline designed to skim the collar bones. All that's missing is a martini and a copy of *The Great Gatsby*.

'Do you like it?' he asks eagerly.

'Like it?' I whisper. 'It's unbelievable.'

'Good unbelievable or bad unbelievable?' He laughs.

'It's perfect,' I say truthfully, and it is. I'd never have chosen it for myself, but it's somehow both understated and full-out glamour all at once – the perfect wedding dress in a very unobvious and clever way. I'd never have suspected his plan if I didn't already know it.

'I've got something else for you, too,' he says. 'Go over to your top drawer – your underwear one.'

Feeling as if I'm in a trance, I do as I'm told and slide it open.

'Can you see a box in there? Dark blue with a light blue ribbon?'

I reach in and rummage around and, sure enough, there it is. As I pull it out, I glance at Mum and remember her messing around there earlier. She smiles at me and I turn back to the small package, which has G. Collins & Sons stamped across it.

'Got it?' says Marc. 'Open it up.'

I put the phone under my chin and pull the ribbon. As it slips silkily to the floor, I lift the lid. Nestling on a velvet pad is a delicate art nouveau platinum bracelet. Eight panels are entwined together, with a diamond set at the centre of each one.

I lift it out and Imogen exhales sharply. Alice says, 'Shit!' and Mum's mouth falls open.

'It's beautiful, Marc,' I say quietly. 'I can't believe you've done this for me.'

'Well, don't get too excited,' he says. 'Richard Gere isn't waiting in the bathroom, but I wanted you to have a really fun, fairytale day. The whole works. Oh, damn – I nearly forgot! Tell Imogen, the shoes!'

'Marc says the shoes...?' I say faintly.

Imogen nods importantly and vanishes, before coming back with a shoebox that says 'Sass Taylor' on it. I've never even heard of him or her. Inside is a pair of preposterously high silver and rose-gold leather platform sandals, with an art deco fan over the toe. I don't think I'm even going to be able to balance in them, let alone walk.

'I can't wait to see you later,' Marc says. 'You're going to look amazing. And I love you very much. Happy birthday!'

'Thank you.' It's all I can manage to say – again – and he laughs at my stunned reaction.

'You are very welcome. I've got to go, OK? See you in a bit!'

I hang up, and look again at the dress, shoes and bracelet. Peering at the label, I realize it's Oscar de la Renta. Good Lord… I must be looking at the best part of twenty grand's worth of outfit. That's absurd. 'I don't know what to say,' I blurt.

'Er, "Thank you, God, for my amazing fiancé?"' exclaims Imogen. 'I don't know a single girl who wouldn't *love* her boy-friend to do what yours has just done.'

I hesitate. She's probably right. 'I don't mean to sound ungrate-ful. I'm just a bit… overwhelmed.'

There's silence for a moment, and then Mum says, 'Well, don't you want to try it all on?'

'No!' cries Imogen. 'Not until we've completely done the make-up! You need the full effect. You're never going to get another chance to feel this much like a film star *ever* again – it has to be *perfect*!' She puts the shoes down carefully on the bed, sits down next to me and reaches once more for the make-up box. 'Ready?'

I turn back to her, looking at the dress again out of the corner of my eye as Mum hangs it up on the wardrobe door. It's shim-mering as if it has a life of its own.

'Soph, do you want a drink of water?' Alice says quietly. 'You look a bit pale.'

I nod, and she leaves the room.

'I chose the shoes!' Imogen says breathlessly. 'They were eye-wateringly expensive, but so beautiful, I couldn't not. Do you like them?'

I examine them more carefully this time. That makes more sense. I couldn't see Marc picking them out.

I don't know if 'like' is the right word. They're very impressive in their cool, remote glamour. They look intensely uncomfortable. I glance at the dress. 'Marc chose that, though?'

'Oh, yes.' Mum smiles. 'Very much so. He had very definite ideas about what he wanted.'

'Ready?' Imogen instructs, holding a brush.

Is that really all anybody expects of me today – just to do as I'm told?

Reluctantly, I close my eyes.

CHAPTER FOURTEEN

'There,' says Imogen triumphantly, as Mum walks back into the room having changed into her evening wear: an elegant, coffee-coloured column gown. 'I've finished. No, you can't look, not until you've got everything else on.' She puts the make-up box to one side and stands up. 'OK. Dress time!'

I obediently strip down to my underwear. Imogen looks horrified, opening her mouth, but drawing the line before she can say anything, I hold up a firm hand. 'They're non-VPL – don't worry.'

'But—'

'I won't tell anyone I'm wearing M&S pants if you don't.' I unhook my bra and step half-naked into the dress that Imogen and Mum are holding out. The silk lining slips over my skin, and as they zip and hook me in at the back, the metallic material tightens over me, automatically making me stand a little taller.

'That's so clever,' Mum says admiringly. 'The zip is completely concealed.'

'And look at how well it's lifted her,' says Imogen in amazement. 'That's couture for you. I don't think you're going to need Spanx after all. No, it's not too long, you just need the shoes – and where's the bracelet? Here... oh, *wow*!' she steps back admiringly and Mum puffs with pride. 'You look wonderful, Sophie!'

Even Alice looks impressed. 'Fair dues, Soph,' she says after a moment. 'You've got a pretty amazing figure.'

They stand to one side, and I walk uncertainly over to the mirror. Never mind that they're about 4-inch stilettos, the shoes are also slightly too big.

A tall, armoured woman stares blankly back at me. The surroundings of my bedroom don't seem to fit any more, either – I feel as if I should be in some vast, white, floaty-curtained hotel suite that smells of gardenias, waiting for my close-up. I look nothing like my normal self, but then I don't feel anything like me either.

I'm slightly shocked to realize that, if anyone, I resemble Claudine. Not literally, although now I notice it, I suppose our colouring is similar. But I look polished, confident – a woman not to be underestimated.

I take a deep breath. 'What time is it?'

Mum checks her watch. 'Six o'clock. We ought to leave here in about an hour, girls.' She looks at the others, who nod.

We'll be leaving well before that.

'I don't think I should sit around in this for that long. Can one of you unzip me again?' I am still facing the mirror, looking uncertainly at my reflection. Here goes...

Mum is looking down carefully at the clasp. Imogen has started rummaging around in the make-up box. Only Alice is watching me silently. I meet her gaze for a brief second, and then against every instinct I have, and trying not to break my fall with my hands, I close my eyes, crease at the knees and slump sideways to the floor in an apparent dead faint.

'Oh God! Sophie!' Mum exclaims in panic as I let my head loll forward. I feel the hands of my sisters hauling me up onto the bed, lying me back on the pillow. 'Sophie? Can you hear me?'

I turn my head away from her. I feel so guilty I can't meet her eye – but it must only serve to make it look as if I really am confused, because she says, 'Alice, call 999, ask for an ambulance. Now! Get this blasted dress off her, she can hardly breathe!'

132

I can already hear Alice's urgent voice in the background. 'It's for my sister. She injured her head earlier today and she's just collapsed.'

I can't actually remember the other symptoms that I'm supposed to be displaying. 'My head hurts,' I announce lamely.

'What's that, darling?' says Mum worriedly, still trying to undo the clasp of the dress. 'What did you say? I think she's slurring slightly,' I hear her mutter to Imogen.

What? No, I'm not... But then I stop concentrating on Mum, because I realize I actually do feel quite nauseous. 'Um, I need to take this off *now*,' I say, starting to panic for real. 'I think I'm going to throw up.'

The zip flies down and I yank my arms out, stand up and step out of it, like some kind of schizophrenic lap dancer, naked apart from my ridiculous shoes and very sensible pants. Kicking them off, I push past Alice and lurch out into the hall before slamming into the bathroom.

'Go after her!' Mum exclaims. 'She might pass out again!'

I'm already hanging over the loo, however, and to my huge surprise, I *am* sick, for real, as Alice appears behind me. 'You all right?' she whispers anxiously, then grimaces as she catches sight of the vomit in the bowl. 'Urgh. Did you just stick your fingers down your throat?'

I hesitate, then nod quickly, wiping my mouth with the back of my hand.

She sits back on her heels. 'I had no idea you were such a good liar. I'm slightly freaked out, to be honest. MUM!' she yells. 'She's just puked!'

I hear the sound of footsteps, and Mum and Imogen crowd into the small space with us.

'Lift her up. We need to get her into some clothes before the ambulance arrives. Sophie? Can you walk, darling? We're going back to your bedroom, OK?'

The letter. I *cannot* forget that. 'I'm fine. I can get dressed on my own.'

'No,' insists Mum. 'We're coming too. Imogen, go downstairs and open the front door so they can see which house it is when they arrive.'

Alice and Mum, supporting me under an arm each, lead me back and sit me down on the bed. 'Can you pass my jeans, Mum?' I nod at them on the floor as I reach for my earlier discarded bra. 'Alice, my mouth tastes horrible. Could you get my toothbrush for me?'

I wait for her to disappear off back to the bathroom. As far as Alice is concerned, I now have no need for the party clothes at all.

As soon as she's gone, I turn urgently back to my mother. 'Can you put the dress and the shoes in the overnight bag that's under the bed?'

'But darling…'

'There's still a chance I might be able to get to this wedding. He's worked so hard, you know he has! I have to at least be able to try!'

She looks at me doubtfully, but then hurries to the dress. As she's carefully folding it, I stand and reach for my bag, still hidden behind the chair. Mum is so distracted, she doesn't even notice as I slip the letter into the overnight bag, before putting the shoes in on top of it. Mum gently lays the dress over them, like a metallic shroud, then looks around for the bracelet box while I pull on my shirt.

Alice reappears with a loaded toothbrush. 'Thanks.' I start to clean my teeth just as we hear Imogen call from downstairs: 'They're here!'

My heart thumps as I take the brush out and pass it back to Alice. I can't believe I'm about to lie to paramedics. This is so wrong – what if someone else needs this ambulance and because

134

it's here with me, something dreadful happens? I sink down onto the bed again and start to do my shirt buttons up just as two middle-aged men dressed in dark green walk in, one of them clutching some sort of case.

'Hello there,' one of them says, walking up to me. 'What's your name?'

'Sophie Gardener,' I say, and he smiles at me.

'Hello, Sophie. I'm Frank – and this is Steve.' His colleague nods from the doorway. 'What's happened to you, then?'

'I, er, hit my head this morning.' I lift my hair. 'I'm not sure there's much to see, though.'

Frank inspects it impassively. 'What did you hit it on?'

'A massage table.' I feel ridiculous saying that.

'Did you pass out before you hit it, or because you hit it?'

'Um, *because* I hit it, I think?' I look at him worriedly, unable to remember suddenly, I've got so much flying around my brain.

'She was out for no more than a few seconds,' says Mum, 'but she fainted again just now, before we phoned 999. Literally just fell to the floor.'

'OK,' says Frank, turning back to me. 'How are you feeling at the moment? Does your head hurt?'

I nod, truthfully. 'I've still got a headache.'

'How long have you had that?'

'Since this morning.' Which is also true, but then, I've had a few things to deal with.

'I'm just going to check your eyes and ears, OK, Sophie?' He opens his case. 'Are you on any medication at the moment?'

'No.'

'No allergies or anything?'

'None,' I confirm, as he shines a light in my eyes.

'Except cats. She gets sneezy around them,' cuts in Mum anxiously.

Frank nods kindly. 'Thank you. But nothing like this has ever happened to you before?'

'No.'

'No tingling in your fingers or pains in your arms?'

'No.'

'And you've no medical history of any problems? No surgery or conditions?'

'No.' I can't lie about *that*. 'I was sick just now, though,' I add, slightly desperately.

'Sophie is due to go to her fortieth birthday party in about an hour, which she's very anxious to attend, and we're concerned she's deliberately downplaying how she's really feeling,' Alice says. 'She told us earlier that she had a very stiff neck, and she was slurring a little after she fainted.'

Well done, Al. I feel relieved.

'We wanted her to see someone this morning when the accident happened, but she refused. She's been quite confused at times, and behaving erratically. She's been very irritable, too, which isn't like her at all.'

All right. I frown at her. Let's not go crazy.

'No alcohol, anything like that?' asks Frank.

'No,' I say. 'Half a glass of champagne at lunchtime, but that's it.'

'She was drunk last night, though,' chips in Mum.

'Look, I had a beauty treatment today, which I think dehydrated me,' I explain. 'I stood up quite quickly, and that's when I fell. I couldn't put my arms out because I was trussed up in cling film.'

To give him credit, Frank's face remains impassive. 'OK, Sophie. Well, I think we'll take you into hospital, get them to check you over, all right? Can you stand up for me, and we'll go down to the ambulance? Who's coming with you?'

'Mum, please,' I say quickly.

'Don't you need to immobilize her head?' says Mum, picking up the bag.

'I'm confident we're not dealing with a spinal injury here,' says Frank. 'I think you're probably concussed, Sophie, but because you've passed out twice, I'd like the A&E team to check you over.'

'Shouldn't we phone Marc?' says Alice pointedly. 'He ought to know what's happening.'

'No, please don't ring him.' I put a firm hand on her arm, and understandably she gapes at me, spluttering, 'But he's going to want to come to the hospital with you, Sophie!' before giving me a furious 'And I thought that was the whole bloody point?' look.

'Given the circumstances,' I say slowly, 'he's going to panic, especially as he's got Isabelle and Olivier with him. They don't know anyone else at the party, there's no one he can leave them with. Could *both* of you go to Goldhurst Park and tell Marc in person?' I look between my sisters. 'Then one of you can stay and look after Isabelle and Olivier – maybe you, Gen, they know you best – and Alice, you could drive Marc to the hospital. She can drive your car, can't she?' I turn to Imogen.

'Um, yeah, I suppose so,' Imogen says slowly, and looks at Mum, adding carefully, 'What makes you think the children are coming, though?'

I flounder around for a moment, before managing: 'I heard them talking in the background while I was on the phone to Marc earlier. Don't worry, I haven't said anything. Whoa!'

Frank reaches out to help me as I wobble to my feet and ushers me towards the door. I ignore Alice glaring at me mutinously and, thankfully, she stays silent.

As we make our way out into the street, I can already see a few curtains twitching curiously. I glance up and down the road. No white transits.

'We'll see you at the hospital, then,' Alice snaps, as Mum struggles to climb into the back of the ambulance in her long dress. Steve and Frank help her in.

'Up on the bed,' Steve says cheerfully, strapping me onto the trolley.

'You've got my bag, haven't you?' I ask Mum anxiously. 'Shit! My keys!'

'I picked them up while you were putting your trainers on. Everything is right here.' She reaches for my hand. 'It's going to be fine, don't worry.'

I try to smile at my sisters, still watching as Steve makes sure I'm secure. 'I'm so sorry about all of this.' I look beseechingly at Alice.

She sighs. 'Don't be stupid. I'll see you there with Marc in a bit,' she says, as Steve starts to close the doors on her and Imogen's frightened faces.

'Right, ladies.' Frank turns to Mum and me. 'I need to warn you, these aren't the comfiest of vehicles.'

I look at Mum, perched on the edge of her seat, one hand clasping the bag handles tightly, the other holding me. I've never seen her so pale. She wobbles as the ambulance pulls away. 'I've got you.' I try to smile.

I feel so guilty for doing this to her. I *hate* you, Claudine.

'I should be saying that to you,' she says faintly. 'I'm the mum.'

'I really am sorry for this.'

'Don't be ridiculous!' Dismissing me, she turns to Frank. 'Sophie is actually supposed to be getting married in an hour and a half. Her fiancé has arranged it all as a surprise. Obviously she knows about it, but that's why she's so anxious not to be going to hospital.'

Frank looks taken aback. 'Riiight…'

'But you can't be too careful, can you, Frank?' Mum looks at me.

'Not with head injuries, no,' he says, without hesitation. 'I'm sure they'll be happy to let you go after they've given you a once-over, but we always have to consider the risk of bleeding inside the skull, or bruising to the brain, which can have very serious implications.'

'By serious, do you mean fatal?' Mum looks horrified.

'It's because Sophie's passed out twice and vomited – that's why we need to check it out.'

'Well, then.' Mum turns shakily back to me. 'You see? Marc will understand. *Everyone* will understand. Don't give it a second thought.'

'I'm going to be OK, Mum,' I say quickly. She looks so frightened. I start to feel sick again, though, and have to concentrate on not throwing up. I think it's travelling backwards that's doing it. I close my eyes briefly and try to concentrate on my breathing.

'Sophie,' says Frank sharply, 'we're nearly there. I need you to stay awake, OK? Not long now...'

I know, Frank, that's what I'm afraid of.

CHAPTER FIFTEEN

I'm wheeled from an ambulance on a stretcher bed straight into A&E, where the busy staff move calmly around me, taking me straight into a small, curtained-off bay. I wonder how they can't see the big neon sign above my head that reads, 'FRAUD!' I should not have done this. This was very, very wrong.

But as the triage nurse assesses me, she doesn't say anything like, 'Hmmm. Something's not right here. Are you making all of this up?' She simply tells me a doctor will be along shortly, and do we need anything else?

'We're fine. Thank you. There, that's good, isn't it?' Mum turns to me weakly, once the nurse has disappeared and pulled the curtain back around us. 'I must say, I'm very impressed with how quickly they've seen you. Not that I think we should read anything into that,' she adds hastily. 'You wait, it'll be hours before a doctor arrives now.'

Her phone starts ringing in her bag. 'Oh, blast!' She panics and starts to fumble for it. 'I forgot, you can't have mobiles on in hospitals, can you?' I've not seen her so flustered in a very long time.

'I think it's OK these days,' I say, 'although you probably want to put it on silent after this call.'

She nods and looks at the screen. 'Oh, it's Alice. Hello, darling!' she booms, and I close my eyes briefly with embarrassment, before pleading, 'Don't shout!' in deference to the people on either side of us. It doesn't make any difference, though, as she's not looking at me, and she has her finger in the ear her phone isn't clamped to. 'Yes! We're at the hospital! What's that? Oh, of course! Here she is.' She holds the phone out to me. 'Marc wants a word.'

Alice has arrived with him already? What? It can't even be seven o'clock yet! I reach for the phone. 'Hello?'

'Hey!' Marc sounds calm, but with tight worry in his voice. He's also walking somewhere fast; I can hear his footsteps. 'We're on our way, Soph. Just leaving the hotel now. We'll be there just as soon as we can.'

So they'll be here in half an hour? That's too early!

'How are you feeling?' he asks.

'I'm OK,' I manage, trying to think of a way to delay them further. 'I've not been sick any more, or passed out again, so that's good. I'm sure this is nothing to worry about.'

'Alice said you hit your head on the massage table, of all things?' He gives a nervous laugh.

'I know,' I mumble. 'What a prat, eh?'

'She also said only the massage girl saw you fall and she's being vague about it – probably terrified we're going to sue her,' he says. 'Make sure you tell them everything, Sophie. It could make a big difference to how they assess you, and what tests they give you, if they know *exactly* what happened to your head. Promise me?'

'OK,' I say warily. I don't want him doing his lawyer bit and worrying away at things. My story is not going to stand up to close scrutiny. 'I'm really sorry about having to drag you away from the party before it's even begun.'

'That's not important,' he says anxiously. 'The main thing is that you're all right and you're not hurt. You must—'

But I miss the rest of what he says because the curtain is pulled back and a doctor appears. Already? My eyes widen and I glance at Mum worriedly. That really is ridiculously fast.

'I have to go, Marc. They want to speak to me. Please tell Alice to drive safely and *don't* rush. I'm not going anywhere.' God is going to strike me down for such lies.

'Will do. I love you, Sophie,' he says, adding slightly desperately, 'I'll sort everything out when I get there, OK?'

'I love you too.' I hang up. He sounds completely overwhelmed, which, given what he's about to walk out on at the hotel, is understandable.

I look up at the doctor, waiting patiently for me, and I'm struck once again by the utter lunacy of what I'm doing. 'Sorry about that.'

'No problem,' she says. 'I'm Dr Forrester. I understand you've had an altercation with a massage table.' She speaks drily, reminding me a bit of Alice – they're probably about the same age. I like her instantly.

'Yes. I fainted, fell and hit my head.'

'Do you remember falling?'

'Um, I'm not actually sure. When I came round, the beautician said she thought I might have banged my forehead.'

'OK. I'm just going to check your eyes, Sophie – can you look straight at me? Thank you… How have you been feeling since the accident? Nice hair and outfit, by the way.' She nods and grins at Mum. 'Do you both always make such an effort for trips to A&E?'

I give a faint smile. 'It's my fortieth birthday today. We're meant to be on our way to my party right now.'

'Oh, I'm sorry to hear that,' she says instantly.

'Thanks. In answer to your question, I feel fine, apart from a headache that I can't shift, and I've been sick once.'

'She passed out again this evening,' Mum says helpfully. 'She had slightly slurred speech, too.'

Dr Forrester's eyebrows flicker slightly. I don't miss it. 'Can you sit up, Sophie? I'm just going to check your pulse and breathing... OK, good... An ambulance brought you in, did it?'

'Yes,' I say quietly.

'Can you do this?' She brings out her index finger in front of her, as if she's pointing into space. I copy her. 'Great. Now, place your finger on your nose.'

I do as I'm told.

'And can you put your finger on mine?' She starts to move her finger around slowly, as if tracing an imaginary figure of eight in the air.

'I feel like ET,' I mumble, feeling a little awkward as I touch her.

She smiles. 'OK, now push on my hand with yours, as hard as you can... Good. Let's just do your reflexes... Well done. Now, can I ask you to stand up and walk over to me? Sorry, it's a crazy small space in this bay – have you got enough room?'

I get up a little stiffly, and in three steps I'm there.

'Thanks, Sophie. You can sit down again on the bed now.' She gives me a considered look for a moment. 'Much as I want to just let you go to your birthday do, I think we ought to do a CT scan.'

'The paramedic already told us bumps to the head can be fatal,' blurts Mum.

'He didn't say that at all. Dr Forrester is just being thorough,' I say quickly.

Mum ignores me and looks pleadingly at the doctor.

'The skull is essentially a closed box, so if there is any swelling within or pressure on the brain, we'd need to address it,' she says. 'But your daughter is right – I'm erring on the side of caution.'

'Is that what makes it so dangerous?' Mum persists. 'Because if that pressure or swelling isn't alleviated, the brain stops working properly?'

Dr Forrester hesitates before answering. 'Yes.'

'Oh my God.' Mum is horrified. 'I should never have let them book that bloody girl to do that treatment. This is all my fault!'

'Mum!' It's almost frightening seeing Mum so uncharacteristically in freefall, and my resulting guilt makes me snap at her. 'Stop it! Of course it isn't your fault. I got up and fell over, that's all. I'm going to be fine.'

She swallows and I realize she's fighting back tears. This is awful.

The doctor looks between us sympathetically. 'We'll get everything organized and then someone will be back to get you in due course. I'll ask them to bring you a gown, too, Sophie.'

'Thank you.' As she vanishes, I turn to Mum again. 'See? "In due course." I'm hardly being rushed down there right now, am I? They wouldn't be delaying anything if they were really worried.'

'But you're not going to get married!' Mum says miserably. 'Everyone is going to be arriving now!'

What on earth is she going to do when I disappear off in a minute? I can't leave her here on her own like this... But I have no choice. I *have* to go to the hotel – that's non-negotiable, for all our sakes. I reach out to take her hand again. 'Don't, Mum,' I plead. 'None of this is your fault, OK? What time is it now?' I tense, dreading her answer.

'I'm sorry, I'm so sorry, you're right. I need to calm down.' She looks at her watch. She's actually trembling – Christ. 'Coming up to quarter past seven.'

A cold wash of fear surges over me. I have to go.

'I suppose when Marc gets here, we could call the registrar and see if they can be persuaded to stay on a little longer?' Mum clears her throat. I can tell she's trying to get herself under control. 'They can't exactly have any other weddings to do this late in the evening, can they? Imogen is there already, and Alice can drive back to help her. They can explain everything to the guests, if need be. It might just be a question of everything happening a few hours later. And maybe don't let on to Marc when he gets here that you know about the wedding, just in case.'

'I promise, I won't.'

'Good. I think I might just pop to the loo.' She gets unsteadily to her feet. 'Will you be all right? Maybe I ought to tell a nurse so you're not on your own?'

'Don't be silly,' I say immediately. 'I'll be fine.'

She pulls back the curtain.

'Mum,' I say quickly, 'if they come to get me for the scan while you're gone, just wait here until I'm back. I'm sure they won't, but in case they do, I don't want you to worry.'

'All right,' she says obediently, and suddenly I feel like the parent, about to sneak away from playgroup while my child's back is turned.

I watch her walk down the ward and pause at the nurses' station. For God's sake, Mum! I said don't tell them! But then she points uncertainly towards a door, and I realize she's just asking for directions. The second she disappears through it, I get up from the bed and grab the overnight bag. Putting it quickly on the bed, I pull back the zip. I haven't let it out of my sight since we climbed into the ambulance, but I can't risk leaving without checking the letter is still there, under the dress and shoes.

It is.

I shut it again and take a deep breath. Here goes. Picking up the bag, I begin to walk towards the nurses' station, past the rest of the bays. It's busy, with patients and their relatives talking to other doctors. The nurse and doctor that assessed me are nowhere to be seen. Blood is squishing in my ears because my heart is beating so loudly, but I lift my head up confidently and don't make eye contact with the nurse that just spoke to Mum. She doesn't even look up anyway. I turn left and push straight out through the double doors, following signs to the exit, and very quickly find myself in a hectic waiting room. No one looks at me as I walk straight through to the main doors and into the foyer, before heading outside.

I breathe out. When Mum gets back, hopefully, like I said, she's going to assume I've gone for my scan and just sit there. Even if she does ask someone, they're probably going to think I'm *being* scanned and not actually check. I should have at least twenty minutes, maybe more, before they realize I'm gone. But I need to get going, especially as, without my phone, I have no idea what time it is.

Now, I need a cab...

I look around, but to my surprise there is no obvious rank, which is also when I realize I have no money on me – no purse, no nothing. Shit! But once I get there, someone will pay for me, surely? Biting my lip as I clutch my bag containing my couture dress and ludicrously expensive bracelet and shoes, I try to think. The nearest rank will be down at the station, but that is at least a ten- to fifteen-minute walk from here. I don't have time.

I'm just starting to panic when, unbelievably, a taxi rounds the corner and indicates to turn left, starting to slow down. I can see someone in the back. It's dropping someone off! My heart lifts and, as the car comes to a stop by the pavement, I move hurriedly over, hovering as the rear passenger door opens and an older lady gets out. She fumbles in her bag for money as the taxi driver opens his electric window, then she passes over a crisp note, for which she gets no change. 'Thank you very much,' I hear her say politely, before she steps away, looks up and notices me. She smiles and I smile politely back, before hurrying over to the passenger door as the window begins to close again.

'Excuse me!' I say desperately, and it judders to a halt, leaving just a small gap for me to speak through. 'Could you take me to Goldhurst Park? It's really urgent that I get there as soon as I can.'

The slight, shrunken driver in his fifties scratches his loose nylon trousers with nicotine-stained fingers, and is already shaking his head firmly like I'm an idiot before I've even got my words out. 'Fully booked,' he says, from behind a horrible moustache. I hardly see his lips move. 'Have been since midday. It's all the early evening lot now, for the pubs and restaurants. You could call the office but they won't have anything until at least half eight.'

'I'll pay double the going rate.'

He doesn't react – just reaches forward and gets a card from the glove compartment. 'I just go where I'm told. Like I said, you'll have to call the office.'

I straighten up miserably. 'Thank you, but I don't have my phone with me and past eight is much too late.'

He shrugs like it's no skin off his nose, then does his window up all the way before indicating to the right and driving off. Frightened, I watch him disappear off up the road again. What the hell am I supposed to do now?

'Excuse me?'

I jump. The older lady is standing right behind me.

'I couldn't help overhearing,' she says. 'Would you like to use *my* phone?' She holds out an ancient mobile. 'You'd be most welcome if there is someone you need to call to come and get you? Please, take it.' She pushes it into my hands. 'I can see you're in a hurry for something. I love the pins in your hair,' she adds. 'My mother had some that were very similar.'

'Thank you so much!' I blurt, but then discover I am at a complete loss as to who to call. All of my friends and the rest of my family are at the hotel waiting for me – by the time they got here it would be too late and, in any case, I'm shocked to realize that I don't know anyone's number off by heart. Not a single soul.

Well, all except *one* person.

I swallow, close my eyes, and start to dial.

CHAPTER SIXTEEN

It rings and rings. Oh, please, *please* answer your phone!
Still nothing...

Maybe he's changed his number? But surely he wouldn't – it was always his business one, too.

'Hello?'

I catch my breath. 'Josh? It's me, Sophie.'

I can practically feel him sitting up straight. 'Wow.' There is long pause, and finally he says, incredulously, 'How are you?'

'I'm not great, actually.' My voice starts to tremble. 'I need your help. I know this is going to sound totally mad, but do you think you could come to the hospital and get me, then drive me to Goldhurst Park?'

'As in the big posh hotel?' he says, confused. I hear a female voice in the background murmur something. 'No, it's not' – he half covers the phone – 'it's someone else... Sorry, you were saying? You're at the hospital, yeah?'

'Outside A&E, yes,' I say, wishing with all my heart there was *any* other number I could have rung. 'I wouldn't ask unless it was an absolute emergency.'

'I know you wouldn't. You need me to come right now?'

'Yes. Er, you do still live in Middlebridge, don't you?'

'Yup. I'll be there in five minutes.'

Relief floods through me. 'Oh, thank you so much! Actually, I'm going to walk up to the main road and turn left into that road that runs down towards the park.'

'Hopewood Gardens?' he says. 'Where they've built that new block of flats on the corner, opposite where the guitar shop used to be?'

'Exactly,' I say. 'I'll wait down there. Is that all right?'

'Of course.'

'Oh, and this isn't my number either. I've borrowed someone's phone, so don't call me back on it.'

'All right,' he says slowly. 'I'll just wait until I see you on the roadside if you're not there when I arrive. It's a black BMW. I'm leaving now.'

He hangs up, and I turn back to the older lady, who is waiting a few steps away from me, politely not listening.

'Thank you so much.' I hasten over to her. 'I can't tell you how grateful I am.'

'It was no trouble at all. I do hope you managed to arrange something.' She reaches out, puts a hand on my arm and squeezes it very briefly. It's such a simple gesture of support, but I am very grateful indeed for her kindness. 'Goodbye.' She smiles, and walks off through the automatic doors of the A&E.

I stare after her for a moment, then turn and start to stride quickly up the hill. The absolutely last thing I want to happen is for Alice and Marc to drive past me. I'm hurrying so much, I practically break into a run, prevented only by the awkward bulk of the bag, which I am having to keep by my side because the straps are too short for me to put it over my shoulder.

I approach the left turn. He's right, it is Hopewood Gardens.

I walk far enough down so that I can't be seen from the main road, and come to a stop outside what obviously used to be a private house, but has now been converted into a vet's practice. It's closed, and the small, tarmacked car park is empty. I sit down on the low brick wall to wait and put the bag at my feet.

*

When the black car appears over the brow of the hill, it is the strangest feeling to watch Josh slowly drive down towards me, indicator flashing; just like the hundreds of times he'd come to get me from work over the years, albeit now in a much nicer car than we ever could have afforded back then.

'Hi,' Josh says, as I open the car door nervously and get in, rather awkwardly balancing the bag on my knees as I slam it shut. Breathing in the familiar smell of his aftershave, I turn to him. He gives me a slightly quizzical look, and there's a horrible pause where I wonder if I should give him a kiss on the cheek or something... but then I've hardly bumped into him socially, so I don't, and instead quickly reach for my seat belt, face flaming.

'All in?' he says, and I nod silently. He glances over his shoulder and pulls smoothly away. 'I thought I'd go the back way, down Sector Lane – as you're in a bit of a rush.'

'Good idea.' He's filled out a little in the four years since we last met – I bumped into him in the shopping centre while he was with his mum – and his once dark hair is now liberally flecked with grey. He's also sporting quite a bit of stubble but, other than that, he looks exactly the same. He's even wearing an old sweatshirt I recognize. This is so, so odd.

We drive in silence for a moment, then he glances sideways at me.

'I'm sorry,' I say. 'This must seem completely mental.'

'A bit surprising, maybe,' he agrees.

'It's just literally everyone else I could have asked is already at the hotel waiting for me, and I *have* to be there by eight o'clock... It's my birthday today,' I explain, embarrassed. 'Well, my fortieth, actually.'

His mouth falls open. 'No! But it's not the fifteenth today?'

'Er, no, it's not, but my birthday isn't the fifteenth.'

'Oh.' He pulls an awkward face and says hastily, 'Wow! Well, happy birthday!'

'Thanks.'

Still obviously confused, he says, 'So what were you doing in A&E then?'

'Head injury.'

'Shit!' He glances at me in concern. 'You're all right?'

'I'm fine,' I say quickly. 'It's just everyone has gone to a lot of trouble to make this evening really special, and I don't want to ruin it for them by making a fuss I only realized once I left the hospital that I didn't have my purse or my phone with me – I was literally stranded.' He doesn't say anything, just listens. 'I tried to get a cab, but I'd forgotten what it's like on a Saturday night here. They said it would be more like nine and I couldn't wait that long.'

'Soph,' he says. 'What's going on?'

I look at him, frightened. 'Nothing! I told you, I have to get there, that's all.'

'You wouldn't have called me because you were late for a party, fortieth or not. Are you in some kind of trouble?'

'I'm getting married tonight,' I blurt, opting for the same diversion tactic that I've been using all day.

His eyes widen. 'Jeez. OK...'

There is a long pause, and he shifts slightly in his seat as he stares at the road, taking one hand off the steering wheel and resting his elbow on the window, rubbing his head lightly. 'This just got a lot weirder. *That*'s why you called me?'

I whip around, horrified. 'No, no, no! Nothing like that, I swear to you! What, you think I'm having some last-minute doubts and I'm just checking to make sure you don't want to sweep me off into the sunset after all?' I laugh, but he doesn't. Oh God – that's exactly what he thinks. 'Josh, I've not seen you or spoken to you for over four years! That'd be insane of me!'

There's a pause, and then he clears his throat. 'One of the things you said, the morning I came to get my stuff out of the house, was that I had to be sure I was doing the right thing, because if we ever walked into each other's lives again, it would only be by chance, and we'd probably both be with other people by then anyway, and was I prepared to take the risk?'

I give a more awkward laugh this time. I absolutely remember saying that. Mostly because of the pain I felt when he rather sullenly replied that yes, he *was* prepared for that. I'm amazed he recalls it so clearly, though. 'I think in fairness we both said quite a lot of stuff back then that we probably didn't mean. I promise you, Josh – this isn't about me desperately "creating" a moment for us to meet again, before the door closes for ever.' I turn in my seat to face him full on. 'Look, my husband-to-be has got a completely psychotic ex-wife. And I mean actually unstable – not just your average wacky texts and letting tyres down. I can't tell you more than that, but I really needed to get away from the hospital fast, and I've only told you I'm getting married so you understand why it's so important I get to the hotel.'

He looks appalled. 'She put you in *hospital*?'

I close my eyes briefly, suddenly so exhausted that all I want to do is curl up and sleep for a thousand years. 'No,' I say wearily. 'I hit my head on a table and I knew everyone was going to say I had to stay at the hospital to be treated, but I can't, for reasons I can't explain. I know how it all sounds, and if I could tell you any more, I would.' I pause and add, 'If you want the honest truth, I called you because yours is the only number I can ever remember off the top of my head. That, and I thought there was a chance you might still live nearby.'

'Hmm,' he grunts. 'Well, that was predictable, I suppose.'

I look at him in surprise. 'Nothing wrong with that. I'm still in Rainshill.'

He smiles. 'Same house?'

'Yup.'

He looks pleased. 'I wondered if you might be, but I'm not on Facebook or anything—'

'Oh, right,' I say politely. As if I've never tried looking for him, not once.

'—and I've pretty much lost touch with all of the old lot, so—'

'You're still with Melanie, then?' I say, not thinking, and have to add quickly, 'Not that she's why you're not in touch with everyone now,' although that's exactly what I mean. Several of our mutual friends have remarked to me over the years that they no longer see much of Josh since Mel – his very tall, attractive and fiercely possessive new girlfriend – arrived on the scene.

He looks amused. 'Yeah, I am. Still bumbling along.'

Yes, well, if I remember rightly, Melanie's quite a bit younger. She won't be hitting the 'No bumbling beyond this point' fork in the road for about another year or so.

'Are you still teaching?' he says.

I shake my head. 'Nope. Gave it up.'

He looks genuinely taken back. 'But you loved it.'

I shrug and grip the bag more tightly as we go round a corner. 'Things change.'

'Well, that's a real shame,' he says. 'I've never seen anyone as passionate about their job as you were about yours. Do you miss it?'

I hesitate. 'Bits of it. The actual teaching – very much.'

'What are you doing instead now, then?'

'I work in London in sales. Some of my clients are children's charities, though.'

'Oh, well, that's good,' he reasons. 'You're still putting your skills to use, then. And at least it's an easy commute from Rainshill. You were so smart to buy there when you did. The house must be worth a fortune now. Do you know Rainshill's got the most millionaires per square foot in the whole country? I thought you'd have sold it to go and live abroad and set up your own school.'

I smile briefly. He remembers that too? 'Are you still working in town?'

'Yeah. It's a living, and loads of people want us at the moment because so many of them are building extensions but, to be honest, I'd happily never fit another kitchen for the rest of my life. Plus we're covering a wider area now, so I spend most of my time in the bloody van.'

'Sorry,' I say, 'and now you're playing taxi on your night off.'

He looks at me in surprise. 'Don't give it a second thought. Anyway, I'm pleased you asked.' He hesitates. 'I'm sorry about my comment before, when you said you were getting married. That was a really stupid thing to say.'

'Oh, I don't know,' I say. 'It's hardly your average Saturday night call, is it?'

'You don't know my average Saturday night,' he deadpans, and it strikes me suddenly that's true. I knew this man better than anyone for almost a decade. I know the only thing he won't eat is egg white. I know his mum's middle name. I know what all of his family pets were called and which one he loved best. I know that he would cheerfully punch a man called Chris if he ever saw him again, and why. I know we were once everything to each other... But I know nothing about his life now. He is practically a stranger to me, yet he's held me naked in his arms.

'Hello?' he says, and I look at him, blinking. 'I said, "Actually, all I was doing was watching TV" and you didn't say a thing. You all right?'

'I'm fine,' I answer automatically, then turn away and look out of the window. 'We're making good time. Thank you.'

'Well, we'll have to drive around a bit, then,' he says. 'The bride's meant to be slightly late, isn't she?'

'Not this one.' I smile tightly.

He looks puzzled, but doesn't pursue it. 'Is that what you're wearing?' He nods at my jeans and shirt.

'Of course not, I've got everything in my bag. In fact, that's a point. How the hell am I supposed to get changed without anyone seeing me?' I realize aloud.

He shrugs. 'Just do it here. I don't care.'

I look at him like he's mad. 'Don't be completely ridiculous!'

'It's not like I haven't seen it all before.'

'Josh!'

'What?' he protests. 'It's true, isn't it?'

'That's hardly the point. You don't get to see it now, do you?'

'Look, if it makes you feel better,' he says reasonably, 'I'll pull over and shut my eyes. Although when did you become so prudey?'

'Do you mean prudish? "Prudey" isn't actually a word,' I correct, and he bursts out laughing.

'Wow, it's been a while since I last heard you say something like that!'

'Oh, shut up,' I say, smiling, while also looking around and glancing at the clock. It's coming up to quarter to. My smile vanishes. I have no time to play with at all. 'OK, yes, can you find somewhere we can stop, please...'

'Certainly, ma'am.' At the next lay-by, he swings the car in and keeps the engine running. We are clearly visible to any other passing cars. 'Go for it.'

I have no choice. I unzip my bag and start to unbutton my top. I look over to him and he smiles pleasantly back at me. 'Close your eyes?' I say pointedly.

'Sorry, gotcha.' He leans his head back on the headrest and

sighs happily, as if settling in for a nap. I slide off the shirt and then start to wriggle the jeans out from under me.

'Da da daaa... da da da daaaa...' he starts humming under his breath.

'Josh, you're really not helping.' I become flustered and get my foot stuck in my haste to free myself. 'I'm not stripping, I'm getting into my *wedding* dress.'

'Sorry, sorry.' He holds a hand up, eyes still shut. 'I'll stay as quiet as a mouse.'

He's true to his word, and I pull it on – only whipping my bra off right at the last minute – and slip my arms in, before putting on the stupid shoes and the bracelet. I turn my half-bare back to him, sitting up as straight as I can, and ask uncomfortably, 'Can you zip me up, please?'

He doesn't say anything. I feel his hands lightly brush my skin, and the material tightens over my body again. 'Done,' he says quietly.

'Thank you.' I dart away from him and clip my seat belt back in.

He pulls out onto the road again and we drive for another moment or two in silence, before he says, 'That's one hell of a wedding dress.'

'Thanks. I didn't choose it. Marc did.'

He glances at me. 'What?'

'My fiancé has organized the wedding. It's meant to be a surprise for me. Oh, we're here!' My heart thumps as the gates to Goldhurst Park and the long private drive appear on our right.

'You drop that just as we're arriving?' he says incredulously. 'He chose your dress and sorted the whole wedding?'

'Yes, well, I wouldn't expect you to appreciate it. Right, have I got everything?' I peer down into the footwell, shoving my trainers and jeans back into the bag, checking that the letter is still there. I feel nauseous as I spy its now horribly familiar seal, just visible under my scrunched-up shirt.

'Actually, I wouldn't think *you* would appreciate having everything done for you like that.' He looks at me curiously. 'I take it you do *want* to marry him?'

I deliberately don't look at him. 'Relationship advice? Seriously?'

'Fine, fine...' He holds up a hand.

'Can you just pull down into that overflow car park?' I say anxiously. 'I don't think I ought to risk anyone seeing me getting out of your car, if that's OK... Although they're probably all inside by now. Oh God, ten to eight.' My stomach flutters with panic again.

He turns down quite a steep little hill and takes me right to the back of the car park. 'You sure here's all right? It's getting dark.'

'Yes, it's fine.' I turn to him, realizing suddenly that this is goodbye. 'Well.' I give him a big smile. 'Of all the people that I imagined would drive me to my wedding...' I trail off, not knowing how to finish that. 'But genuinely, thank you for helping me.'

'It was a privilege,' he says. Then he leans over and kisses me gently on the cheek. 'Be happy, Sophie.' My eyes close briefly at his touch and my heart tightens involuntarily. As he pulls back, I just sit there stupidly and stare at him for a moment. I really have to get out of the car.

I turn and pull the handle. Stepping out, I reach back in for my bag. 'Goodbye, Josh.'

'Bye, Soph. All the best.'

I physically wince as if someone has just given me a sharp dig right on a scar. All the best? Nine years decanted into one trite throwaway nicety. I shouldn't even notice, but I do. I have to straighten up and shut the car door, looking away quickly so that he can't see the expression on my face.

He spins the car around, and I watch him drive off slowly as I stand alone in the quiet car park, clutching my bag, the shimmering dress catching the last rays of evening sunlight.

He speeds up at the last moment and I hear him roar off up the hill.

Then he is gone.

CHAPTER SEVENTEEN

I have to take an extra second to wipe my eyes furiously, before gripping the bag and starting out towards the hotel. It is impossible to walk in my stupid shoes; I can barely totter. Kicking them off, I reach down and grab them by the straps, then pick up the bottom of the beaded hem of my dress so it doesn't drag in the damp grit.

Wincing slightly as some sharp bits dig into the soles of my feet, I clench my jaw, lift my head higher and keep walking. Marc will be at the hospital by now. They will have realized I'm missing and, in five minutes, I'll be opening the letter. I must keep focused. There is no time to think about anything else. I swallow and force from my mind the warmth of Josh's hands on my back. I am strong enough to do this. I've come *this* far. I've also met all Claudine's conditions: I've not breathed a word to anyone about what she's done, and I'm here. I am not going to fall at the final hurdle. She can ruin me, that's fine – but I *will* protect Marc and the children from public humiliation. I owe them nothing less.

I hitch up the dress more determinedly as I approach the main car park. It's not, of course, designed for striding uphill, only small, delicate, red-carpet steps. Squeezing in between two cars, I'm now on the main lawn in front of the hotel. The grass feels much softer under my feet, and slightly soggy with the dusk dew beginning to settle, but I'm able to pick up a little more speed, puffing slightly with the effort.

Hurrying across the open space towards the former stately home, I can see the elegant façade all lit up and figures gathered in the vast hall. My head starts to swim a little. How am I going to play this? They are all going to be hideously confused to see me. Maybe I'll just open the letter and worry about everything else afterwards...

The grass runs out, and with the gravel drive still between me and the door, I drop the shoes, reluctantly stepping back into them, before crunching towards the stone steps that lead up to the entrance.

As I appear in the doorway, everyone is chatting busily. They've all got glasses of champagne and, at first, only a couple of the guests closest to me glance up then do a double take, but before anyone can say anything, I hear a voice call, 'Sophie!' and realize Lou is practically barging a path through the crowd. 'Marc said you'd been rushed to hospital!' she exclaims. 'Soph?'

Oh God, she's here... I open my mouth to answer her, but more and more people are realizing I've arrived; the whispers are spreading like waves of dominos and heads begin to turn. My eyes flit instead to the oversized clock face that is hanging on the wall, next to the entrance to the library.

I watch the long hand click elaborately, straight to twelve. It is exactly 8 p.m. Ignoring the stares, I let the bag drop to the floor, bend quickly and undo it, reaching for the envelope and pulling it out, before zipping the bag back up and handing it to Lou. 'Can I give you this to look after, please?'

I offer her no further explanation as, cutting through the crowd, I head for the clock, until I am standing right under it, back against the wall.

Turning the letter over in my hand, I take a deep breath and break the seal.

Inside the envelope is a single sheet of paper, folded in the middle with a knife-edge crease. Sliding it out, I realize it is wrapped around several, much smaller envelopes, simply numbered one to four. The second envelope has 8.05 p.m. written on it, the third 8.10 p.m. and the fourth 8.20 p.m.

Sophie, reads the neat type of the letter,

> *As I am sure you already know (I would certainly be prepared to stake your life on it – !) everyone is here for your wedding. Forgive my cynicism, but then it's almost impossible these days to keep anything a secret, isn't it, Sophie?*
>
> *I wonder if you have you come across this Dorothy Parker poem before?*
>
> *By the time you swear you're his,*
> *Shivering and sighing,*
> *And he vows his passion is,*
> *Infinite, undying,*
> *Lady, make a note of this –*
> *One of you is lying.*

It will now be two minutes past eight.
Open envelope number one.
>   *X*

Tearing at the first small envelope, I pull out what almost exactly resembles a Monopoly 'Chance' card.

What WILL your parents say?

'Sophie!'

I look up to see my father marching towards me, with my stepmother in hot pursuit. He's holding his phone.

'What on earth is going on?' he demands, not even bothering with hello. 'Alice told us all you'd been in some accident and were in hospital, and now' – he waves the mobile at me – 'your poor mother is in a complete state wanting to know if you're here.' He pushes the phone into my hand.

'Sophie? Hello?' Mum sounds terrified. 'Alice, please slow down!'

'I'm here, Mum.' I say.

'Oh, thank God! We've been trying and trying to reach you! Hang on – Marc wants a word. I'll pass you over.'

The phone line crackles slightly with the movement, but then goes dead.

Before I have a chance to do anything else, the handset vibrates on my palm and I instinctively look at the screen, only to see it's displaying a text from **Sophie (daughter)**

What?

My heart stops. I open it quickly and scan the message.

Exposing a lying little whore.

Underneath are three small attached pictures. I peer at them more closely and my mouth falls open. It's a couple in bed. I tap on the first and it enlarges.

The duvet is half-covering an apparently naked man facing away from the camera. I can see his bare back, the back of his arms and the back of his head. Beneath him, the head of a brunette woman is just visible.

I instinctively tip the phone towards me so that my father and Margot can't see what I'm looking at – because there is no mistaking that this is a couple having sex. I scrabble to the next image. This is a clearer shot – the photographer has moved slightly to the right. The man's head is hanging slightly, his arms and shoulders taut with his body weight, and this time the torso and bare breasts of the woman under him can be clearly seen. She has her arms loosely above her head, her head twisted to the side and her eyes shut. Her mouth is also slightly open and she looks like she is gasping.

Horrified, all I can do is stare at the image.

'Sophie?' My dad starts talking again, but I don't register what he says as I am totally focused on the face of the woman.

It's me.

My chest tightens as I start to breathe faster and rush to the last picture. It's almost identical to the one before, but this time my leg is half out of the duvet, wrapping around Rich. My back is arching and Rich has lifted his head heavenward, his eyes closed. We very obviously have no idea there is anyone else in the room with us. The rest of the world has ceased to exist.

Clenching my jaw so tightly my head starts to thump and my teeth hurt, I grip the phone like a live wire I am unable to let go of.

How, *how*?

I start to shudder involuntarily. Someone watched me having sex. I hear the noises in my head and see through the eyes spying on us from the bedroom doorway: me being drunkenly fucked, none the wiser to either the act or being watched.

It is both disgusting and utterly degrading in equal measure.

I don't know how my legs continue to hold me up. Somehow I manage not to slither to the floor in my silver skin-like dress. I am completely unable to stop staring at the picture. Dad is still in front of me, speaking words I don't hear, as I begin to realize that had it not been for sheer luck, he would be looking at these images now.

My earlier determination that Claudine could ruin me as long as Marc and the children were not forced to witness it gushes away like someone pulling a plug on a sink full of dirty water. I don't want *anyone* to see pictures of me like this...

Oh, Jesus. The card said 'parents'.

This has gone to Mum too.

167

Deleting the images with fumbling fingers, I scramble for Dad's recent call list. **Maura** appears on the screen and I hit it instantly. Please don't have looked at your messages. *Please.*

'Hello, Sophie? We just got cut off I think. I gave the phone to Marc but you weren't there.'

'Mum, listen. Have you had any texts from me?'

'No... Should I have done?'

I feel faint with relief. I might just have got there in time. 'This is very, very important. When you get off the phone, there will probably be one waiting. I want you to delete it *without* opening it, do you hear me? I can't stress this enough, Mum. You have to promise, on my life, that you don't look at it.'

There is a pause.

'Mum, *please*,' I beg.

'I promise,' she says finally. 'We will be there shortly. Stay exactly where you are.'

I hang up, distraught. She's going to look. Of all people, she will look. There is no time to block my phone again. And what's the point, when whoever they are has successfully reactivated it twice already?

'Sophie!' repeats Dad. 'Can you *please* tell me what's going on?'

I look up at him, stricken. No, Dad, I can't, apart from Claudine is going to annihilate me. I silently pass him back his phone and, uncurling my fingers, select the second envelope. I check the clock.

It's 8.05 exactly.

So, who's next? Let's go and find Lou!

Lou? So Claudine *has* had someone follow and investigate me. She must have done. Oh God, this is going to kill Lou. It's going to destroy everything! I whirl around in panic, but my best friend is nowhere to be seen. 'Lou!' I shout, ignoring everyone's worried glances.

Rich suddenly appears out of nowhere, in knife-sharp black tie. 'She's over at reception checking your bag in. What the hell is going on? And how exactly was I supposed to keep her away?' he adds in a low voice. 'Sophie, can you stop a minute? I need to talk to you!'

Already hurrying to the desk, I see he's right. Sure enough, there is Lou with her back to me.

'Lou, I need a phone. Right now,' I pant. 'Can I have yours, please?'

She turns around, surprised. 'Sure.' She reaches into her clutch bag, taps at it and says in surprise, 'Oh, I've got a text from you!'

I reach out and snatch the phone away from her, deleting it immediately. Lou gives Rich a 'What the hell?' look and he shrugs helplessly.

Thank God he *didn't* manage to convince her not to come. If he had, she'd be looking at those pictures right now. I practically fall over at the thought of what almost just happened, and have to be helped to a chair, still clutching Lou's phone and the envelope.

'Can someone get her a glass of water?' I hear Lou say, her voice sounding curiously distant. 'Sophie?' she says worriedly. 'I don't think she can hear me. Does anyone know if Marc's arrived back yet? We should call him.' I feel her gently slip the mobile from my grasp.

'I'm fine,' I say, dazed, and stand up. I have two more envelopes to go.

'Sweetie, you're really not.'

I push past her, ripping into envelope three, vaguely aware of Rich trying to reassure her while also blocking her path.

Papa, what's Sophie doing with this man?

I gasp aloud. Claudine's going to use her own *children* to tell Marc what I have done? That's beyond sick – it's abusive.

I begin to shove past everyone, looking for my brother-in-law. I need to find Imogen and the children *now*.

'Is Marc aware you're here?' Someone – Marc's father, I think – shouts. 'Should we call him?'

'Don't worry!' I yell back. 'He's on his way.'

'You look lovely, Sophie,' comments a woman I don't recognize as I pass by. Actually, I think she's one of the partners at Marc's firm.

'Thank you!' I say, smiling manically. 'Thanks for coming!'

Finally, in a deep armchair by the fire is Ed, happily holding a glass of champagne, which he has just raised to his lips. He freezes at the sight of me. 'Sophie?' he says in astonishment. 'We thought—'

'Where's Imogen?'

'Upstairs in our room. Gen needed to feed Evie and she thought it would be best if they all just watched some TV. She didn't want Isabelle and Olivier getting upset after Marc left so suddenly.'

'What room number?'

'Two eighty-eight.'

I spin around and hurry away.

'You guys are unbelievable!' taunts Philip, another one of Marc's colleagues, appearing to my left as I reach the main stair-case. '"Piss up" and "brewery" spring to mind!'

I briefly consider punching his fat, smirking face, but move past him and up the shallow, red-velvet stairs.

Outside room 288, I knock smartly on the door, and Imogen's voice shouts, 'Hold on!'

'Sophie!' I hear her exclaim as she looks through the peep-hole. 'Er, you can't come in right now, I'm afraid.'

'Imogen, I know the kids are there! Open up!'

The door unlocks to reveal Imogen dressed in a long, flowing, pale green dress. 'Why are you here? What's going on?'

I ignore her and march past her into the room. Olivier and Isabelle are sitting very close to each other on the bed in a page-boy suit and a primrose-yellow bridesmaid dress, quietly eating sweets while watching TV. They look a bit small, lost and incredibly cute, but while I smile genuinely for the first time all day to see them, they understandably regard me warily as I approach – a very unfamiliar version of myself, what with the dress, make-up, swept-up hair – and shrink back into the pillows behind them.

I slow down and make a conscious effort to appear calm. '*Salut! Ca va?*' I sit on the end of the bed, not so close to them as to make them more nervous, holding the cards tightly in my lap. '*Papa est en route. Il a... quitté l'hôpital.* OK?'

They both nod slowly.

'*Les bonbons – c'est bon?*' I try, my French already practically exhausted. '*J'aime les vetements... Vous êtes tres jolie.*'

Isabelle gives a thin smile. 'You look very shiny,' she says in English.

'Yes, I do, don't I?' I agree, looking down at myself. 'We're going to wait here for Papa, OK? Do you need anything else? A drink, maybe?'

They shake their heads.

'Isabelle, do you have your phone with you?'

She nods. 'It's in my *sac...* bag.'

'Can I borrow it?'

She gets up without a word, walks over to her backpack, rummages around and silently hands me her iPhone before scampering back to the bed.

I switch it on.

As it updates, sure enough, a message comes in from my number. I exclaim aloud in rage, which makes them all jump. There are no pictures. Just a message.

Ask Daddy what Sophie was doing in bed with Richard.

How can Isabelle's *mother* be prepared to use her like this? She's only a child! A switch suddenly flips within me and, hands shaking, I go straight to the contacts list. 'Mama' is one of the only numbers in it.

'I'm just going to make a quick phone call,' I smile. 'You stay with Imogen and I'll be right back.' I don't want them overhearing any of this.

I close the door firmly behind me and walk silently down the hall, across the thick carpet, until I come to a quiet alcove window that overlooks the front lawn. I hit 'Call' and wait.

She answers almost immediately. '*Chérie! Ça va?*' She has a lighter voice than I expected, softer – although I can hear the concern in her voice, before she adds, '*N'êtes-vous pas à la noce?*', which I don't understand.

'This is Sophie.'

'*Sophie?*' She is astonished. There is a pause and then she says in perfect, albeit heavily accented, English, 'What's wrong? Are the children OK?'

'Oh, you do care about them, then?'

There is a longer silence this time. 'Excuse me?' she says slowly.

'Don't!' I interject. 'You have to stop this. OK, so you hate me—'

'Hate you? I've never met you!'

'You've spent eight months making my life a misery.' I talk over her, determinedly. 'Dragging out the divorce, doing your best to wreck everything. That's fine. Trail me, snoop on me, you can do your worst, but don't involve them. It's—'

'Hey!' Claudine interrupts sharply. '*I* dragged out the divorce?' Her voice tightens. 'Are you out of your mind? Marc contested *everything*, every tiny detail, any delay he could find, he exploited. He tried to have me fired from my job. Why would I want to stay married to him?'

And here come the lies. I lose my patience completely. 'Stop it!'

172

I shout. 'I *know* what you've been saying to him, how you feel about him!'

'Whatever he's told you, it's not true.'

'Right. So you didn't have an affair with his boss?'

She hesitates. 'It's not like it sounds—'

I give an incredulous laugh.

'It isn't!' she insists. 'I'm certain he didn't tell you he would give me a divorce only if I signed a contract promising never to marry Julien? That's the kind of vindictive man you are involved with.'

'This is bullshit,' I say slowly. 'This is what you do. You twist everything, you manipulate it all. I've been there when you've called! I've heard you shouting at him on the phone myself.'

'You heard me shouting in frustration because he refused to agree to any of the very generous terms I offered him!' she retorts. 'I don't care about money – just let me be. All he said over and over was, "I can't do that". You say *I* manipulate? He is a lawyer, Sophie – how naïve are you? I mean, really? You know what I think I should say to you? *Run.* Run as fast as you can. I don't want him back! I wouldn't wish him on my enemies. He may appear charming, but he is a very damaged man. You have no idea.'

I close my eyes. 'You say you don't want him back, and yet you are deliberately and maliciously wrecking our wedding, intent on humiliating me. The crazy thing is, you didn't need to do any of it!' I take a breath. 'I'd already realized I shouldn't be marrying him by myself, thank you.'

There is a stunned silence. 'I don't know what you are talking about.'

'I saw the pictures on at least one of the phones! What are you planning to do – send them to everyone and see who tells Marc first? You're sick! You must realize there is another family you're about to wreck? Two children who are going to lose everything?'

'The pictures?' When she finally speaks again she sounds a little frightened. 'Sophie, Marc told me you had an injury to the head and he was on his way to the hospital – in case the children called me and they were upset. Perhaps you are... confused right now, I don't know. I don't mean to be rude, but I think I should go. I hope you feel better.'

She hangs up.

I stand motionless in the corridor. She actually sounded quite normal. But isn't that what they say about people who do mad, deranged things? '*They were so nice, so ordinary...*' Marc has told me all along that this is exactly what she does – spins everything.

'Sophie?'

I exclaim and jump so badly with fear, before whirling around on the spot to discover someone standing right behind me, within touching distance.

'I think you've got something to tell me, haven't you?' he says.

CHAPTER EIGHTEEN

'Is it true?' Rich demands. 'Are you pregnant?'

I shake my head. 'It was just a misunderstanding in the restaurant. I promise you, I'm not.'

He looks sick with relief and nods. 'I got your message, but I couldn't keep her away. I tried, but she didn't buy it. I told her one of the kids was ill and we had to go home, but she just phoned her mum straightaway, who said she had no idea what I was talking about. It just looked dodgy as hell. As it is she's got to start suspecting *something* sooner or later – what was all that grabbing her phone business about?'

'I can't tell you but, trust me, you have to get her away from here.'

'You keep saying that, but how?' he explodes. 'What possible reason could I have for taking her away from the wedding that she's helped organize from start to finish for her best friend?'

'I don't know!' I exclaim. 'Perhaps if you'd *told* me that this was a wedding, I might have had the chance to think of something a bit sooner!'

'It was none of my business,' he says flatly.

There is a pause. 'Fine. I take your point,' I manage. 'But in the interests of now saving *your* marriage, you might want to do whatever you can to leave, before it's too late.' As the words leave my mouth, I see a movement out of the corner of my eye.

I turn to see, through the leaded window, Alice hurrying across the illuminated lawn towards the hotel. On one side of her is my mother, and on the other, in full morning dress, is Marc. 'Oh, God, they're here. You have to go, before anyone sees us talking like this.'

'But what is it that's going to—'

'GO!'

He stares at me, then turns and walks smartly down the corridor before disappearing around the corner. I spin back to the window, just in time to see Alice and Marc also disappearing out of sight below, about to come into the front hall.

Hitching up my dress, I run as quickly as I can back to the children's bedroom. Reaching the door, I hammer on it and, as Imogen swings it open, I push straight past her, lurching into the bathroom before slamming the door behind me. Flicking the lock, I check the time on Issy's phone – 8.19 p.m. – and tear open the last envelope.

Time for the ceremony.
Walk down the aisle and take your place next to your fiancé –
don't forget to smile!
But wait – does everyone *have objections?*
Speak now or for ever hold your peace!

Everyone? Dear God, the pictures are going to go to the whole congregation? In fact, couldn't those pictures potentially go to everyone in my contacts list, including my email and Facebook? I moan softly. What can I possibly do to prevent *that*? I begin to rip up the cards and envelopes, scattering them down the loo like confetti, as a muffled male voice sounds on the other side of the door. Marc. My fingers fumble as I frantically speed up. Chucking it all in, I pull off some tissue, ball it up, throw it on top and flush.

There is a knock at the door. 'Sophie? It's me. Are you all right?'

'Just a moment!' I call, checking myself briefly in the mirror before exhaling shakily, then undoing the lock.

Imogen is sitting on the end of the bed, holding Olivier's hand, as Isabelle peers curiously around the doorframe. Alice and Mum are standing in the middle of the room... and Marc is right in front of me.

I look at him, terrified, trying to gauge his expression – and just for a second, I picture *him* standing in the dark doorway of our bedroom as I lie in the bed in front of him, having sex with someone else. He's the only other person that has keys to the house... But then, what about the open front door – it could have been anyone! No! It wasn't Marc. It just can't have been!

His mouth has fallen open. 'Wow, you look amazing,' he says, seeming to gather himself and shaking his head slightly before taking two urgent steps to me, placing his hands either side of my shoulders, making me flinch. 'How are you feeling?'

'Why did you leave the hospital? I don't understand,' Alice interrupts before I can say anything. 'Mum thought you'd gone for your scan, but one of the nurses realized your bed was still there and you would have been wheeled around in it if they'd come to get you.' I realize she is trembling with anger. 'What the *fuck*, Soph?'

'Alice!' Mum remonstrates, as Isabelle gasps in shocked delight. 'I had to explain everything to Marc,' Mum turns back to me desperately. 'About you knowing this is a wedding. You do understand, don't you? It's only that once we discovered you were missing, I was certain you'd be coming back here.'

'Let me see your head.' Marc gently lifts my hair and peers anxiously. 'We have to get you back for that scan. I'm sorry you found out. I tried so hard to keep it a secret... But you know what? It doesn't matter, Soph. We can do it another time. Come on. We should go.'

He is a lawyer, Sophie – how naïve are you?

This calm and sensible man is a pathological liar and control freak, who has been waging a hate campaign against his ex-wife that I knew nothing about? Not only that, but he saw me in bed with another man, took pictures of it, then planned a secret wedding for us, hired someone to break into the house and is now set to publically humiliate me? That's what you want me to believe, Claudine? Marc is guilty of no more than trying to surprise me with the ultimate romantic gesture – an amazing wedding.

'Shall I take Issy's phone?' he says gently, and I realize I'm still gripping it. 'It's OK. I spoke to Claudine. And don't worry, I don't believe her. She called you, right? Not the other way round. I'm sorry she picked today of all days. I hope she wasn't too vile.'

There's another knock at the door, and we all jump. Imogen gets to her feet and hurries over, only to discover two anonymous women on the other side, both dressed in trouser suits, one clutching a file and looking pretty fed up.

'I'm sorry to interrupt.' The taller and more smiley of the two speaks directly to Marc; she obviously knows him. 'It's just that we were wondering if you still need, um, *everyone*' – she nods at the other woman – 'to stay, or if...' She makes an awkward face.

'My fee is non-refundable, regardless,' the shorter woman snaps.

'You must be the registrar,' Alice says. 'What a ray of sunshine.'

'Alice!' Marc cautions gently, before turning to the two women. 'My fiancée could be seriously ill right now. We need to get her to a hospital, and I don't know how long that's going to take. So while I understand about your requiring payment – which I'll honour – we are leaving now.'

'But I can't!' I say immediately, and everyone looks at me. 'I can't let you do this, I mean,' I say quickly to Marc.

'How long will the ceremony take – ten minutes at the most?'

Mum says suddenly, witheringly addressing the registrar, who sniffs and reluctantly nods.

'No, Mum!' Alice rounds on her. 'Are you crazy? Sophie could have some massive blood clot building up *right now*! Couldn't you, Sophie?'

'Sophie knew the risks, and yet she did everything in her power to be here. It seems very clear what she wants, and I think we should respect that. Please' – Mum turns to the registrar and the other woman – 'go downstairs and tell everyone we urgently need them seated in the main room. Alice, where are the flowers?'

'What is wrong with all of you?' Alice gives me a look of panic, and I have to turn away from her. She knows I overstated my symptoms, so I get what she's trying to do, but she has no idea of the very real risk to *all* of us if I leave now.

I have to follow the instructions, and that means actually walking down the aisle and facing my public humiliation during the ceremony. I will have to somehow live with the personal consequences, but – I think of the photograph of Evie, tiny and vulnerable in her car seat – I will do anything to keep us safe.

'We are going to make this happen for you. I promise,' Mum says. 'Alice, FLOWERS!' She practically shouts. 'Marc, you go too.' She is starting to appear almost frenzied in her doggedness.

I watch her worriedly. Did she open those pictures after all?

'Are you sure you want to stay?' Marc asks me. I swallow, and nod silently. He grins, grabs me, and gives me a quick kiss. 'I love you.' He dashes over to kiss the children as well and rushes from the room.

'YES!' Imogen squeaks excitedly. 'You're going to get married! Let's go! Oh, Lord!' Her eyes widen. 'Evie!' She dashes over to the travel cot and scoops up her sleeping daughter. 'Mummy hadn't forgotten you,' she says hurriedly as Alice reappears, her arms full of flowers, which she hands out expressionlessly.

'Hurry up!' says Mum anxiously. 'Everyone ready? Right, follow me.'

We all burst into the corridor. Mum is leading, at the front, and Isabelle suddenly speeds up, slipping her small hand into mine so she can trot importantly by my side. My heart breaks, and I just manage to give her hand a brief squeeze as she smiles up at me eagerly.

This will be the price I pay for what I did. I have completely and utterly failed to protect her, Olivier and Marc, and Lou, from a now inevitable and very public demise.

As we reach the top of the stairs I see that, true to her instructions, the lady organizer has emptied the hall of our guests. Only she and Dad remain, cutting a rather lonely figure as he waits outside the large, closed double doors that lead to the ballroom, beyond which waits my fiancé.

Dad looks quite choked as we all carefully make our descent.

'Now, now. Man up,' says Mum, but she pats his shoulder as she passes him and slips into the room ahead.

'Shall we?' Dad smiles, offering me his arm. I take it in a daze, and the doors in front of us swing open.

CHAPTER NINETEEN

Everyone turns around. A sea of beaming smiles. I stare straight ahead so I don't have to pick out individual faces, but there is Marc at the front, looking so happily back at me I can hardly bear it. I can't even feel the floor as we start to walk towards him – it's as if I am stepping through clouds in slow motion, about to fall through a gap and start hurtling to the ground.

He is a good man who does not deserve this. We shouldn't marry, I don't deny that – but *this* is so cruel and unnecessary.

We arrive alongside him. He takes my hand. Someone else, I don't even notice who, reaches for my flowers. Dad melts back and I glance over my shoulder to see Mum standing next to him, and Margot and my stepfather, Derek, standing awkwardly in the row behind them. Mum gives me a brief, determined nod. I look up wildly into the faces of our friends and other members of both our families, and then I see Lou grinning at me, fit to burst with excitement. Rich is standing alongside her, eyes downcast. So he has failed too, then.

The registrar has started talking and I turn back quickly. She's welcoming everyone, asking them to please make sure that their mobile phones are switched off. That will make no difference – no one ever actually does that, they'll all just put them on silent. She tells them the hotel has been duly sanctioned, and that this ceremony will unite Marc and me.

'We are here to celebrate their union and to honour their

commitment to each other.' She speaks warmly, with no hint of her earlier ill humour. I don't know what is genuine any more. 'Today they will both proclaim their love for one another.'

I stand ramrod straight, my back to the firing squad, craning to hear if the whispers have started. It's way past eight twenty. Who will be the first person to get the pictures? Will they be brave enough to stand up and say something? Marc's parents' numbers are both stored in my phone. My family would jump up if the shoe were on the other foot. Will Lou be sent the images again? Will it be her cry that stops everything dead? The whole congregation is about to have grounds for an objection. This is surreal. Who knows, perhaps Josh, too, is right now driving back here at full pelt, ready to burst in through the doors...

'I am required, however, to ask that if any person knows of any lawful impediment to this marriage they should declare it now.'

Here we go... My muscles lock and I focus hard on a spot on the wall above the registrar's head. Technically I suppose it's not a *legal* impediment, but I still feel my lawyer fiancé is going to have a problem with the photographs of my having sex with someone else. I start to sway slightly.

Someone coughs suddenly and there is a ripple of good-natured laughter as I visibly jump. Marc turns around and gives the perpetrator a mock, fierce glare. My nails are digging so hard into the fleshy part of my hand it starts to throb, but then he turns back, the registrar smiles easily at us and *smoothly moves on*.

The shock makes me catch my breath.

'The purpose of marriage is that you love, care for and support each other through both the joys and sorrows of life.' My dress feels incredibly tight, suddenly several sizes too small. I physically can't exhale. Why has no one said anything yet? 'Today you will exchange vows that will unite you as man and wife, and it is my duty to remind you of the solemn and binding character of these vows that you are about to make. I am now going to ask you each in turn to declare that you know of no legal reason why you may not be joined in marriage. Marc, please repeat after me: "I do solemnly declare…"' She busily addresses him, and then the next minute, I too am saying aloud, stunned, that there is no legal reason why we can't marry.

'And so I ask you both: Marc – do you take Sophie to be your lawful wedded wife, to be loving, faithful and loyal to her for the rest of your life together?'

It's going to happen now, surely?

'I do,' he says firmly, and turns to me to earnestly repeat the rest of his vows. 'I call upon these persons here present to witness that I, Marc Turner, take you, Sophie Gardener, to be my lawful wedded wife, to love and to cherish, from this day forward.' He smiles at me, then looks excitedly at Isabelle and Olivier and winks. He is a good dad. I turn to see them both smiling up at us – Isabelle looking so genuinely happy, my heart tightens painfully.

The registrar turns to me. 'Sophie, do you take Marc to be your lawful wedded husband, to be loving, faithful and loyal to him for the rest of your life together?'

All I hear in response is my own stammering voice in the silence: 'I do.' No one shouts 'Liar!' It resounds only in my head. The room is pregnant with silent excitement.

'Please repeat after me: "I call upon these persons here present…"'

What's happening? Why is *nobody* speaking up? I don't understand.

'Sophie?' says the registrar firmly. 'Please repeat after me: "I call upon these persons here present to witness that I, Sophie Gardener—"'

'Sorry,' I say, dazed. 'I call upon these persons here present to witness that I, Sophie Gardener… Take you, Marc Turner…'

I slowly repeat all of the vows, and nobody says a single word. We exchange rings, and the next thing I hear someone say is: 'I now pronounce you husband and wife!'

There is a spontaneous cheer as Marc scoops me into his arms and kisses me. Issy and Olivier are giggling and pulling faces in embarrassed delight.

What the hell just happened?

We got *married*?

CHAPTER TWENTY

I look across at my sisters incredulously. Imogen is wiping away tears, and blowing kisses at Ed and Evie; Alice gives me a sad little smile and mouths, 'Love you'. I swallow, in shock. Mum sits down heavily in her chair and fans herself lightly, in apparent relief.

'Congratulations to you both,' says the registrar, before raising her voice to address everyone else. 'Ladies and gentlemen, this is the conclusion of the marriage ceremony. You may take some photographs now if you wish, but we would then ask you to be seated for the signing of the register.'

Out come the phones immediately, waving in the air as everyone cranes for a good shot. Lou has tears running down her face as she snaps away.

If the images were going to arrive, they would have done by now. Everyone would be staring right at them.

So they weren't sent? Marc reaches for my hand and leads me over to a table. I sit down and a pen is pressed into my hands, the registrar pointing at where I am to sign. I automatically scribble *Sophie Gardener* before panicking suddenly that perhaps I was meant to sign it as Sophie Turner.

'Is that right?' I ask her.

She looks at it and nods. 'Yes, you use your maiden name.'

I pass the pen to Marc and watch him sign it too. My husband. Dad and Marc's mother step forward as witnesses. I've only met his mother twice before. A tall, too-thin woman called Olivia, she is wearing a raw silk lilac shift dress and matching bolero encrusted with crystals around the stand-up collar, as if it's been dipped in egg white and Demerara sugar. A vast amethyst twinkles on her finger as she signs carefully, before looking up at me stiffly. Her rather dated feathered fascinator is perched on the side of her ash-blonde hair like a dead owl chick caught in a bit of netting. I glance away quickly and stare down at the floor. I think I am going to be sick.

'Sophie?' says Marc immediately. 'Are you OK? You've gone very pale.'

'I don't feel well.'

'Shit. We shouldn't have risked this.' He pushes the chair back in alarm and hastens over to the registrar. I let my head hang as the events manager hurries over to join them.

We just got married?

I see them look at me in concern and nod. Marc quickly makes his way back to me as the registrar clears her throat pointedly, killing the excited chatter in the room.

'Ladies and gentlemen, due to unforeseen circumstances, the bride and groom will now be leaving. They very much hope to return shortly to celebrate with you, but ask you in the meantime to stay and enjoy yourselves! I'll hand you over to Amanda Knights, the events manager of Goldhurst Park, who will be acting as master of ceremonies, as it were, in their absence.'

She gestures to the organizer, who gives everyone a little wave, and does a curious little curtsey before saying loudly, 'I'd like to invite you all to make your way out to the library immediately for a champagne reception!'

Everyone looks worried, rather than their confusion of earlier, but they all dutifully stand and begin to move slowly en masse to the doors behind them, one or two of them unable to stop themselves from giving me an anxious thumbs-up and a 'You OK?', to which I do my best to nod and smile reassuringly.

'Oh, and everybody,' continues the manager, 'a lost mobile phone has been handed in at reception. If any of you has mislaid yours, do go to see the girls at the front desk.'

I stiffen instantly, just as Marc's mother helpfully grabs him, wrapping him in her arms as she holds him with inappropriately tight fervour, her eyes closed, while Isabelle and Olivier look around them uncertainly at everyone leaving.

'Alice,' I call quickly, and she steps straight over to me. 'I have to go to the loo. Tell Marc I'll be right back. Stay with Papa, you two, OK?' I look down at the children, and Isabelle nods.

'Sophie?' I hear Marc call worriedly, but I ignore him and hurry up the left-hand side of the room, placing hands on people's backs and saying loudly, 'Sorry, can I squeeze through?' Of course they let me. It's like the parting of the Red Sea.

'Can I see the mobile that was handed in, please?' I blurt to the girls at the front desk. 'I think it's mine.' One of them reaches under the counter and brings out an iPhone – *my* phone, complete with the scratch down the front of the screen that happened the day I got it and dropped it in the car park at Waitrose. I inhale sharply. 'Who found it?' I reach out to take it. 'I'd like to thank them.'

'Um, I'm not sure, actually,' says the younger of the two. 'I know it was in the ladies loo, by the sinks, but that's all.'

I switch it on and Evie pops up on the screen. As everything else loads up, I go straight to my sent messages.

There are only two. The first was sent from my phone eighteen minutes ago, to my own number. It reads:

07679857154
Congratulations. We're done.

I want to scream aloud. *How* can we be? What the hell was the point of sending the pictures to my parents, Lou and that horrible message to Issy, only to *not* send them to everyone else at the last moment? It makes no sense! I open the other message, sent at 1.47 a.m. last night.

It's a picture of me, sleeping peacefully, taken from right alongside my bed.

'Soph?' Marc appears at my right shoulder, holding Olivier and Isabelle's hands. I immediately hide my phone. 'What are you doing? We need to go right now! Imogen is lending us the car, but I want to bring the kids this time, if that's OK. They're getting a bit freaked out.'

'I've got a bag,' I say blankly, 'with some clothes I can change into. I think Lou checked it in for me—'

'I'll sort that out, Marc.' My mother appears behind me. 'You take the children and get the car. I'll bring Sophie out to the front steps and then we'll follow on separately behind you.'

'Thanks, Maura.' Marc dashes off gratefully.

As Mum retrieves my bag, the people closest to me offer me smiles of support, but evidently don't know whether to congratulate me or wish me luck. The female partner at Marc's firm is one of them, coughing awkwardly as she says, 'Well, in case we don't see you again later this evening, pass our best on to Marc. He's so cool in a crisis – we'll miss that! Do tell him to stay in touch, won't you?'

Mum stares at her for a moment, my bag now in her hand, and says icily, 'Come along, Sophie,' before leading me firmly towards the main door. 'Honestly. Some people have no social skills *whatsoever*. You're doing very well, darling. That's it, hold on to me.'

Gen's car is already sitting outside. 'You're going to be absolutely fine, Mrs Turner,' Mum continues as we walk down the steps. 'It'll be nothing to worry about, I promise! See you shortly, darling.' She turns away quickly as I climb in, and hurries back to the hotel.

I place the large bag on my lap just as I did in Josh's car an hour or two earlier and turn to Isabelle and Olivier, forcing a smile as we pull away sharply. 'All right, you two? Got your seat belts on?'

'Yes, Sophie,' Isabelle says obediently before asking curiously, 'You're our stepmother now, aren't you? So what do we call you?'

'Just Sophie, like you usually do.'

Marc gives me a subtle thumbs-up.

'Hmm,' says Isabelle. 'Helllooo,' she mimics me. 'I'm Sophie Gardener...'

'Hush, Issy,' says Marc quickly. 'Soph's got a bit of a headache.'

'Sor-ry,' she says slightly grumpily, and we lapse into silence for a minute.

'What about when Mama marries Julien?' persists Isabelle. 'What do I call him?'

I look at Marc, surprised.

'You'll just call him Julien, like you do now,' says Marc.

'OK.' Isabelle nods and, after a moment or two, she and Olivier begin to chatter to each other animatedly in French.

'Is that imminent?' I ask Marc quietly.

'Apparently.' He shrugs. 'Claudine told me yesterday when I went to pick them up.'

'Wow. Well, it's a good thing, I guess, isn't it? She's finally moving on.' And what she said about Marc not 'letting' her marry Julien was also clearly rubbish.

'Papa,' announces Isabelle suddenly, and says something in French, to which Marc answers in French, but then insists, 'And now back to English, please, Issy.'

'Urgh.' She tuts in disgust and slumps back into her seat. 'Why? I don't like it.'

Something occurs to me suddenly. 'Marc, can Issy read English?'

'No,' he says regretfully. 'She would have been able to – I bought them both English reading books – but it wasn't followed up, if you get my drift.'

Why would someone send that message to Issy in a language she couldn't understand?

Wouldn't Claudine have written it in French?

'You know what?' Marc reaches for my hand. 'I don't want to think or talk about that woman. This is our wedding day and, with a bit of luck, we might actually get to celebrate it later, once the scan is done.'

Unless the sender didn't *want* Issy to be able to read it, and it was really intended for *my* benefit... My hand sits loosely in his.

'Before I forget – that partner at your firm, she said to tell you to stay in touch and she'll miss you being calm in a crisis. What did she mean?'

'Oh, right.' He looks rather nonplussed. 'Yeah, she's leaving. Going off to another company. Bit of a rubbish one, if truth be told. But, far more importantly, how are you feeling? All right?'

'I feel... completely disorientated.'

He glances worriedly at me. 'OK. Well, we're nearly there. Not long now.'

Sophie – how naïve are you? I mean, really?

He's a damaged man.

I wish I could stop hearing her voice in my head.

We get the formal report on my scan result at 10 p.m. I have concussion.

'That's it?' Marc says. 'There's no fracture or anything like that? Thank God.'

'We'll keep her under observation for the rest of tonight anyway,' says the earnest young male doctor alongside my bed.

'Losing consciousness and vomiting are not common symptoms, so I think we ought to be certain of no further complications developing. But, all being well, you'll be able to go home tomorrow.' He beams at us, and looks a bit crestfallen when no one reacts positively.

'Well, let's face it, even if we left now, the reception is pretty much over,' Marc says after a moment. 'But what about the honeymoon? We have long-haul flights booked. Is that OK?'

'You'd have to check with your insurance company,' says the doctor. 'I'd expect that if Sophie doesn't experience any further problems in the next forty-eight hours, then it will be fine.'

'We're meant to be leaving tomorrow,' Marc says bleakly.

'Daddy, aren't we going on holiday any more?' Isabelle tugs at his sleeve.

'Shhh!' Marc says gently, then turns to me. 'Dubai for a week with the kids, then a week in Barbados for us,' he explains to me. 'Surprise!'

'Oh, Marc, I'm so sorry. We could just go anyway,' I suggest. 'I'm sure it will be OK.'

He looks appalled. 'It might invalidate the whole policy. No.' He exhales. 'I'll call them tomorrow and sort it. Forty-eight hours, you say?'

The doctor nods.

'Fine. I'd better get these two back to the hotel now we know you're going to be all right.' He reaches out for Isabelle and Olivier. 'It's getting pretty late.' He bends over and kisses me. 'Happy wedding day. I love you.'

'You too,' I reply.

The children wave uncertainly and I try to sit up a bit to wave back as he ushers them from the room.

Finally I am left alone. Gasping, I collapse back onto my pillow. If I hadn't just experienced it, I'm not sure I would have believed any of it had happened. I look down at the thin platinum band sitting on my finger.

But it did, and we *are* married.

CHAPTER TWENTY-ONE

'Can I have the first and second letters of your password, please?'

I shift position slightly on the hospital bed, trying not to pull the charger that Alice has just brought in for me out of my practically flat phone, while at the same time making sure the wire doesn't get caught up in the detritus of my breakfast that has yet to be cleared away. 'K and I.'

'I'm sorry, but I'm afraid that doesn't match with my records. Could you give me the third and sixth characters of your password?'

'N and O.'

'That doesn't match either. I'm sorry.'

'That's *definitely* my password.'

'Can I take your full address and postcode?' the mobile phone employee says patiently.

I tell him, and then he asks for my date of birth. 'Could you also tell me how you pay your bills?'

'Monthly, by direct debit from my NatWest account,' I answer.

'And how much was your last bill?'

'It's always about £36. I'm on a payment plan.'

'OK, Ms Gardener, I'm happy to pass you through security. How can I help?'

I take a deep breath. 'Yesterday, someone pretending to be me reactivated my phone after I'd lost it and had it blacklisted, so I called and had it blocked again – and changed my password – only for them to call up and repeat the whole process. I'd like to know how this person kept being given access to my phone.'

'The phone you're calling from?' he says, confused.

'Yes, I've found it now,' I explain.

'Right,' he says, clearly not understanding at all. 'Let's look back through the notes. Now, I can see a password change was requested at one twenty-seven yesterday.'

'I know.' I picture myself at the restaurant. 'That was me.'

'You then called back at one thirty-two and said you hadn't requested that password change or the blacklist request.'

'No, I didn't! That was someone else.'

'It says here "Customer received text alert to phone that password had been changed, which they hadn't instigated."'

'You sent a text to the phone saying I'd changed the password?' I say incredulously. 'You *alerted* them to the fact I'd changed it? Why would you do that? I didn't need to be told I'd changed it – I *asked* for the change! And how would I have got that text alert anyway, seeing as I'd lost the phone?'

'It's company policy to send a text alert when you have a password change, so if it's not you who has requested it, you know that someone is trying to access your records... Although I can appreciate, in this case, it wasn't relevant.'

'Well, even that aside, what's the point of my setting up an obscure password if you don't ask people to use it – which you obviously didn't when whoever it was called you back?'

'But if we only gave account access to customers on the basis of correctly supplying a password, I wouldn't be speaking to you now, because *you* don't know what the current password is,' he says, maddeningly yet correctly.

I grit my teeth. 'So this person, they just passed security anyway, did they?'

'All my colleague has written is "Confusion over new password, customer passed additional security."'

'What additional security?'

'It would have been the same sorts of questions I've just asked you.'

'You have *no* idea what happened to me as a result of that phone being reactivated.'

'I can only apologize that losing your phone caused you so much inconvenience, Ms Gardener.' He says it sincerely, he's not trying to be sarcastic. 'Is there anything else I can help you with?'

'Yes.' I hesitate. 'This is going to sound a bit odd, but if the person who called yesterday and said they were me was in fact a child, do you think it's possible one of your colleagues might have not realized and dealt with her? Say if she gave the password and then passed the phone to someone to speak on her behalf?'

'Um,' he says uncertainly, 'you mean like a four-year-old or something?'

'No! A girl of about—'

Alice appears back around the curtain, having returned from the loo.

'Never mind!' I stop hastily. 'Thanks anyway. Goodbye.' I hang up.

'Sorry about that.' Alice gives me a slightly delicate smile. 'I've drunk waaay too much water this morning. It's obviously not in your league, but my head has been *banging*. Your husband picked a good band.' She flops down onto the end of the bed. 'You were saying? You're feeling better?'

'Much.' I swing my stiff legs carefully off the bed.

'Good. I'm disappointed to see you're not wearing your beaded number today.' She nods at my shirt and jeans. 'It must have caused a stir when you arrived last night.'

'They didn't bat an eyelid, actually, and I gave it all to Mum to take home. Where on earth is she parking? She's been ages.'

'She didn't take the shoes then?' Alice reaches under the bed and pulls out the art deco platforms. 'Unless that's the combo you're planning to wear home?'

I give her a 'Ha, ha' look. 'I hope I never have to wear them ever again.'

'They *are* pretty monstrous. So, how's your husband?' she says. 'In Paris yet? Nice that Claudine made him take the children back even though it's only going to be for one sodding night. She's such a bitch.'

My husband. She keeps saying that. I glance at her.

She waves a hand. 'Don't. We're over it. I'm just happy that you're OK. I literally can't believe you spent the majority of yesterday with concussion. It'd almost be funny if it weren't so bloody scary. I mean, you read about people not knowing they're pregnant and then suddenly going to the bathroom and having a baby, but you had your hair washed and styled, for crying out loud. Didn't you feel anything?'

'I just mistook the headaches and being sick for me being stressed out.'

'You actually *were* sick?' She looks at me incredulously. 'If you weren't already in a hospital, I'd brain you just for that.'

'Yeah, well,' I mumble. 'It's all OK now anyway, so…'

'So you were lucky,' she says pointedly. 'Hey…'

I look up.

'Did Rich say anything to you yesterday in the end?'

'No, not really.' I rub my nose. He must have been totally confused too when, despite my dire warnings, nothing came to pass.

'Why *did* you rush back to the hotel yesterday, Soph? I still don't understand.'

'It doesn't matter now.'

'Well,' she says, as I start to look around for something to put the stupid shoes in, 'I want you to know, I respect your decision, whatever motivated it, and I'll support you one hundred per cent.'

'Morning, darling.' Mum suddenly appears, to my relief, clutching a plastic bag. 'Oh, you look *much* better today. Alice, get up off Sophie's bed.'

'She's not even on it,' Alice sighs, getting to her feet.

'You know if everyone just stood correctly, the world would be so much slimmer.' She looks pointedly at my sister, before reaching into the bag and pulling out a pair of socks. 'I brought you these. And a flannel.'

Alice wrinkles her nose.

'What?' demands Mum. 'She'll want a little freshen-up before we get in the car. Let me take those shoes for you, Sophie.' She reaches out and slides them into the bag. 'Have they said you can go?'

'Yes, I'm all signed off. I've got my painkillers.' I hold up the small bottle. 'We're free to leave.'

In the car park, Mum opens the back door of an immaculate Jaguar so that I can climb in. I lower myself down gingerly until I'm sitting on the tartan rug that always covers the back seat of the car to keep it clean. In the driver's seat, Derek folds up his copy of the *Sunday Telegraph* as Alice walks around to the front and climbs in.

Once Mum is in the back next to me, Derek says cheerfully, 'All aboard?' and eases away at a snail's pace. He is sweetly determined not to bump or jolt me in any way at all while we are in transit, so the journey actually takes quite a lot longer than it needs to.

It's a bright day and my head is splitting by the time we finally pull up onto the drive.

'There we are,' Derek says. 'Home sweet home.'

I don't look at the house. 'Thank you very much for coming to get me. Do you want a cup of tea before you go?'

'Go?' Alice says. 'What, you think we were just going to drop you off and leave you on your own? We're staying until Marc gets home.'

'Let's get the kettle on,' says Mum firmly, presumably expecting me to protest that I'll be fine. But I'm relieved and put up no fight.

We all stand on the front step while Derek, who has taken the keys from me, fiddles about with them in the lock. 'Sorry.' He frowns. 'I can't seem to get it to work.'

Mum purses her lips and manages to wait for about point five of a second before exclaiming, 'Oh, for goodness' sake, Derek – stand aside!'

He steps back as she grabs them firmly, and the front door swings open.

'There,' she says, and steps in, the rest of us following. 'Right – tea,' she calls over her shoulder as she bustles off to the kitchen. 'Sophie, go and sit down and I'll bring it through.'

I actually just want to go to bed, but do as I'm told, exclaiming aloud as I walk into the sitting room. It looks like a funeral parlour. There are white roses everywhere – what must be about twelve separate arrangements on every surface. Leading through into the dining room, I can see some wrapped gifts on the table and a few opened cards. I wander over and pick up a couple.

'That doesn't look much like sitting down to me,' Mum says severely, reappearing with a mug. 'Here. Careful, it's hot. I do hope you're not going to be a disagreeable patient. Now, I'm going to make you some soup, and then I think you need to go upstairs and have a lie down. Chicken or tomato?'

'Chicken, please,' I say bleakly, reading: *Marc and Sophie – congratulations! What a wonderful journey to be starting out on together!*

'One slice of toast or two?'

'One, please.'

Five minutes later, Mum brings it through on a neat little tray with a napkin in a napkin ring that I didn't even know I had. I eat it dutifully, then she stands to accompany me up to bed.

'See you in a bit,' Alice says with a wave, flicking the TV on as I get up. Derek has resumed his position behind the *Telegraph*. It all feels reassuringly normal.

In the bedroom, however, I discover that Mum has hung the dress on the front of the wardrobe door. 'Do you mind if I just put it away?' I reach up, but Mum gently takes it from me.

'I'll do it.'

I get under the covers just as I am. Mum frowns when she comes back in. 'You don't want a shower first or anything? Even just a clean pair of pyjamas?'

'No, I'm too tired.'

I can see she wants to argue, but kindly doesn't – just draws the curtains before tucking me up properly, like I'm about five again. 'There we are,' she soothes. 'You snuggle down and have some rest. I'll come up and check on you in a bit.'

'Mum... yesterday, *did* you open the message with the pictures attached? I really do need to know.'

'Sophie, I promised you I wouldn't, and I keep my promises. In any case, no such message came through.'

'You swear on my life?'

'Shhh,' she says. 'Close your eyes. I'll be downstairs if you need me.' She strokes my hair briefly and then disappears off.

I lie there and stare at the ceiling, before glancing at the empty chair where that man was sitting the last time I was in bed like this.

All last night I thought about the person who did this to me. Claudine tells me Marc is damaged and dangerous, that's he tried everything to stop them from getting divorced. He says she is manipulative, devious and will stop at nothing to get him back.

Claudine knew I would be in the house alone on Friday night. Marc says she hates me. I saw the photos on Dad's phone myself. Lou would have got them too if I hadn't deleted them first. Did Claudine get halfway there in executing her plan? Was it my phoning her that made her realize it was in fact real, not a game – that she'd gone too far? Did she scare at the last moment and decide not to go through with it after all? Or is she right, and I *am* horribly naïve? Marc knew I was holding Dad's phone when the pictures came in, that Dad wouldn't actually see them. Mum says she never received a message. He knows Issy can't read English, so she was at no real risk…

Ultimately, I waited for something that never happened, and we got married.

Was it him in the bedroom watching me and Rich? Has he known all along that I have cheated on him? Was he so frightened that I might be about to call off our engagement and wedding – as indeed I would have done, without the letter – that he did this?

Either way, I was violently threatened into attending a wedding I only knew about at the last moment, and wound up married when I shouldn't have done. That much I am certain of.

But do I believe my now husband, or his ex-wife?

It's surely a no-brainer. Marc would never physically hurt anyone and, in any case, if his motivation was to trick me into marriage by making me believe, right up until the last moment, that the wedding *wasn't* going to happen, why send the pictures to Lou and jeopardize everything?

It wasn't him. I'm *sure* it wasn't him.

I try to concentrate on the low hum of the TV filtering up from below, the opening and closing of doors as my family move around beneath me. Exhausted, I fall asleep.

*

When I wake up, at first I have no idea where I am. It's dark in the room and quiet. I think I hear the low whisper of voices downstairs and the click of the front door. I blink a few times and try to sit up. My face is itchy from the residue of Imogen's make-up that I have only washed off rather than properly removed. Feeling a bit grubby, I push back the covers, shiver and just lie there for a moment, slightly dazed.

The bedroom door opens silently, just an inch, as if drifting in a draft, but when I look up, there's the silhouette of a man in the doorway, watching me.

This time my instinct doesn't let me down. I scream instantly. He fumbles for the switch on the wall, flooding the room with light. 'Soph! What's wrong? It's me!'

'Oh, Jesus! Marc!' I gasp. 'I thought...' I trail off, trying to get myself under control.

He steps smartly around the edge of the bed, sits down and draws me straight into his arms. 'I didn't mean to scare you! I was just trying to make sure you were all right without waking you up, that's all.'

I pull away from him. 'How come you're back? What time is it?'

'Half eight.'

What? I've been asleep that long? My tummy rumbles automatically, as if to prove that things are woefully out of sync.

'Your mum has left us some supper downstairs,' he says. 'They've only just gone. They didn't want to disturb you. Alice said they've been checking on you all afternoon and you've been sleeping like a baby. I'm so pleased.'

'You got Isabelle and Olivier back then?' I swallow, my heart still racing. I need a drink of water; my mouth has gone completely dry.

'Yeah,' he says. 'They were really teary. It's so bloody ludicrous that she made me take them home when she's going to be turning around and bringing them straight back again on Monday afternoon. I said to her, "This is crazy! We fly on Tuesday!" but she wasn't having any of it.'

I stand up unsteadily, aware suddenly that I must smell disgusting. 'I'm just going to get my toothbrush.'

He follows me, still talking. 'She just kept saying she wanted to make sure they were OK. I only took them to the hospital, for Christ's sake. What was I supposed to do? Leave them at the hotel?' Leaning on the bathroom doorframe, he watches me squeeze some paste onto the brush. 'You look better for some sleep.'

I smile faintly and start to brush.

'Do you mind about us having the week in Dubai with the kids first, Soph?'

'No,' I say truthfully.

'It's just Claudine wants them with her for the whole of their spring break, which starts the week after next, so I wouldn't have seen them for ages otherwise. I know Dubai is a bit tacky but—'

'It's fine, Marc. Honestly.'

'No, you don't understand. *I* wanted us to go to South Africa on safari with them, but she went ballistic about malaria, and them not being old enough. Dubai was the safer bet. We're going to the Atlantis Palace, which has got a huge water park and aquarium, so the kids will be happy, and the temperature won't be crazy hot. You can just lie around and sunbathe and I'll keep them entertained. In hindsight, it'll be better for you anyway, rather than bouncing around in a jeep on rough terrain.'

I spit out the toothpaste and straighten up. 'I've just thought – what about work?'

'Oh, that's all arranged. I booked the time off for you ages ago.'

'What?' I'm astonished. They said nothing to me at all – not even Nadia, and she can't keep a secret to save her life.

He holds out a hand. 'Let's go and eat. I think I might open a bottle of wine. You probably shouldn't have any, but do you mind if I do?'

I slept with Rich, and we shouldn't have got married.

'No, you go ahead,' is what I actually say.

'OK. See you down there.'

He heads off downstairs whistling, just like it's any old ordinary Sunday night.

CHAPTER TWENTY-TWO

'I'm just going to pop out for a bit.' Marc appears in the sitting room the following morning as I'm eating some toast on the sofa.

'OK. But hadn't you better do some packing at some point?' I say absently, not turning away from the TV. 'You've got to get the children from the station later this afternoon, don't forget.'

'It'll be fine,' he says dismissively. 'There's just something I want to arrange. I've asked your mum to come and sit with you so you're not on your own, in case that's what you're worried about. Just wait there a sec...' He hurries over to the sideboard and reaches into the cupboard. 'Do you think you could sign here?' He places a covered piece of paper resting on a hardback book in front of me. Only a blank signature box is visible. He pulls a pen from his back pocket and holds it out.

I set down my plate and look up at him. 'What is it?'

'A surprise.' He smiles.

'Another one?' I say slowly. 'What sort of surprise?'

'I can't tell you or it'll ruin it! Just sign your new signature and don't let it touch the sides.' He waits, but still I hesitate. 'What's wrong?' He looks confused.

'I don't feel comfortable not knowing what it is.'

He blinks a couple of times. 'Oh, I see,' he says quietly. 'No, you're quite right. Call myself a lawyer!' He pulls the sheet of paper back. 'It's a passport application form to amend it to your married name. I'm sure you don't want to use Turner on everything like bank cards and your driving licence, but it's useful for ID to have it on *something*, and your passport is quite a fun one to have.' He looks completed deflated.

'I'm sorry. I didn't mean to—'

'No, no,' he says quickly. 'You're absolutely right to have asked. I thought I'd put it through their one-day premium service.'

I look at him in astonishment. 'But Marc, we fly *tomorrow*. And don't you need photos of me – that sort of thing?'

'There were some in your admin draw,' he confesses.

'From when I lost my driver's licence?'

He shrugs. 'I have no idea.'

'Marc, it's crazy to try and do this now! You're going to go all the way into central London, only to turn around and go back in later to get the children?'

'It's only eight in the morning; I don't have to get them until half four.' He sighs and sits down again on the edge of the sofa opposite. 'I want to keep my mind occupied, OK? I haven't told you, but I had a row with Claudine yesterday. She went off on one about not being sure it's such a good idea after all for the children to come with us. Some excuse about your head injury and you being unstable because of it. I'm not one hundred per cent sure they'll even turn up this afternoon and it's really stressing me out. Soph, what's the matter? You looked weird when I just said that.'

'No, I didn't. I'm fine, Marc, honestly. I promise you, there's nothing wrong.'

He frowns, unconvinced. 'Look, I know this hasn't been the best of starts, and I get why you're disappointed. But marriage is about more than a wedding. And actually, even though we were only there for about ten minutes, it was everything I wanted it to be. I felt like we were the only two people in the room.' He smiles suddenly. 'Didn't you?'

'Er, not exactly.'

'Well, I suppose it was different for you, with your head and everything.' He stops for a minute and draws back. 'That's not why you're being a bit funny with me, is it? You think I should have just taken you to hospital?' He looks devastated. 'You think I put you at risk?'

'God, no, of course not!' I instinctively reach out, realizing I really don't think that.

'Then what is it?' he says. 'Is something else wrong? Please, tell me.'

'It's nothing, Marc. Here – give me the passport paper.' I grab it and sign quickly. 'There you go. All done. I'll see you later then, shall I?'

'*Another* message?' Mum says later as I put down my phone, having just received more kind, well-wishing texts. 'I don't know how you manage not to hurl it out of the window with all of that constant bleeping.'

'I can turn it off if it's bothering you.'

'No, no,' she says from the opposite sofa, where she is knitting a summer cardigan for Evie, the needles whizzing away. I have no idea how she does it so fast without even looking. Years of practice, I suppose. 'I'm fine. Although you shouldn't rest it on your lap like that. It's not good for your ovaries.'

I ignore that, along with yet another message that pings in from Lou, wanting to know how I am, if we're still going on honeymoon. I know I should text her back, but...

'Did Dad phone you to see if you got home from hospital all right, by the way?' Mum interrupts.

'No.'

'Oh, well, never mind. I rang to say everything was fine, so I expect he didn't want to disturb you in case you were asleep. I thought he looked quite tired on Saturday, didn't you?'

'I honestly can't say I noticed, Mum.' I wriggle down into the sofa a little more, exhausted, and not wanting to go down this conversational route.

'Hmmm.' She glances at me. 'He's a funny old stick, but I do love him.' She sighs and pauses for a second before starting to knit again, even faster. 'It would have been our forty-second wedding anniversary tomorrow.'

'Would it?' I say, surprised.

She nods and we fall silent again.

'I'll tell you a secret,' Mum says conversationally. 'When I walked into the church to marry your father, I panicked. I suddenly thought, "I don't think I should be marrying this man."'

I look across at her. Well, *that*'s comforting to hear. 'And twenty years later when you wound up divorced, you realized you had been right all along?' I say tersely. 'What's your point, Mum?'

'Actually, my point was exactly the opposite,' she says. 'We had twenty very happy years together, despite my reservations in the church. You just both have to be prepared to put some effort in, that's all. The divorce was totally your father's fault. If he'd never told me about his affair, I wouldn't have had to do something about it. At the time he said he couldn't live with the guilt and the lies. He *had* to tell me. That's just another way of saying he wanted to feel better about it. He needed me to tell him it was all right, which was very weak of him.'

I sit very still.

'If you're going to do something like that, you'd better be prepared to live with it. That's the price you pay, I'm afraid.' She pauses and inspects the row carefully, counting under her breath, then adds, 'Every couple has secrets, Sophie.'

'But what if someone else had told you, and not Dad?' I say eventually. 'You'd have been devastated.'

'That's true, but we'd at least have lengthened the odds of our staying together. Is there a risk that the other person in your situation might say anything?' she asks innocently.

There is a very long pause before I eventually say, 'No. None at all. Someone else knows, but if they were going to do something, they would have done it by now.'

'Well, there you are then.'

'But isn't that dishonest and making decisions for Marc? And what about me? You're saying I'm just supposed to live with knowing that we shouldn't have—'

'Sophie,' she interrupts again, 'there are few chances in life at happiness. Marc was the proudest man in the world when you married him on Saturday, and you made your bed. Now enjoy lying in it. Let's make a fresh cup of tea and go and pack, shall we?'

After lunch, I'm busily removing from my suitcase pointless things like the winter cardigan Mum insisted I take, when Marc appears in the bedroom doorway. 'Can I ask a favour?'

'Sure. What is it?'

'Will you come with me in a bit to meet the children?'

I look up in surprise. He's never asked me to accompany him to a drop-off or collection before.

'Do you mind? After all, I suppose you have to meet Claudine sometime.'

'Um. OK.'

'Thanks.' He looks relieved, and disappears off again.

I sit down on the bed. I absolutely do *not* want to see her. And I can't imagine for one moment that she will want me to be there either.

I go downstairs and find Marc in the sitting room, on his laptop. 'Actually, would you mind if I don't come?'

He looks up, dismayed. 'I do, really, yes. What's the problem?'

I hesitate. 'I've still got loads of packing and…'

'The thing is, Soph, if you're there, she won't make a scene in front of the kids, which they, and to be honest I, can so do without.' He looks at me pleadingly. 'I wouldn't ask if it wasn't important. Please?'

We end up arriving at the train station slightly too early and decide to kill some time in Costa. 'I've never appreciated until now the carbon contribution divorce is responsible for,' I remark nervously, trying to appear totally relaxed.

Marc looks up from the paper. 'Sorry, what?'

'Well, Claudine is bringing Isabelle and Olivier from Paris to London, so we can fly with them from Heathrow to Dubai – and then we all come back again to London, for Claudine to collect the children and take them home, so that we can fly straight out to Barbados. At least it's a one-off, I suppose – we're unlikely to ever be so jet-set again, are we?' I try a smile and pick up my cappuccino.

This is ridiculous. My being here isn't going to prevent Claudine from saying anything, should she decide she wants to. We both know that. So why…?

'OK.' Marc exhales, looking at his watch for the millionth time. 'We ought to go and wait on the concourse now.' He's completely on edge.

'Marc, I'm sure she'll be there. She wouldn't—' I begin, but he's already on his feet and making for the door.

I follow him out of the coffee shop as he begins to march in the direction of the platform, like he's going into battle. I practically have to trot alongside him to keep up.

'Marc,' I pant slightly, 'can you slow down a bit?'

He turns back impatiently. 'Sorry, I just don't want to be late in case—'

'Papa!' We hear an excited shout and Marc spins around eagerly. There they are, running towards us – Isabelle's fair hair flying out behind her, an enormous smile on her little face and Olivier struggling to stop his backpack slipping off his shoulders as he tries to keep up. Isabelle flings herself at Marc, and he laughs as he gathers her into his arms. She clings to him like a monkey, burying her head in his neck. Olivier catches up and jostles to be hugged too. Marc attempts to engulf him as well, but overbalances, and has to set them both down amid lots of kisses.

'Hello, you two!' I say.

'Hello, Sophie!' Isabelle says breathlessly, breaking free of Marc to give me a happy smile. I am distracted, however, and don't give this positive reaction the full attention it deserves, as Marc has begun to straighten up slowly.

His expression completely changes as he stares over Olivier's shoulder and I follow his gaze anxiously... to see Claudine walking towards us.

I tense up immediately as she gives us a wide smile, which makes her eyes crinkle attractively at the edges – the sign of a woman who is happy often. Her dark hair is piled loosely up on her head, curls escaping here and there, and she's wearing a midnight-blue, tightly belted coat over skinny black trousers and what must be at least four-inch suede ankle boots that are all zips and buckles, with a toe so pointed they look dangerous. They are the only angular thing about her though, and I would guess she's worn them for height, as she is also absolutely tiny. It's hard to imagine anyone less threatening than this pretty little doll, but still I take a wary step back.

Her lack of stature is accentuated by the taller, older man accompanying her, pushing a trolley loaded with cases. He has greying, slightly unruly, thinning hair and lugubrious jowls. His overcoat is sharp and expensive, however, and as they arrive right in front of us, I notice that on the proprietary hand he places around Claudine's waist is a dynastic-looking signet ring. He could be any anonymously powerful career man that one might easily walk past on the street without knowing that he runs half the world. He is, I imagine, Julien.

Claudine clears her throat. 'Marc.' She turns to me. 'And you must be Sophie. It's a pleasure to meet you. This is my fiancé, Julien.' He reaches out his hand and smiles at me. As he does, his face completely changes, lighting up warmly, and just for a second I think I see what Claudine might find attractive about him.

'Many congratulations to you both on your recent marriage,' he says, and *then* I completely get it. His voice is a million clichés: melted butter, chocolate, liqueurs, late nights, and far, far too many cigarettes. I could listen to him speak all day.

Marc, however, remains mute. He just stares at Julien, who raises an eyebrow and drops my hand before simply looking away.

'Thank you,' I say, looking at Marc and willing him to say something.

'I hope you are fully recovered from your accident now, Sophie.' Claudine turns to face me, speaking with concern. 'It's incredible that it was concussion all along, but you were walking around and…' She trails off uncertainly.

Phoning you? 'I'm much better, thank you,' I say firmly, silently challenging her not to disagree, or to say anything at all. We're done, remember, Claudine? Let's both of us just walk quietly away. 'Very excited to be heading for a bit of sun. You know our terrible reputation for bad weather.' I laugh lightly, but no one else does. Even the children have fallen silent as they stand next to Marc.

'Indeed,' she says politely. 'I have packed everything the children will need for pretty much every eventuality in their suitcases.

212

Here are their passports.' She holds them out and Marc takes them. 'I'd be very grateful if you could make sure they only use the sun block I've provided you with, as Isabelle has very sensitive skin and most creams give her a rash.' She looks at me as she says that, and I nod.

'Of course, that's no problem.'

'There's easily enough for the whole week,' she says, suddenly anxious. 'And please keep a hat on them at all times, particularly in the midday sun.'

'Claudine…' says Julien quietly.

'Sorry. It's lucky you're *not* going on safari – then I really would be a complete mess, hey?' She laughs but looks horribly flustered, for a moment just a nice mum who is worried about things being done as she's used to doing them, because she loves her children. It seems that is *all* she's worried about right now.

'We'll take very good care, I promise,' I assure her automatically in my best teacher voice.

She looks at me quickly and, after a pause, says, 'Thank you. And please make sure they drink lots of water – only bottled, though.'

'We should go now,' says Julien firmly.

Claudine nods and smiles brightly. I realize she's trying not to cry and instinctively take a respectful step back to busy myself with looking in a newsagent window while she hugs them both fiercely and whispers to them in French, kissing them repeatedly, before forcing herself to straighten up and let them go. 'Have fun!' she says. 'Say a nice goodbye to Julien.'

Marc visibly stiffens as Isabelle steps forward and dutifully kisses Julien's cheek, and Olivier follows suit. 'Come on!' Marc says, taking the trolley and beginning to walk away. He doesn't even say goodbye.

My eyes widen. I find myself giving Claudine and Julien a silent wave – I can't not, it's too rude – before turning to follow him, but Claudine doesn't notice me anyway. She's only watching the kids already trotting after Marc.

I don't know how *any* divorced couple does it. I can't think of anything worse than having to let your children go off for a week with your ex and his new wife, who you don't know from Adam. I hope Imogen never divorces Ed. I don't think we'd all cope. I am still reeling slightly – trying to reconcile the woman I've just met with the one who sent me that letter – as we climb into a cab. The children are already bouncing around and have started gabbling away excitedly in French. I wait for Marc to ask them to start speaking English, as he usually does, but although he is smiling, he's also noticeably still very wound up, and I decide it would be better just to let it go.

It takes Marc an absolute age to get them into bed after supper. I'm about to offer to go up and help when the doorbell rings.

To my horror, I open the door to find Lou on the other side.

'Oh, that's nice!' She laughs. 'Don't worry. I'm not stopping long. Glad I've just driven all the way over here to make sure you're all right because you weren't answering any of your texts… Jesus! I won't bloody bother next time.'

'Sorry,' I say automatically. My face must have completely given my shock away.

'You should be. I've been really worried.' She walks in past me. 'Also, I know you're probably up to your ears in packing for tomorrow, but I really did just want to check in before you go. You *are* still going, I take it?'

'Yes, we are. And I'm really sorry, Lou. You're right – I should have called you back.'

'Ah, don't worry about it.' She waves a hand, goes into the sitting room and flops down on the sofa. 'It gave me a good excuse to get out of the house. It's fine, honestly.'

There's a moment's silence, until I remember myself. 'Do you want a drink? Tea, coffee?'

'Have you got wine?' she says. 'But just a small one, I'm driving. And I'd rather red if it's—' She stops, interrupted by a loud ringing coming from her bag. She closes her eyes briefly. 'Excuse me…' She reaches in, answers and says, 'Hi, darling!' brightly. 'Everything all right?'

'Not really, no,' Rich says crossly – loud enough that I can hear every word. 'The girls are saying they can't get in the bath without bubbles, and I can't find any. Where have you put them, please?'

'Hey!' We hear a small voice shout in the background. 'That's mine! Daddy, Tilly stole my rod!'

'Give it back, Tilly, please – and don't touch that either.'

'If there aren't any on the side of the bath, there might be some in the cupboard under the sink,' Lou says.

'Nope!' he barks. 'Already looked and there's nothing. I said don't touch that!'

'Well, there's not much I can do from here,' Lou says calmly. 'Can I leave you to sort it out?'

'I hardly have much choice, do I?' he says tightly. 'You're not going to be back late, are you, because I've— MATILDA, *DON'T* TOUCH THAT, I SAID!' A high-pitched wail begins in the background. 'Well, it's your own fault, you were winding her up! I've got a presentation to finish for tomorrow and it's already half seven. I really would appreciate it if you could stay no more than half an hour. This is about *work*, Louisa, I've got to be able to—'

'I want to speak to Mummy!'

'Well, you can't, unfortunately, she's busy. Right, I'd better go.'

'Daddy, I need to!'

'Bye,' he says tersely, although he's almost completely drowned out by a roar of 'MUMMYYYY!'

'Good, well, he's got everything under control, then.' Lou hangs up. 'Sorry, I was saying red if you've got some open, wasn't I?' She smiles at me. 'So how *is* your head?'

'I'm still getting some headaches, but painkillers are keeping them under control.'

Lou whistles. 'Who knew massage tables could be so lethal, hey? Still, all you've got to do as of tomorrow is lie in the sun. Excited?'

'Of course,' I say uncomfortably. This is horrible. She's my best friend and I don't want her here any more than Rich clearly wants her alone with me. Why didn't I just text her back earlier? 'Let me get your wine.'

When I come back in, she has kicked her shoes off, folded her legs up underneath her and is frowning at her phone. 'Thanks.' She beams at me and takes the glass. 'To marital bliss.'

Feeling sick, I raise an imaginary glass and chink with her.

'What gives with you taking the children on honeymoon, by the way?'

'Well, they break up from school in a week or something. You know how Marc usually has them for a bit of every holiday? This time Claudine wants them for the whole thing, apparently, so it's more us doing something with them first, then having our honeymoon, rather than we're taking them on honeymoon with us, if you see what I mean.'

'I do,' she says. 'Talking of which – can we very briefly discuss how amazing your wedding was? Weird to say the least, because you weren't there, but amazing. Congratulations.'

'Thanks.' I sit down.

'The food was the best I've had at a big bash like that and Marc chose such a great band. I don't think I've danced that much in ages. The thing is' – she drinks some more – 'it was pretty subdued until we all got the news that you were OK, then everyone went a bit crazy and just got plastered. Rich was *completely* hammered. It was like being back in uni again! You looked incredible.'

'Thank you.'

'Did you like the bracelet?'

'I loved it.'

'Well, you're very welcome,' she twinkles.

'You helped Marc choose it?' I can't help my surprise.

'Help him? Love, I went down there and viewed the whole collection, the works! It's very you, isn't it? You have *no* idea how hard it's been not to say anything – I've had to tell random strangers about the wedding instead, to try and work it out of my system! Everyone has just been blown away that romance is still alive and well after all. It's made for some pretty pissed off blokes though.' She laughs. 'Marc has raised the bar very high for the rest of them. There've been plenty "You'd never do something like that for me" accusations flying around.'

'Did you choose the dress, too?'

'I may have pointed him in the direction of a few select places,' she murmurs. 'Do you want to see some of the pictures I took?' She sets her glass down, gets up and sits down right next to me instead. I can't help flinching at her proximity, but she doesn't notice. 'This is you arriving. You look so stunning! Although I almost shouted, "Shoulders, Soph!"'

'Sorry?'

'Your posture! You *know* it drives me nuts. When you get back from honeymoon, we'll have to start Pilates or something, sort you out. Here, these are some of the bits you missed. This is all of us dancing – very badly. God, Rich's got his tie around his head. Idiot. Which of your friends who were there do you think will be the ones you're not talking to in five years' time?'

'What?' I stammer.

'It happens to everyone,' she says, not looking at me but peering at the screen more closely. 'I think Rich is starting to go bald. Lord, that's all I need. Something else for him to start ranting about. Mine was a good friend from school. She got pregnant just before me and she wanted a girl, only she had a boy. When Sadie was born, she stopped speaking to me, because *she'd* wanted the name Sadie.'

'I didn't know that. Which one?'

'Caroline, her name was.'

'I remember. Bossy. A bit shouty.'

'Yup,' Lou says. 'That's the one. I mean, I had a tiny baby to concentrate on, I hadn't got the energy to make it OK for her, you know? I was her bridesmaid when she got married, funnily enough, and I'm in *loads* of her photos. Which is quite satisfying.' She grins. 'That's one of the things you realize as you get older, though, isn't it? Some friendships just aren't meant to last the distance. You think they will, you can't imagine not having them in your life, but then they just walk out of it. Weird.' She shakes her head.

I can't do this. I can't sit here talking to her about friendship. It's too much.

'But you're a much nicer person than me, Soph. I'm sure *you* won't lose anyone! Forget I said anything.' She puts the phone down. 'So are you completely packed for Dubai?'

'Um, yes, I think so,' I say. My head is starting to pound again.

'I bet the kids are beside themselves. I noticed at the wedding how they seem to be very pro their new *maman*. Good work, babe. You've done so well. I'm so proud of you.'

I clear my throat. 'Thank you. I'm determined to do everything I can to make it work for them. I've been really lucky with my step-parents, and I'd like to try and give Isabelle and Olivier that same stability. After all,' I take a deep breath, thinking about what Mum said earlier, 'I'm going to be around in their lives for a long time – I've made a commitment to them too.'

'Well, they're very lucky to have you,' says Lou sincerely. 'Madame Nut-job didn't manage to kick up a stink at the last moment, then? I had visions of Marc going to Paris to collect the children and her flinging herself under their departing taxi, or something wacky like that.'

'She's getting married, actually.'

'No!' says Lou incredulously. 'Well, there you go then. All's well that ends well. Next thing you'll be telling me you're all going on holiday together, *en famille* – isn't that how the French do it? They're so much better at that sort of thing than us. And on the subject of family,' she says innocently, 'are you *sure* what your sister said at the restaurant wasn't her hitting the nail on the head by accident?'

'I'm absolutely not pregnant.'

'Oh, well, never mind, hon.' She gives me a sympathetic look. 'Plenty of time yet. I know a woman who fell pregnant at the drop of a hat aged forty-three.'

'Well, I quite literally need to get my head sorted out first.'

She shrugs. 'No time like the present. A honeymoon baby might be nice, don't you think?'

Before I can say anything to that, Marc reappears, looking shattered, and then rather taken aback to find Lou sitting on the sofa.

. 'I'm just going!' Lou laughs again. 'Blimey, you two are as bad as each other!'

'Sorry,' I say for the third time, embarrassed. 'We've just been—'

'You don't have to say anything!' Lou gets up. 'You didn't know I was coming, it's fine. I just wanted to satisfy myself that you really were OK, that's all, and to say have an unforgettable honeymoon. You deserve it.' She pulls me into a tight hug. She releases me just as quickly and turns to Marc. 'Bye, Mr Turner!'

'Bye, Lou, and thank you so much for all your help with everything,' Marc says sincerely.

'It was a pleasure. No, don't worry, I'll see myself out. Call me when you're back.' She blows me a kiss and disappears off.

I exhale as we hear the front door close.

'I didn't know she was popping over.' Marc sits down heavily.

'Neither did I. Sorry.'

'It's fine.' He yawns. 'We ought to have her and Rich round properly soon. She really was a huge help to me with everything.'

'So I hear,' I say as lightly as I can. We are absolutely not having them here. There is no way I could cope with that. No way on earth. It would be dreadful.

'I forgot to show you this earlier. Ta da!' He reaches behind him into his back pocket and pulls out a passport.

I take it and flip to the back page. There I am – Sophie Turner. 'Wow. Thank you.'

'You're very welcome,' he says. 'Now, can I have it back, please, so I can put it with the others in my special clear plastic "holiday documents" wallet?'

I roll my eyes. 'I swear, you couldn't be anything but a lawyer. Except maybe an accountant.'

'I'll pretend I didn't hear that,' he says over his shoulder, making his way over to the sideboard and slotting it away. He comes back and sits down again, reaching for the TV remote and flicking it on. But after a moment, I realize he's just staring into space.

'Are you OK?'

'Just tired. That's all.' He mutes the sound on the TV.

We sit there for a minute and I wait.

'I fucking hate him, Soph,' he says after a moment more. 'I can't help it. I know I ought to be OK with it by now – and it's nothing to do with feeling anything for Claudine, I promise you. I just hate him being around the children. She didn't tell me he was going to be there today and when I see him with them like that, it makes it impossible to pretend it isn't happening most of the time.' He puts his head in his hands. 'I know him, you see, I know what it's like to work for him – what an out-and-out shit he is. That tortured intellectual vibe is just crap.' He clenches his fists. 'Underneath all that is a completely ruthless, very sharp thug. And, even at best, he's just so old. I don't want my kids being told "Don't touch this" and "Don't say that", living in some kind of museum of beautiful objects. He collects things but he doesn't value them. I wish, *I wish* she'd chosen just about anyone else but him.'

I don't know what to say. I just reach out and squeeze his hand.

He sits there for a moment, then shakes his head slightly. 'Sorry,' he says. 'I'm really sorry. I shouldn't let it get on top of me. We're going to have a brilliant week, all of us, let's just focus on that.' He stands up. 'I might just go to bed, if you don't mind. We've got a long day tomorrow and the kids are going to be up at the crack of dawn, just so you know.'

'I think I'll come up now too,' I say, suddenly feeling a little overwhelmed.

'Can I talk to you about something else quickly?' Marc says, as I finally climb into bed beside him. 'It's nothing bad,' he laughs – I must have visibly sagged. 'I just wanted to say, I know we've never been hugely specific about it, but I meant what I've said all along about children, and I've no objections to having more. I'm not one of those, "Been there, done that" blokes. Just so you know, now we're married, if you *do* want a baby, I'd be cool with it. That's all.' He turns back to his book.

I stare at him for a moment, and think about the bracelet and my dress. 'Have you been talking to Lou?'

'Er, about us having a baby?' he says, puzzled. 'No. Because that would be weird.'

'Earlier, she pretty much asked me outright if we're going to start trying for children.'

He puts his book down and turns onto one elbow to face me. 'What did you say?'

'Um, what I *wanted* to say is I honestly don't understand how people think it's acceptable to ask that question.'

'She's your best friend!'

'Even then. There ought to be a law against it. I might not be able to have them.'

'I'm sure you can, and that's the good thing about kids. They make you feel *younger*, trust me. Well, except in the middle of the night.' He frowns. 'Then you feel about double whatever age you actually are. Look, don't worry about Lou, or anyone else. I know you've always said you're happy as you are, and that's fine, but if you want to change your mind, as far as I'm concerned, it's really no big deal – I'm OK either way. You want them, we'll have them. I love you, Soph. You know that, don't you?'

He pauses suddenly, giving me one of his full-on stares. I have never met a man so unafraid of direct eye contact. Having become more used to it, I secretly like how it makes me feel – like he literally can't take his eyes from me. Except tonight, something about him holding my gaze as if he can see into my soul makes me very uncomfortable. 'I love you, too.'

He leans across and starts to kiss me. I pull away from him before I even realise I've done it.

'Head still hurting?' he says, concerned. I nod, mutely, feeling like a complete bitch. He pulls a sympathetic face. 'No problem, I understand.' He turns off the light instead. 'Wake me if you need me.'

'Marc?' I suddenly whisper in the dark, moments later.

'Yes?'

'Thank you for our wedding – for doing all of that for me.'

'It was a pleasure. Goodnight, my sweetheart. Sweet dreams.'

But I am still awake, long after his breathing gently slows, dreams of any kind eluding me.

CHAPTER TWENTY-THREE

The children appear by the bed at 6.30 a.m., announcing proudly that they're ready to go to the water park now. By the time we've wrestled them through breakfast and into the cab, double-checked the house is locked (me), got to the airport, gone through Customs, messed around in duty free, texted Mum, Alice and Imogen to say we're about to board and that we'll let them know when we land safely, bought a load of magazines and books, sweets, bottles of water and a toothbrush (me), and a new phone charger (also me), I'm ready to drop.

The children settle down quite happily once we're on the plane, however, selecting a movie pretty much as soon as we take off. In fact, they are as good as gold the whole way. I find myself watching them at one point, Olivier frowning at the screen while Isabelle colours in a picture and absently eats a packet of Mini Cheddars.

'They're a credit to you,' I say to Marc, who takes his earphones off and says, 'What, sorry?'

'Isabelle and Olivier,' I say, nodding over at them. 'They're such good little kids.'

He smiles proudly and watches them. 'I'm a very lucky dad.' He gives me a kiss and puts his headphones back on.

I look back at them. If we *were* to have a baby, would Isabelle and Olivier be OK with it? That's one thing Imogen, Alice and I were always very glad of: no half-brothers or sisters to come to terms with. Marc and I would have to make sure they were really involved, so they didn't feel shut out. I'd actively want them to be the baby's big brother and sister. Especially as it would, in all likelihood, be our only child.

I flush slightly. The baby... not even *a* baby. Do I even have a right to be thinking like this? It's incredible how fast my life is changing – a married woman on my way to Dubai on holiday with my stepchildren. Whirlwind doesn't come close. I'm feeling pretty lucky too.

By the time we land nearly six hours later, I am mostly feeling pretty headachy, but the warmth as we step off the plane – just getting off full stop and being able to stretch out – lifts us all, and the children begin to chatter again. Isabelle wants to know how long it's going to take until we get to the hotel, and I'm relieved to hear it will only be about an hour. What with the time difference, it's now half past nine at night, and I really want to go to bed. Thankfully Marc has arranged a private transfer, which means we don't have to mess around with finding coaches or anything, and once we're through passport control, which is very quick – Marc happily remarks how efficient it is as he zips all of our passports back into his clear folder – and we've got all our suitcases, it's barely any time before we're walking through into Arrivals.

I look around for a placard that says 'Turner', but nothing leaps out at me. I can see Marc scanning everyone too.

'Hmmm,' he says, when it becomes apparent that there is no one there to meet us. 'That's not a great start. I'd better give them a call.'

The kids have stopped being excited and are becoming increasingly whiney and tired. Isabelle leans against Marc, scuffing her shoe on the ground, and Olivier starts climbing on the back of the trolley.

'Don't do that, Ol,' says Marc absently, phone to his ear. 'Oh, hi. Is that the Atlantis? I'm a guest and I've just arrived at the airport with my family and there's no one here to meet us. Could you – Yes, I will… They're transferring me,' he says to me. 'Yes, I'm still holding… Hi there. Oh, OK. We will, thank you.' He hangs up. 'Great. They're…' He frowns suddenly at his phone.

'They're what?' I say, when he doesn't finish his sentence.

'Hang on, please.' He is focusing intently on the screen and, just as I'm about to ask again, he looks up suddenly and stares unblinkingly at me for a moment before saying, 'You've got a smudge on your face, did you know? Just *there*.'

'Oh, really?' I reach up self-consciously. 'Here?'

He shakes his head. 'You need a mirror.'

I wipe my face again. 'I might just pop to the loo then. I've got time before they arrive, haven't I? It sounded like you've sorted it.'

'Yes. It's done. And yes, you've got plenty of time.'

'Isabelle, do you need to go? Want to come with me?' I ask, but she shakes her head and shrinks back.

'I want to stay with Papa.'

'OK,' I say equably, turning and walking off in search of the ladies. Once there, I grimace as I look in the mirror. I must have got the bit he was talking about, but I'm still horribly shiny and faintly appalled to see how flat and lank my hair appears. How do A-list stars do it, jumping on and off planes, looking fresh as daisies. Maybe I'm just a bad traveller. I'll feel better after a shower once we get to the hotel. I grab a tissue and blot my face, before trying – and failing – to shake some life into my hair.

Yawning as I wander back out and over to where I left Marc and the children, I discover they're not there. I've probably started a chain reaction of loo-needing and they've all had to go.

I'm so tired, I really hope the transfer car doesn't take long to arrive. I turn to my right to make my way over to the nearest seats to wait for them, which is when I notice a lone suitcase propped up at the end of the row – *my* suitcase. I frown and walk over to it. It's definitely mine – I can see the luggage label written out in my own handwriting. *Marc!* Everyone knows you don't leave suitcases unattended in airports! I hurry over and drag it close to me before sitting down to wait for them, but I'm now on alert and looking around anxiously.

Marc knows not to leave a case by itself. Of course he does. He's Mr Detail. Did it maybe fall off the trolley and he didn't notice? Surely not – and why would he have been rushing anyway?

I wait for them to come back from the loo for a five further minutes.

They don't reappear.

I reach into my handbag and pull out my mobile. My call goes straight to his voicemail. He must be actually talking on the phone, because he definitely has it on – he just called the hotel.

I get up and, starting to wheel my case behind me, try him again. Still nothing. I make my way over to the nearest gents and hover outside, but although a couple of men go in, Marc doesn't come out before they do. One of them stares at me as he re-emerges and I think he was on our plane, so I ask him if he wouldn't mind just seeing if Marc and the children are in there?

He looks. They aren't.

Feeling now far too concerned to even be embarrassed that I appear to have lost my own family, I thank him, turn and hurry away. One of the children must have been taken ill or something. But how can that have happened so fast? They've been fine all day.

I hurry over to the airport information desk and explain the situation to the two male staff on the desk. They are very nice, but tell me they are not aware of there having been any medical emergency. Would I perhaps like them to make a customer announcement for Marc and the children? I say gratefully that yes, I would, please – and listen as the tannoy request resounds through the airport.

But still they don't come.

The two men look at me a little more curiously. Where have I just flown in from? 'London,' I reply absently, looking around me, scanning the faces of strangers, looking for Marc, or Isabelle's long hair, Olivier's backpack... I reach for my phone again and Google the Atlantis in Dubai, selecting the phone number straight away.

'Hello? My name is Sophie Turner. My husband and I are staying at the hotel with our children, and we're waiting for our collection at the airport, only I know my husband rang to see where the car was, and now I can't find any of them and my husband's phone is off. I'm so sorry' – I give a small, desperate laugh – 'but is it possible for you to call the mobile phone of the driver, so I can track them all down?'

'Of course,' says the man on reception. 'One moment, please, Mrs Turner.'

I hold, and then he comes back on the line. 'I'm sorry, Mrs Turner, what name did you say the reservation was under?'

'Marc Turner. Marc with a "c".'

There is an agonizing pause, but then he says pleasantly, 'Ah. I can see you on our system now. One moment, please.'

I start to breathe again as the line goes quiet, and eventually he returns. 'I'm afraid the driver is not answering his phone, Mrs Turner, which leads me to think he must be driving still. I am sure he will be with you very shortly though, and I apologize for his late arrival.'

'OK, thank you.'

Well, that was useless. I hang up and try Marc again. It goes straight to voicemail.

Taking a small step back as someone else tries to speak to the men behind the desk, I accidentally knock my case over. It falls to the ground, and as I bend to set it back onto its wheels, something small and metal clatters to the ground, having apparently slipped out of one of the side pockets. As it bounces on the hard floor, the person next to me bends helpfully and passes me the shiny object.

It's Marc's wedding ring.

My mouth falls open in surprise as my phone simultaneously buzzes in my hand. It's Marc! But why is he *texting* me? I open it – to be confronted by the image of Rich and me.

The one with my leg around him.

Every one of my muscles locks into a spasm of complete shock. I am unable to move – I simply stare at the picture, transfixed with horror, before snatching my head up and looking desperately at the people walking past me; purposeful strangers on their way to their destinations.

Neither Marc, nor the children, are anywhere to be seen.

CHAPTER TWENTY-FOUR

Clutching his wedding ring, I have an overwhelming urge to shout 'MARC!' at the top of my voice, but I notice, as I'm wildly scanning faces, that the staff behind the desk are now openly staring at me. They've realized something is very wrong and instinct tells me to proceed with caution. I pretend to dial a number on my phone and, holding it to my ear, wait a moment, then say, 'Ah! There you are!' I roll my eyes. 'Found him!' I mouth, and they smile widely. I put my hand on my case and pull it away, still talking.

I make sure I'm well away from the desk before wobbling over to the nearest seat. Crashing down, I try to blink away the frightened tears that are pricking the back of my eyes.

He knows. He knows everything.

I'm not sure how long I sit there waiting – another half an hour? – before I realize he is not coming back. He must have found the driver after all and gone on to the hotel without me. I'll have to make my own way there, try and talk to him, attempt to explain.

I somehow manage to work out, by reading TripAdvisor reviews, how much money I am going to need to get to the Atlantis from the airport, and where to get a taxi from. Just as the reviews warned, the traffic is terrible, and it takes more like an hour and a half, but I barely register a thing. I am silent in the back of the car, as bright, gaudy lights flash past us. I cannot believe this is happening.

Once I arrive at the hotel, I hurry straight to reception and ask for our room numbers.

'Certainly. What name is your reservation under, please?' the receptionist asks pleasantly.

'Turner.'

'Thank you. Ah, I see you're checking in today. Welcome! Could I ask you please to fill out these details, Mrs Turner?' She passes me a sheet of paper. 'And your credit card, please? It won't be charged until the end of your stay. Also, if you have your passport, may I—'

'My husband will have already have done all this,' I interrupt her, having scanned the form she's passed me. 'I just need to know what room number we're in.'

She frowns and looks back at her screen. 'No, he's not checked in.'

It's my turn to be confused. 'He must have! He left the airport long before me. One of your drivers picked him and the children up.'

'Um, OK...' She types something and then, hesitating, says, 'Would you excuse me a moment, Mrs Turner?' She disappears through a door behind her, and then, moments later, re-emerges with a smartly suited man who smiles at me politely.

'Good evening, Mrs Turner,' he says smoothly. 'I can confirm that your husband and children have not checked into your reserved family suite. You are, however, most welcome to do so yourself, of course.'

I stare at him foolishly for a moment, and he lowers his gaze respectfully.

'But your driver collected them. That's right, isn't it?'

'Er, yes, madam,' he answers evasively.

'And brought them here?'

'Ah, I'm afraid I am unable to confirm that detail for you, Mrs Turner.'

My heart skips a beat. 'They're *not* here?'

'I can't confirm that for you, Mrs Turner,' he repeats. 'I'm so sorry.'

'He's booked in under a different name and he's asked you not to tell me, hasn't he?' I say slowly.

He doesn't answer. We all stand there in silence, apart from the sound of my heart thudding so loudly in my ears, I start to feel sick. I reach for my purse in my bag and fumble out my credit card. 'I'll just check in now. It's fine.' I try to keep my voice steady.

'Of course,' he says. 'Could I take your passport, please?'

I glance up at him in horror as I remember. 'I gave it to my husband,' I whisper, and sudden tears rush to my eyes. 'I don't have it.'

He hesitates, and then says kindly, 'No matter, Mrs Turner. You can confirm that detail with us later. OK, so here are your keys – your suite is on the third floor. We will have your case brought up to you immediately. Enjoy your stay.'

I give him a quick glance as he says that, and realizing his glib, force-of-habit oversight, he at least has the grace to look embarrassed.

'*If* my husband is here, or arrives later,' I say quietly, 'will you please tell him to contact me urgently?'

'Of course,' he says sincerely, but I am certain I feel him and the other receptionist staring and whispering once my back is turned and I am walking unsteadily towards the lift.

In the large, anonymous seating area, just off the bedrooms, I wait over by the window for my case to arrive, locking it inside the second it does. Heading straight back out, I walk up and down endless plush corridors and through the public areas looking everywhere for Marc and the children. They *have* to be here... But it's vast, with rabbit-warren corridors, and I quickly realize I stand little or no chance of stumbling upon them, particularly given he evidentally doesn't want to be found.

Back in our room, I resort to trying his phone over and over again, but it remains switched off. Isabelle's mobile is too. I try to think rationally. Claudine... She will know where they are, but I don't have her number. Could I reach her via Julien perhaps? The Paris office, if it's anything like Marc's London one, will have a 24-hour switchboard. I Google him under 'Julien' with the company name and there he is, instantly – Julien Calvel. I hesitate, but this is undoubtedly an emergency. I have to find Marc.

I tell the receptionist – one thankfully does pick up my call – that I need to get a message urgently to Mr Calvel, regarding his stepchildren on holiday in Dubai, and I leave my name and number.

Then I wait.

In less than ten minutes, my phone begins to ring.

'Sophie?' It's Claudine, panicking. 'What's happened?'

'Marc is very angry with me, and he left me at the airport. I need to get hold of him urgently. He's at the hotel, I assume, but I don't know where. Can you reach him for me please, and explain I really want to talk to him?'

'He abandoned you at the airport?' she repeats blankly.

'Yes. We arrived, got off the plane, I went to the loo, and when I came back, he and the children had vanished. He'd left behind my suitcase, and' – I take a deep breath – 'his wedding ring.'

There is a long silence. 'They've vanished...' she says slowly.

'Marc was phoning to see where the car was and the children were playing with the trolley. I came back and they had gone. I waited for a long time but they didn't come back, and now the staff won't even tell me if he's here or not. You must know – please tell me!'

'I haven't heard from him since yesterday. You're sure neither of the children has been taken ill? Have you checked anywhere?'

'I asked at the information desk at the airport, and they said there were no reports of a medical emergency – and Marc would have called me by now if they were at a hospital and that was what this was about. I know it's because of something I've done, and he's very angry, but I have to speak to him – only he's gone!' I can hear hot, frightened humiliation bubbling up in my voice.

'It's OK, Sophie,' she says automatically. 'Don't worry, we will find them. Stay where you are and I will call you right back once I've spoken to him.'

'Claudine,' I blurt suddenly. 'It *wasn't* you, was it? That letter, the flowers, the pictures – any of it?'

'You're asking me about pictures again?' She sounds exasperated. 'I've told you! I don't know what you are talking about, whatever Marc has done or said to the contrary. I need to find my children. I said I will call you, OK?'

She hangs up. I open my other hand slowly, looking at Marc's wedding ring and the small red marks on my palm from where I have been gripping onto it. I should never have agreed to marry him. If I'd only said no that morning when he—

My mobile goes again. It's Claudine. Her voice is strained, but she's trying to hide it. 'Only Isabelle's phone is ringing, although there is no answer, but, as Julien says, it's quite late at night with you now, isn't it? Marc has probably put the children to bed. Maybe you should try to get some sleep too and we will call you in the morning your time when we know more, and everything is calmer.'

'I am so sorry for all of this, Claudine.'

There's a pause, then she says, 'It's OK. I'm the only other person who understands what it's like to be married to Marc, remember? I will call you, I promise.' Then in a rush, as if she can't help herself, she adds, 'I tried to warn you about him, Sophie. You can't say I didn't!'

When she is gone, I stare at his wedding ring afresh, her words echoing in my head. Once again, I picture Marc stood silently at the foot of our bed, watching me have sex with Rich. He can't possibly have known all along?

Can he?

CHAPTER TWENTY-FIVE

'He hasn't returned *any* of our calls. Isabelle's phone is now switched off. We do not know where they are.' Julien's voice pours down the line, but it offers me no comfort at all this time, curled up in the chair of my air-conditioned hotel room, looking out at an almost plastic-blue sky. 'It's now been almost forty-eight hours since Claudine has had any contact from the children, and that is unprecedented. Sophie, I have to tell you that we have now reported the children as having been parentally abducted by Marc, both to the police here in France and to the authorities in Dubai. At the moment, all Immigration can confirm is that the children legally entered the country last night, and that they have not left. We know no more than that. Claudine tells me that Marc has your passport. I think you must assume that you will need to visit your embassy to obtain a replacement so that you can return to the UK.'

'Parentally abducted?' is all I can repeat, horrified. 'But this is—'

'He has removed them from their place of habitual residence, and that is illegal.'

'No, Julien, wait! I'm sure this is just about something *I've* done, it isn't—'

'Please,' he interrupts firmly. 'I am not trying to belittle your very valid and distressing situation, but I think you need to accept that this is much, much bigger than you and Marc. I don't believe this is an impulsive decision on his part – I think he has been planning this for some time. I have spoken to the managing partner of Marc's office. Did you know Marc left his job in London the day before you married, having worked out a three-month notice period?'

'What?' I gasp.

'I've done some asking around. It seems he's been taken on by another London firm and is due to start there in two weeks. But I don't think he will be there.'

'You don't know that,' I say quickly. 'I'd say that's a *positive* sign. He must be intending to—'

'You are defending him?' He talks over me. 'A man who abandons you in a strange country? And you are not concerned that your own husband didn't tell you that he had left his job? You also need to understand what I have been advised today by a specialist in this field. The United Arab Emirates is not party to any of the international conventions that provide many other countries with a legal framework within which a child abducted by one parent can be returned to another. Only the local courts in Dubai can order the return of Isabelle and Olivier. Despite all of my legal contacts, if Marc contests us when we find him, the progress will be, at best, long and slow. The help that the French authorities can provide is limited. I have had to warn Claudine that she may not see her children again for years. You think Marc didn't know this? I don't believe it, even if you say otherwise.'

I am reeling. He's left his job and abducted his own children? 'But Julien, originally he wanted to go to South Africa. It was Claudine who put pressure on him to change the destination.'

'Yes, which was very clever. Make us feel relieved about not taking them somewhere so dangerous, so we don't suspect anything when you say Dubai instead.' He is becoming angry. 'I don't think you understand. Listen to me! *We may not see the children again.*'

At that, words fail me completely. I hear someone else shouting something in French in the background, a female voice. Julien covers the phone and there is a muffled, heated conversation, the sounds of a struggle, then suddenly Claudine is on the line.

'Sophie? You tell me what you know,' she demands breathlessly. 'Everything! You said he was enraged with you at the airport. Why? Did he tell you his plan? Did you try and stop him?'

'Of course he didn't!' I'm appalled. 'Marc knows I would never agree to anything like that. We didn't argue, there was no "plan". We were waiting for the driver to collect us. We had reservations at the hotel!'

'So everything was ordinary? I don't believe you. Why did you say he was angry if that is true? You told me he left his wedding ring behind.'

I hesitate and she hears it. 'You have to tell me! Please! This is important! It might help me find Isabelle and Olivier.'

I close my eyes, and I don't know why, but all I see are Isabelle's shimmering fish in her bedroom back at mine, suspended from the ceiling, twisting silently in the empty room. Oh Marc... What have you done? They are just children.

Claudine's right. I *have* to tell her.

I take a deep breath. 'No, it hasn't been ordinary. I cheated on Marc recently. Somebody took pictures of me in bed with this other man, and then used them to blackmail me into getting married. Part of what they did was hire someone to break into my house and physically threaten me in the middle of the night. Marc sent me the pictures at the airport and then just disappeared.'

'You think it was Marc who did all of that?'

'I don't know,' I whisper. 'I have no proof that he did, and why would he marry me, only to leave me at the airport? It doesn't make sense, but then I would never have believed he would be capable of doing this to the children either.'

Everything goes quiet. For a moment I'm not even sure she is still there.

'There's something else,' I confess. 'On Saturday night, Marc was very distressed. He referenced your plans to marry Julien, then he told me how much he hated Julien being around the children. How he wished you'd chosen anyone but him.' I realise I'm crying. 'You're absolutely *sure* he's done this? Taken them, I mean.'

'There is no doubt.' Claudine's voice is shaking too. 'I don't think you know Marc at all, do you?'

Three Months Later

CHAPTER TWENTY-SIX

I sit in silence, my cup of coffee untouched on the table in front of me as Claudine does her best to stop the sudden tears from running down her cheeks. 'I'm sorry,' she says furiously. 'This is how it is now.'

She has lost so much weight I almost didn't recognize her when she opened the front door. Her hair is scraped back and she's wearing no make-up. Seated by the window of the vast, bright Paris apartment, every line and shadow on her exhausted face is illuminated by the unforgiving summer sun.

'Please don't apologize,' I beg.

She doesn't hear me. 'It was ninety days yesterday. How can that be possible? What is he telling them about where I am – because they *will* be asking for me.' Her voice cracks again. 'I know they will, and I'm not there! I have always been there! When Issy was little and she started school, she used to cling to me sobbing every time I left, and had to be prised off me. I'd feel her little hands trying to keep hold of my coat, but I'd leave anyway because they said she would settle, and it was normal, you know? And after-wards, every day, she would say to me, "You always come and get me, Mama," over and over and over again, as if that was the only thing that had got her through. And I'd say' – Claudine has to stop, breathing back more tears – 'I'd say, "I *always* come and get you. Always."' She closes her eyes and her face screws up in pain. 'What will she be thinking now? It's killing me.'

I half stand to get up and hug her, but she carries on talking, so I awkwardly sit back down.

'I know I have only myself to blame. This is my fault. I keep asking myself over and over again, *why* did I trust him? After we formally separated, I placed legal restrictions on Marc and his access to the children. It was with Julien's help. I don't deny that, but it was because of *my* fears about what he might do. Marc was unstable at that point, and he was very, very angry with me. I didn't want him taking the children out of France. Then he met you, and things seemed to begin to calm.' She reaches for a tissue and blows her nose. 'I was anxious when he first said he wanted the children to come to England, but I agreed on the condition that I brought them over, retained their passports and stayed in London while they visited you, and then I took them home again. Did you know that?'

'No.' I am incredulous. 'I had no idea. He never once told me that you were staying nearby in a hotel all the time the children were with us. He'd be gone for hours after they left – I assumed bringing them back here to you.'

She doesn't look surprised. 'When he asked me if the children could come away with the two of you for the week, it was very, very hard for me, but you were getting married, so I didn't feel I could say no. I wanted you and the children to bond – for their sake, of course. It seemed wrong to try and prevent it, but you know, when you rang on your wedding day...' She shakes her head. 'I had my doubts, I'm sorry but I did. Only he brought them back here safely, and it was all fine... I felt badly when he explained about your accident and Marc seemed only to want to make everything better. We actually talked properly for the first time in years about how best to go forward with ensuring the children's future was happy, what with all the change that was going on. I relaxed and I let my guard down. And all along he was planning *this.*'

She gets up and walks over to an elegant writing desk in the corner of the sunny room, picking up a folded piece of paper and carrying it back, before handing it to me. 'This is what I knew you'd want to see. It arrived via his legal team two days ago.'

To whom it may concern,

I wish to state for the record that my decision to keep my son and daughter in UAE was made solely on the basis of their making me aware of incidents of cruelty at the hands of Julien Calvel, the fiancé of my ex-wife Claudine Dubois; a situation that Claudine seems to have been either prepared to ignore or tolerate. It has been alleged that my actions were planned and premeditated. I refute this. I had travelled to the UAE with my son and daughter, and wife, Sophie Turner, for our honeymoon. Upon arrival I received shocking photographic evidence of my wife having been unfaithful to me, and while it has been made clear I can no longer trust anyone, my primary concern when we separated at the airport was that my children be prevented from witnessing an unnecessary and painful confrontation. My wife subsequently, I believe, returned to the UK. Our marriage is now in the process of being annulled.

'He insists that's true?' I ask slowly.

'Which bit?' Claudine says sarcastically.

'That someone sent him the pictures. That he hadn't, in fact, had them for months.' I hesitate. 'That it wasn't premeditated.'

'He's lying, trying to go for the sympathy vote,' Claudine says in a flash. 'But so what? Premeditated or not, abducting your children, whatever the circumstances, is illegal and what he did is wrong. You cannot argue that what he has done is acceptable. It isn't! It can never be!'

'I'm not condoning his actions,' I assure her sincerely. 'I promise you.'

'And you cannot deny it is an inescapable fact that he left his job without telling anyone, you included, which is just bizarre. I found out last week that his parents have "relocated" to Dubai now too. Did you know that's very common with male abductors?' she demands, and I shake my head. 'The parents go to help with the childcare. Ostensibly they've gone there to "help find him", but they've bought a house – they are going to build a life there. They disgust me.'

I don't know what to say to that.

'And I have never, *ever* had any concerns regarding the children's safety and Julien,' she continues. 'What "acts of cruelty" are these, exactly? It is all so clear to me now. You being a married couple allowed him to travel abroad with the children as a family without raising any suspicions. You told me yourself the lengths he went to in changing your passport so you were "Mrs Turner". This, the same man that gave a hired thug keys to your house and wanted to hurt and punish you for what you did, like he wanted vengeance when *I* dared to fall in love with another man.'

'You believe that's what motivated him to send me that letter?'

'Of course! He's a sociopath,' Claudine says, her voice suddenly flat. 'I've told you. My whole married life he dominated everything. It was always about him. I was weak. I should have ended it long before I did, and when I finally had the courage, he made my life a misery. That's another thing about Marc – he always wants what he can't have.'

'But—' I nearly tell her about our excited plans, him talking about us having our own children, but thankfully catch myself first. How could he have lain there in bed with me and discussed us having a baby – messing with my head, when that was a part of my life I had made my peace with – unless even on the smallest of levels he believed it himself? The alternative is just too devastating and too cruel. 'Could someone really be *that* devious?'

'Yes, Marc can! It's what he does. He is charming when he wants to be, but it lacks any kind of sincerity. He is vindictive and he feels no remorse.' She reaches over, suddenly animated, and grabs the letter, waving it at me. 'Do you know what this goes on to say? It informs me that he has engaged "armed executive protection" to prevent the children from being snatched back. It's not an uncommon practice in the UAE to have guards, apparently, but I risk being fatally hurt should I travel to Dubai independently and attempt a vigilante mission. Only, it seems no one can help us legally, either – so what do I do, Sophie? What do I do?'

She looks at me urgently, but I have no answers. I wish with all my heart I did, but I don't.

'I just want to hold them again,' she says desperately. 'I cannot believe I ever let them go.'

Later, I walk back to the metro station. It's still hot and I have to stop to take my cardigan off. Across the street a mother is remonstrating with her misbehaving toddler, getting down on his eye level and doing lots of fierce finger wagging. I want to go up to her and tell her that I know she's probably at the end of her tether with good reason, but to give him a hug instead and tell him that she loves him, because she can.

I turn away and keep on walking. Please, God, let it be Marc is telling the truth about Julien, and the children are now at least safe, because otherwise, what have we all been left with?

No one wins.

CHAPTER TWENTY-SEVEN

Walking into the almost empty sitting room, my footsteps echo as I drop my bag and keys on one of the last packing boxes. It's only in here that's left to clear now, and Mum and Derek will be arriving any minute to collect the remainder of my things.

I sit down on the floor, leaning against the wall to wait. Getting out my phone, I scan the news pages. Then I click onto Facebook in case Isabelle has re-appeared on there and tried to contact me. Remote, I know, but any chance is exactly that – a chance.

But there is nothing.

I sigh tiredly and put my mobile down for a moment to rest my head on my folded arms. I've still got so much to sort out before I leave in three days' time: lessons to plan... a new passport to collect... I also have to get the keys to the estate agent tomorrow for the new owners – a nice couple who I hope will be happy here. I know pretty much everyone thinks I should be renting out the house rather than selling, but I need to do this properly. No more missed opportunities.

There is a knock at the door and I get to my feet. That'll be Mum. I swing the door open – but to my surprise, Lou is standing there. She holds up a half bottle of champagne and two flutes. 'A final farewell to all that?' she suggests.

I gather myself and stand to one side to let her in. 'You didn't need to drive over for this, but I'm really touched that you have. Thank you.'

'You've been here nearly twenty years. That's a huge thing. When you texted that this was your last day, I couldn't let that go unmarked.' She walks in, looking around in disbelief. 'Wow. This is so weird. It already doesn't feel like your home.'

'I know,' I agree, jumping as she shoots the cork from the bottle and expertly begins to fill the glasses.

'Drink!' she commands, passing one over. 'Here's to fresh starts. You were always meant to be a teacher, Sophie, and in my opinion, the biggest tragedy of that whole Josh debacle was you ending up walking away from the job you were born to do. It's fantastic that you're going back to it.'

'Well,' I say quietly, 'it felt right at the time. It was impossible to stand up there with all of those eyes on me. I wasn't giving my best to the children and that wasn't fair on them.'

She doesn't say anything, just sips her champagne and, after a pause, asks, 'How was Paris?'

'Pretty much as you would expect.'

'Was there a development after all, then? What was in the letter Claudine said Marc had sent?' She perches on the edge of a packing box and waits.

'He alleges Julien has been cruel towards the children, that Claudine knew about it and that's why he's kept them in Dubai – essentially for their own protection,' I say carefully, and sit down on the floor again.

'Well, as a parent, under those circumstances, I can't say I wouldn't have been tempted to do the same thing.'

I frown up at her in surprise. 'Claudine says it's absolutely not true.'

'Well, I guess she would, wouldn't she?' Lou shrugs and plays with the stem of her glass. 'Thing is, Soph, you don't have kids so it's probably hard for you to understand, but when something or someone threatens your children's wellbeing and happiness – with total disregard – there isn't anything you wouldn't do. You'll go to depths you couldn't even begin to imagine, without so much as a second thought. Sometimes even an implied threat can be all it takes. You don't have to actually hurt someone to force people into behaving in a certain way – just them thinking you might is sufficient. When you know someone *really* well, you know exactly how to push their buttons, don't you?' There's a pause as she holds my eye contact unflinchingly.

'But Lou,' I say slowly, 'taking the kids from their mother like that is just *wrong*. There are lots of bits of what Marc supposedly did that I can't actually make sense of, even now, but as Claudine says, it's irrefutable that he *did* abduct them, spur of the moment or not.'

'Yeah, well, like I say – have kids, then come back to me on that one,' she replies, then continues brightly, 'so, that was *all* it said then? She couldn't have just told you that on the phone?'

'She knew I would want to read it for myself because he acknowledged leaving me at the airport' – I clear my throat – 'although he didn't say why.'

'One minute you had a husband, the next you didn't.' Again, I look at her in surprise; the statement hangs in the air as she takes a large mouthful of champagne. 'You've got to wonder how someone could be so cruel as to do that to another. Especially one they supposedly love.' She sighs heavily. 'I feel I owe you an apology, Sophie. I haven't been around for you as much as I would have wanted to be these last couple of months.'

'It's OK,' I say quickly, still watching her.

'No, no, it isn't. There's no excuse. You've had such a difficult time of it. I mean, before all of *this* happened, you couldn't even enjoy the wedding day itself because, all along, you were trying to keep such a dreadful secret.'

Everything slows right down.

'What do you mean?' I whisper.

'Your head injury, silly,' she says patiently. 'The whole day, everything it should have been – it just wasn't. Outwardly, you had the crazily expensive dress, the diamonds, the fairytale... And yet only *you* knew it could be snatched away at any point. That's so hideous. And now, here we are three months later, with you having to walk away from your entire life and cutting all ties.' She shakes her head. 'I'm only sorry my judgement didn't prove better.'

'About Marc, you mean?'

'I gave you all that crap about you just not having met any of the nice men, didn't I? And now I suppose you'll spend the rest of your life wondering if any of it was ever real – if he ever meant any of what he said to you, won't you?'

She drains her glass and gets to her feet. 'Right, I must go. Flying visit – I have to get back to the kids. Rich is working from home today, so he's doing tea, but bath time has got my name on it. Listen, while I remember, Rich isn't going to be able to make your leaving drinks tomorrow night – he's got a work do and although I've booked a babysitter, she's not one of the most reliable. If she doesn't show, I'll be able to find someone from somewhere, but it may mean I get there so late you'll probably have assumed I'm not coming.' She looks at me. 'Just to set your expectations. No, don't get up. I'll see myself out. You take care, Soph. Goodbye.'

She sets down her empty flute on the box, but then appears to hesitate, and with a neatly manicured nail, she deliberately and violently flicks the stem. The glass leaps into the air. Surely that must have really hurt her, I find myself thinking, seconds before it impacts on the bare wooden boards and explodes bright crystals everywhere.

Lou calmly crunches out of the room as, stunned, I stare open-mouthed at the now glittering carpet of glass. The front door closes with a final click behind her, and the house becomes still once more.

CHAPTER TWENTY-EIGHT

'There – all done.' Mum surveys the now empty room with satisfaction, only to immediately frown and peer critically at the floor. Wordlessly, she reaches into her pocket for a Kleenex, carefully unfolds it, steps smartly forward, bends and presses her finger onto a missed mini-dagger of glass.

'I do think the very least Louisa could have done was help you pick it all up,' she says archly, brushing it onto the tissue. 'I know it was an accident, but nonetheless...' She steps over to the open bin bag by the front door and drops it in.

Lou did it on purpose.

I watched her make a split-second decision, and she flicked the glass. She absolutely meant to do it.

One minute you had a husband, the next you didn't...

She meant to do it.

She did it.

'Sophie? I said that's everything now, isn't it? I knew it wouldn't take longer than half an hour... SOPHIE! Honestly, you've barely said a word since I arrived. I know it's hard, darling. You've lived here such a long time, but there we are. I *did* say I wasn't sure selling up was the best idea.' Mum looks around her, sighs and then unexpectedly asks, 'Do you want me to go and wait in the car so you can have one last walk around on your own?'

I shake my head. 'No, I just want to go.' I pick up the bin bag and don't even look back behind me as I walk past her, out into the street. Only pausing briefly to double-lock the front door, once Mum has closed it, I follow her down to Derek's full-up Jag. As he sees us approach he folds his newspaper away, sits up straighter in the driver's seat and starts the engine.

'So you're following straight on behind us back to the house now?' Mum says, gesturing at my equally loaded car.

'No. I've got a couple of things to do first.'

'But tea will be—'

'I'll see you back at the house,' I insist. 'I'll be about an hour or so.'

For once she just lets it go. 'Well, I'll save you something.' She climbs in, Derek waves and they pull carefully away, disappearing off left at the end of the road.

Once I'm in my own car, I sit still in the silence for a moment, before glancing up briefly at the front of what is no longer my house.

Only you knew it could all be snatched away at any point...

She knew EXACTLY what she was doing.

Snatched away.

I see the children running towards us at the station, arms open in delight, and anger finally surges up within me, mixing with the shock still swirling in my head at everything I now realize to be true. How can she have done this? The letter, the photos... But most of all, to Isabelle and Olivier

I pull away determinedly, pausing only at the stop sign before turning right and ramming my foot down.

The traffic becomes rush-hour heavy as I struggle out of the town and onto the bigger main roads, but I barely notice it. I simply stare out of the windscreen, employing auto-pilot reactions: putting the wipers on when it begins to rain heavily; turning up the fan as the windows begin to fog. Eventually I hit the dual carriageway and the traffic eases a little.

I rerun her pointed, parting comment over in my mind – that I might mistakenly assume she wouldn't make it, but she'd be there... I start to breathe a little faster. So, that night at the bar with Rich, she arrived late, but she *was* there – that's what she meant? But nothing happened until we got back to mine! She followed us back to the *house*? I picture the open front door we discovered the following morning and swallow.

But how does she even know anyone like that man who appeared in my bedroom? She told him – *paid* him – to break in when she knew I was alone?

I swing off the dual carriageway. He had pictures of my sisters; he stole my phone; followed me; delivered those horrible flowers... the text messages were all from her too. She would have watched me opening the letter at the wedding, rushing around madly... When I wrestled her mobile out of her hands, it was to stop her seeing pictures she'd sent herself.

I start to shake slightly as I pass an out-of-town shopping centre, then cross over the bridge where the roads become wider and leafier, terraced houses giving way to larger, discreet and comfortable properties tucked back from the road with more than one shiny car parked outside. She manoeuvred everything. That was why she was so heavily involved in helping Marc – she wanted me married and away from *her* husband – no matter what it took to make that happen.

All this time she's let me believe it was Marc! I moan at the thought of him innocently opening the pictures she sent him at the airport, the children clinging to him, tiredly but excitedly waiting to start their holiday. He was telling the truth in the letter Claudine showed to me. That bit he had been unable to prevent creeping in among the legal speak – about not being able to trust anyone any more. What he saw in those pictures must have destroyed him.

I jerk to a stop outside Lou's spacious semi, blocking the drive. Her estate is already back, neatly parked next to Rich's work Lexus, and I can see Rich talking on his phone in the sitting room. I slam the car door shut and begin to crunch over the gravel towards the front door, heart thumping wildly. I have sold my house, I am moving to the other side of the world, Claudine hasn't seen the children in over three months...

I see Rich look up, alarm spreading across his face at the sight of me, and he jumps to his feet.

For all of that double-meaning stuff she said back at the house about being hurt so cruelly by someone you love, doing anything to protect children, how I couldn't possibly understand the depths one might go to when pushed... there was a moment where she *wanted* me to know what she'd done – that's why she broke that glass. She couldn't help herself.

I begin to hammer noisily on the door.

CHAPTER TWENTY-NINE

It swings open and I jump. I'm expecting a frantic Rich — only to discover Lou there instead, as if she's been waiting for me behind it all along.

'Sophie?' she says coolly, with just the right amount of concerned surprise, as Rich appears in the hallway behind her, staring at me aghast. 'Are you all right? What's happened?'

'Don't,' I say warningly, my voice trembling.

'Have you been in an accident or something?' Rich steps forward quickly, before I can say anything else. 'You look like you're in shock.'

I open my mouth, but from the top of the stairs a little voice says, 'Hello, Auntie Sophie!'

I look past Rich and Sophie to see the two small figures of Sadie and Tilly in their pyjamas, twirling shyly on the top step. I falter and, voice cracking slightly, I manage a: 'Hi, girls.'

'Do *you* want to do our stories?' Sadie offers kindly.

'She can't tonight,' Lou says in a level, normal voice. And just for a wild moment, I wonder if this is all some hideous mistake that I've made — and I'm on the verge of destroying another innocent family. 'Sophie'll do it another time,' she adds calmly, turning back to me. But as she finally meets my eye, I realize that I am not wrong, and there is not going to be another time.

She is silently furious.

We stare at each other, neither of us speaking, until Rich breaks in with a nervous, 'Go and get back into bed, girls. I'll be right up.'

'Oh, but I wanted—' begins Tilly.

'You can go and put the *Charlie and Lola* DVD on, if you like, in Mummy and Daddy's room,' he says quickly. The girls' eyes widen at this unexpected bonus, and they quickly scamper off before he can change his mind.

Rich turns back to us. 'So, what *can* we do for you, Soph?' he says desperately, like a drowning man who knows he is swimming against the tide. He puts an arm around Lou's shoulders and she does nothing. Just stands there. They could be a John Lewis advert – both of them side by side in the house they have worked so hard to make perfect... Except they've not had sex in three years and she saw us fucking in my bed.

Tilly laughs distantly somewhere upstairs, and I realize I can't do it. I can't explode the last of what they have left by forcing them to confront the reality of what's happened with each other. But neither am I able to just walk away.

'There's something I have to know.' I turn to Lou, my voice trembling. 'You said earlier that *Marc* acted in such an extreme – some might say deranged and dangerous – way to protect his kids, but how on earth do you think he can live with himself knowing the pain he's caused Isabelle and Olivier? They were totally innocent in all of this!'

She doesn't flinch. 'I'm sure *he* did what he thought was best.'

'Marc wouldn't have done it at all if he hadn't been pushed!' I cry.

'Maybe it would help to try and remember some of the things Claudine told you about Marc?' Lou suggests. 'He contested every part of their divorce. She had to place legal restrictions on him. You just never know what goes on in other people's relationships – we've said it so many times over the years, haven't we? He wasn't the man you thought he was. I think he probably had some sort of breakdown – it happens to a lot of middle-aged men – but, ultimately, if forced to make a choice, I think they pretty much always choose their family first. He just didn't love you.'

I gasp as Rich says uncomfortably, 'Louisa!'

'Shut up, Rich,' she says softly. 'You've got to move on now, Sophie. You've got your happy ending.'

'I've got my *what*?' I look at her incredulously. 'How can you possibly think that?'

'You've sold the house you've held on to for years like some sort of shrine, you're going back to the job you love, you're moving to the other side of the world...' She speaks briskly. 'I almost think Marc did you a favour.'

Tears spring to my eyes as I look at the girl I used to laugh myself silly with. I can see us now dancing uncontrollably to 'Boys and Girls' at the student's union, Lou not caring what anyone thought of her.

'Daddy!' Tilly appears at the top of the stairs again. 'The DVD's stopped.'

'In a minute, Til,' says Rich, looking between us, frightened.

'No, NOW!' insists Tilly.

'Go and sort her out, please,' Lou instructs.

He turns obediently and legs it hurriedly up the stairs.

'I know what you saw is unforgivable,' I whisper eventually, once I'm sure we are finally alone, 'but what you've done is terrifying. How do you even know that man who broke into my house?'

She stares at me stonily. 'I don't know what you're talking about.'

'Yes you do. He threatened my family. And when Marc received your pictures...' I look at her despairingly. 'Isabelle and Olivier are just little kids!'

Still she doesn't react.

I shake my head in disbelief. 'What happened to you, Lou? You used to want to be an artist, you wanted to travel, but now...'

At that, she flushes. 'What happened? I grew up. You ought to try it.' Then she takes a step forward and says, with a seething, quiet energy, 'I'll tell you about a friend of mine, shall I? We've known each other for twenty years. She's always been beautiful, everyone likes her and I loved her. She had it all. Then she slept with my husband. I even thought for one moment he might have got her pregnant! Imagine! She's leaving now, though, moving away – and it looks like I've managed to hold on to my family by the skin of my teeth. But I've got to spend the rest of *my* life wondering if, all along, it's been her he's loved, not me.'

'No!' I shake my head, properly crying now. 'It happened just that once, and I'm so sorry. You know I'm not that person.'

'Just go.' She steps back and puts her hand on the door.

'Wait!' I say desperately. 'Why force me to get married if you were just going to destroy it once we were at the airport anyway?'

She hesitates. 'I already told you. Because I wanted you to see what it felt like to have a husband and then have someone steal him away from you. And in answer to your earlier question – I'll sleep just fine tonight, thanks. Whatever you think, I'm not responsible for Marc's actions as far as his children are concerned. Now, if you'll excuse me, I have to go and put *my* children to bed, so I'm going to close the front of my apparently so offensive, neatly ordered dollshouse' – her voice is full of sarcasm – 'if that's OK with you, and get on with my life.'

She slams the door in my face.

I turn and slowly walk back to the car, only pausing at the last moment before I switch on the engine to wipe more tears from my face. I look to my left and see Lou walk into the front bedroom, then draw the curtains across.

I watch the quiet house for a moment more, then start the car and pull away.

Now we're done.

The End

ACKNOWLEDGEMENTS

My grateful thanks to Maddie West, Joanne Dickinson, Wanda Whiteley, Belinda Budge, Margaret Halton and Zoe Ross for their help and support, as well as all at United Agents and Atlantic for their hard work.

And to Sarah Ballard and Sara O'Keeffe – my first ever champions – thank you both, so very much.